Portrait of Lady Margaret

REGENCY TIME TRAVEL ROMANCE

also by shirley marks

Contemporary Romance

Geek to Chic
Honeymoon Husband
Just Like Jack

Contemporary Holiday Romance

Christmas is a-Coming

Paranormal

What Goes Around - Comes Around
(Contemporary Ghost Mystery)

Portrait of Lady Margaret
(Regency Time Travel)

Portrait of Lady Margaret

REGENCY TIME TRAVEL ROMANCE

SHIRLEY MARKS

ISBN-13: 978-1-946314-02-4 (paperback)
ISBN-10: 1-946314-02-1

ISBN-13: 978-1-946314-03-4 (ebook)
ISBN-10: 1-946314-03-x

Photographs provided by Unsplashed.com
Photographers:
clock- Alexander Schimmeck
Elizabeth Tower - Michael Jin
London Eye - Adam Birkett

www.ShirleyMarks.com

Dedication

Mr and Mrs Lynne

For your inspiration

Portrait of Lady Margaret

REGENCY TIME TRAVEL ROMANCE

CHAPTER I

"Honestly, this is REALLY unnatural."

Peggy Swanson realized her friend had caught her—again.

"You're still staring at that painting. We've been in London for almost four days and that's the only thing you've really seen." Katie entered the front parlor and rounded the Adams style sofa to sit next to Peg.

"That's not true," Peg tried to deny. "We went to Apsley House and the Victoria and Albert Museum the first day we got here. We spent the entire next day at the British Museum. And just yesterday, we went to the National Gallery."

"You didn't spend half as much time staring at any painting there as you do this one," Katie responded. "It's not like it was painted by Gainsborough."

"I know." Peg leaned back into the sofa. She didn't know what it was about this painting that fascinated her so much.

Katie focused on the large, gilt-framed painting of Lady Margaret and her husband, Viscount Alison, probably trying to figure out what Peg saw.

"I can see Lady Margaret was pretty," Katie offered, studying the dark-haired Lady Margaret in an ivory dress.

Peg would admit she was attractive.

"And Lord Alison is hot. Not hot by our standards but Regency hot."

Peg would agree with that too.

The tall, lean Lord Alison was more than handsome. His blond hair combed straight back, accentuated the austerity of his face. She could stare at his dark, piercing eyes...forever.

What was the attraction? Peg wasn't all that sure herself. Drawn to the front parlor, and this painting, more often than she was willing to admit, Peg had the feeling she had met him before and couldn't remember where. And she was sure she would have remembered if she had.

As if that could ever have happened.

"I suspect it's jealousy," Katie theorized.

"What? Please spare me, would you?" But Peg had a good idea what was coming next.

Katie pointed to the woman in the painting. "Of Lady Margaret. You want him for yourself." Indicating Lord Alison with a nod.

"Don't be ridiculous." Peg gave a half-hearted laugh. "You Psych majors are all alike. You think you can analyze everyone."

"But I'm right, aren't I?" Katie's raised brows were not in anticipation of an answer.

How could Peg be in love? She didn't know him, never even heard of him until their small tour group took up residence in this Kensington townhouse earlier in the week.

Him? What was she thinking? He wasn't real. *He* was only a man in a painting.

That reason didn't stop or change what she really felt when she gazed up at the 200-year-old face staring down at her.

Peg hadn't felt this way when she and Katie had sampled the waters in the *Pump Rooms* of Bath, taken tea at *Betty's* in

York, nor when they basked in the summer sun on the shores of Brighton.

It had to be London, and this house, and something about that portrait.

Peg had fallen in love with Ashworth House the minute she arrived, and it would be her lodgings for the next five days until their grand Regency tour came to an end.

A brilliant someone had taken great care to modernize the Ashworth townhouse. Storage areas and closets had been transformed into bathrooms, with what the British called mod cons, modern conveniences, upstairs and down. While the townhouse was completely supplied with electricity, all were available but cleverly hidden, there wasn't a power outlet, light switch, or cord in sight.

In the ensuing silence, the mantle clock chimed the quarter hour. Peg slid her hand from the upholstery on the Adams style sofa to its lion-carved arm. The walls, the furniture, the atmosphere, all emanated history. But what impressed her went beyond the antique furnishings, said to be original pieces from the early 1800s. Something about the house that surrounded her, somehow permeated her, and ingrained itself in her.

Peg imagined the house must have looked very much as it did over two centuries before when inhabited by the fifth Earl of Westchester and his family. But it was the painting in the front parlor of the earl's daughter Lady Margaret and her husband that for some reason continually drew Peg's interest.

When she stared at it...him...she could have sworn his eyes stared back at her. As far as Peg could tell it didn't seem to be happening to anyone else but her.

"It's just a painting, you know," Peg replied.

"Go on, then. Don't mind me." Katie dropped in a well-practiced English accent, looking down her nose at Peg. "For all the time you spent staring at that portrait, you could have posed for one yourself."

Katie was right. Peg had spent a lot of time admiring Lady Margaret and Lord Alison. Correction: admiring him, glaring at her.

Peg's brother would have had a field day knowing she was lusting after a man, not to mention only a *picture* of a man. It would not have surprised Jerry to know it was an Englishman and a titled one at that. Even the day she left for England, he had given her a hard time.

"Give my best to Princess Kate," were his parting words.

And Peg snapped back, correcting him. "I know you mean Catherine, Princess of Wales. I don't think you know her well enough to call her Kate."

"Are we going, or are you going to sit there all day staring at him?" a voice brought her back to Ashworth House and the present.

Feeling slightly embarrassed, Peg blinked and said nothing more that would give Katie any reason to continue their squabble.

"I guess that's what English majors are supposed to do. Study the English," Katie continued, a retaliation to Peg's earlier remark about Psych majors. "Come on, let's get going."

Peg stood, trying to convince herself she wasn't as reluctant to leave the painting as Katie had made it sound.

"The only reason you're leaving without a fight is that we're going to Saffron Hall to learn more about *him*." Katie pointed to the man in the portrait. Peg didn't want to tell her friend that she was more than likely right.

Peg followed Katie outside the parlor and into the large hallway.

In spite of her teasing, it was Katie who encouraged Peg to explore her obsession. The family history display in the back parlor of Ashworth House suggested guests visit Saffron Hall for further information on Viscount Alison and his life.

Whether she liked it or not, Katie would see to it Peg did just that.

"*Margaret*," Paul, another member of the tour group, called out. He mimicked Mrs Taggart the hotel manager who called Peg by her full name *Margaret*. He was only one of many who'd picked up the habit.

"Have you seen..." Paul's eyes widened when he spotted Katie. "There you are." He skirted around Peg, murmuring an 'excuse me' and headed for Katie. "Thanks for the loan." He handed her a folded map of London. "I'm tagging along with Tom and Karen to St Paul's Cathedral. What are you two doing today?"

"We're stopping by a small museum and then some shopping," Katie replied, with a definite twinkle in her eye. "Although, I'm not sure where."

Maybe Katie likes him.

"Do you have a map of the Underground?" Katie asked Peg.

Peg had the impression her friend wanted a bit of privacy and searched her bag and pretended to come up empty-handed. "I'll get another one." She headed for the front desk.

"Somethin' you need, dear?" Mrs Taggart looked up to her elbows in paperwork. Literally.

"An Underground map, if you have one handy."

"Oh, I think I can find one around here somewheres." Mrs Taggart glanced about her area, shuffling through the piles around her. "If I can no' you'll be able to find one at the Tube station." It was amazing how through the pile of papers, which looked to be an assortment of notes, messages, and other miscellaneous bits of paper could, as if somehow by magic, make a Tube map appear. "Ah...here we are!"

Mrs Taggart slid the small, folded map across the counter.

Peg took it and thanked her. While slipping it into a zipped pocket in her jacket, she glanced back at the front parlor. Paul and Katie conversed with soft smiles and quiet whispers.

Maybe Paul liked Katie too.

"Now who's in love?" Peg goaded Katie once they were alone outside.

Katie flashed a smile and replied, "At least he's alive and breathing."

CATCHING the Underground at South Kensington tube station, and one line change, Peg and Katie disembarked at Hampstead Heath and walked a few blocks more to the impressive three-story Saffron Hall.

Peg stepped inside the mansion. A red velvet cord roped off the massive staircase in the entrance area, keeping visitors from moving beyond the Corinthian columns that supported the arch in front of the grand staircase on the first floor.

To one side, a woman sat behind a table handing out information pamphlets about the property, offering audio and self-guided tour maps. Peg and Katie opted for the self-guided tour.

Katie flipped through the pamphlet. "Where's the part about Lord Alison?"

"Don't worry about it." Peg was here and ready to learn more about her Mystery Man and did not wish to appear overly anxious.

Katie gave an exasperated sigh. "I guess we'll get to him eventually. Do you want to see this?" She held out the pamphlet.

"No, you go ahead and keep it. Just tell me what it says."

Pulling the cover and first two pages open, Katie began to paraphrase. "It says Saffron Hall was owned by the law firm of

Bevans, Blake, and Whitfield. They used to entertain clients here." Katie glanced about the entrance hall. "I guess so. This place is pretty fancy. I guess Lord Alison must have been one of their clients." Katie studied the walls, taking in the plasterwork, wood carvings, and gold leaf. "He had the looks and the big bucks too. Lucky Lady Margaret."

Why did Katie always have to bring up Lady Margaret?

Katie noticed Peg glaring at her. "Sorry. I take that back." She consulted the pamphlet and inched ahead, slowly leading the way. "This says the first room is the Front Parlor."

Peg felt a wave of dizziness hit her. Whether it was from watching Katie spin around, taking in her surroundings, or an attack of agoraphobia, by the time Peg steadied herself the feeling had already passed. For the next few moments, she remained still with her eyes closed.

Peg started to follow but paused when an image of a white marble woman flashed in her mind. Then just as quickly, the bare-breasted woman with her arm arched over her head faded and the dizziness left.

That was weird.

Entering the Front Parlor, Katie scanned the room and craned her neck, looking up at the ceiling. "Can you imagine living in a place like this?"

Stepping inside after Katie, Peg stared straight ahead and saw her...them.

There were two. White marble women on the chimneypiece. She stared at the figures posed in mirror images, flanking the fireplace. Their expressions were frozen somewhere between ecstasy and exhaustion from holding the weight of the mantel over their heads for centuries.

Peg looked from one to the other and back again.

This was truly strange.

She must have seen a picture of them in a book. She must have. How else could she explain her feeling of *déjà vu*?

Katie strolled to the portal of the next room. "Wow, look at this. Now, *this* is a big room."

Setting herself on auto-pilot, Peg followed Katie down the Long Gallery. Katie's voice stretched toward her as though she were very far away and Peg could not make out her friend's words.

Peg squinted into the early afternoon light pouring through the large, wide windows lining the right side of the room. And her uneasiness rose while walking past the various chairs, sofas, and small tables set around the room grouped in threes and fours.

Standing in this jammed-packed room filled from wall to wall, Peg felt as if she were suffocating. There should have been half this amount of furniture. It should have been spread out and lined up against the wall out of the way.

The remaining emptiness should have been softened with greenery. Large leafy plants and delicate potted palms, swaying in the gentle air currents created by guests idly strolling by.

Momentarily blinded by the flash of a blade slicing through a frond, Peg covered her mouth, repressing a scream.

"What's wrong?" Katie swung around and faced her.

"Nothing," Peg quickly answered. She glanced around and saw only the over-crowded expanse of the Long Gallery.

"Are you sure?" Katie had stopped for a moment, looking back at Peg with concern. "You look a bit..."

There were no glinting blades or undulating palms here.

Yeah, I'm all right. Peg nodded and flashed the best I-feel-fine smile she could muster.

Katie would probably have thought Peg certifiable.

I'd certify myself.

"Come on, the Dining Room is next." Katie waved for her to catch up.

Peg didn't want to go into the Dining Room.

What if she saw something in there that wasn't there?

She didn't want her increasing discomfort to grow. And she didn't want to make a scene.

She could imagine the headline from the *Evening Standard*: *American Tourist Flips Out in British Manor Museum*

"Come on! What are you waiting for?" Katie called from the next room.

Peg stared at the floor, held her breath and reluctantly proceeded into the Dining Room.

Katie gasped with pleasure. "Isn't this absolutely beautiful? Those vine motifs are so intricate."

At first, Peg was afraid to look. She closed her eyes tight, refusing to see anything. Her curiosity got the better of her and she pried one eye open for a little peek, allowing the view of her surroundings in bit by bit. She soon had both eyes wide open to take in the six ivory-inlaid mahogany sideboards lined against the pale lavender walls, three on the left and three on the right.

She felt the tightness in her stomach subside when nothing, absolutely nothing, looked familiar.

"Look at that table!" Katie cried.

In the center of the room sat a very long, exquisitely set table. Silverware, china, and three crystal glasses per setting waited for guests to take their meal.

"I swear, even a McDonald's burger would taste good on those."

By the time Peg moved on to the Great Salon, she had, for the most part, dismissed her prior uneasiness. Decorated in white and gold, it was clear the enormous, opulent room was used for formal social gatherings.

Peg searched for something familiar, hoping she wouldn't

find it. She felt nothing when she looked at the cream-colored brocade covering the walls. And again, she felt nothing when she studied the white doors, surrounding molding, and ceiling.

She felt much better.

Peg followed Katie through a sitting room and two more beautiful state rooms.

Nothing, nothing, and again, nothing. It was a relief.

The more time had passed, the more Peg could believe that she must have imagined it all.

It was so silly.

Inside the private study, a massive desk sat across from a fireplace, with a less ornate, less decorative, less offensive chimneypiece than the Front Parlor.

Opposite the door leading to the hall was a set of columns supporting an archway to a small alcove with a window. The side where the desk sat had been roped off. The top left drawer of the desk stood open and a false back had been partially removed, revealing a secret compartment in the back of the drawer.

"This says, Samuel Bevans, solicitor, and owner of Saffron Hall, kept the Tontine papers in that secret compartment." Katie indicated the open desk drawer.

"Tontine? What's a tontine?" Peg asked.

Katie studied the pamphlet until she found the explanation and quickly read it to herself. Narrowing her eyes in concentration, she delivered a condensed version. "Basically, it's when a bunch of people get together and bet on who lives the longest. In this case, it was several fathers, each betting their son would be the survivor of the group." She widened her eyes. "That's pretty cold."

"Lord Alison was the winner, and that's why we're here?"

"That's what this says." Katie pointed to the section on the page she'd just read.

Footfalls from behind them sounded, growing louder as the person approached. Peg recognized the woman as the lady who had given out the pamphlets at the information table in the Entrance Hall.

"Just on my rounds, stretching my legs a bit." She smiled in a warm, friendly manner. The small badge pinned on the upper right side of her cardigan read: Mrs Andrews. "Are you ladies interested in the Alison Tontine?"

To hear Lord Alison's name uttered by a stranger and in a native English accent set a chill down Peg's spine.

Katie wasn't shy, and she responded right away. "Yes. We're staying at Ashworth House in Kensington. We've heard we could find more information about Viscount Alison here so we came to check it out."

"Ah yes, Viscount Alison." Apparently, Mrs Andrews was an automated fountain of knowledge on that topic, and Katie had found the ON switch. "The sixth Viscount Alison was the winner of the tontine, you know."

"Was he?" Katie replied all wide-eyed, and in a tone filled with exaggerated interest, encouraging Mrs Andrews to continue.

"Oh, yes. Our Mr Samuel Bevans was the last to oversee the tontine and he continued to keep the matter a secret for his whole life. When the tontine ended, he destroyed the papers, but we've managed to learn some of the details from his personal diaries."

"Really? I didn't see anything about that in here." Katie held up the pamphlet, showing Mrs Andrews the source of their information.

"No, you won't find it in there. That's just an overview of Saffron Hall. There are too many details to include them all." Mrs Andrews looked from Katie to Peg. She must have decided she had an attentive audience and continued. "The Alison

Tontine began with fifteen members. With the mortality rate as high as it was back then, only five survived until the age of twenty."

"Five, that's all?" Peg felt the air thicken. Her concentration started to wane and her hearing faded in and out, catching only portions of Mrs Andrews' discourse.

"...each man dropped a plum on his son..."

Was it just happening to her? Peg couldn't understand why Katie didn't get the heebie-jeebies standing in here.

"...one man named his son *Chance* hoping it would bring him good luck..."

After staring at the door pediment, Peg followed the line of the wall motif, focusing on anything but her growing uneasiness.

"...April of 1813, there was a hunting accident that started a rash of deaths..."

Peg glanced at the heavily draped window. She swallowed and drew in a deep breath.

"...the last three died within the same week of July. One could almost believe..."

Without laying a finger on the long drapes, standing several feet from her reach, Peg knew they were thick and plush to the touch as if she could recall crushing it with her hand.

"...case of food poisoning, from what we can tell..."

She knew the feeling well.

"...at the time, the best estimate was a heart attack, but..."

Peg cringed when she could feel the softness of the velvet curtain crushed in her hand.

"...perhaps a robbery, the injury resulting..."

She rubbed her hands together, trying to erase the unwanted sensation.

Mrs Andrews had stopped talking, she must have finished.

Peg heard Katie thanking the docent for the detailed explanation, and then Mrs Andrews continued her rounds.

"It certainly throws your Lord Alison in a bad light. There's no way all those deaths were coincidences." Katie looked up at Peg.

"You're making it sound as if he's a murderer."

"Not me." Katie pointed down the hallway. "She's the one who said the last four deaths were suspicious."

"He didn't do it," Peg stated with conviction.

"There's no way you can be sure. All that happened over two hundred years ago. How would you know?"

"I don't know..." Peg murmured. "I just do."

CHAPTER 2

ALL THE STRANGE feelings Peg had experienced at Saffron Hall evaporated by the time she and Katie took a tasty tea at Brown's Hotel on Albemarle Street at the end of their shopping.

Nothing rooted one better in the twenty-first century than hours and hours of shopping in modern day London. The newest fashions in European-style clothes, the exorbitant prices to go with them, and nice foreign transaction-free US credit cards to apply the charges.

It really was silly, Peg thought. Believing that weird stuff was happening at Saffron Hall.

This was the twenty-first century for heaven's sakes. The real world. And nothing the slightest bit weird or even on the unusual side had ever happened to her before. She never believed in vampires, ghosts, or any other kind of paranormal hocus pocus, and she wasn't about to start now.

Disembarking at their Tube station, Peg and Katie carried several shopping bags. The guilt in overspending outweighed the number of packages they carried to Ashworth House, so they didn't call for a cab.

They weren't all that far from home. It was only a few

blocks away. Walking to their townhouse had never seemed to take much time as it had today. It was the very same couple of blocks they had always traveled, however, this journey seemed twice as long.

"What do you think about going back to Russell Street tomorrow?" Katie might have gestured if her arms weren't burdened with shopping bags. "We didn't have a chance to browse all the bookstores when we were there."

"Oh, yeah." Peg remembered they had talked about returning to that area while they sat on one of the benches outside the British Museum. They both lived by the rule: So many books, so little time.

"And maybe we can stop by that Mediterranean place we saw for lunch."

"Lunch? Wait a minute." Peg stopped for a second then caught up to Katie. "Today's Monday, and tonight is the re-creation ball. Will we be awake in time for lunch?"

"I know we'll be out late tonight and we'll probably sleep in a bit. I'm sure we'll be up before noon."

"Before we set our plans in stone we should ask around and see what the rest of the group want to do."

"I suppose." Katie's sigh of disappointment could not be ignored. "I guess you're right."

"You always have Paul," Peg suggested. "Since he's alive and breathing, he'll need to be fed. If we don't end up going together, you can take him to lunch."

Katie made an oh-aren't-you-clever face. She paused before turning into the walkway of their townhouse. "Who's the big shot driving the Aston Martin parked in front of our house?"

Peg didn't take much notice of the car and paused on the sidewalk. "Here, hold on to these while I get my keys." She stacked her bags in Katie's arms, blocking her face.

"Hey! I can't see."

"Just don't move." Peg unzipped the front of her purse; she was sure this is where she'd put them. "They're somewhere in here. Why couldn't this place use a keycard like other hotels?"

"Why couldn't this place have a butler?" Katie said from behind the shopping bags. "Or at least a couple of footmen."

"Dream on." Peg snickered, heading carefully down the walkway to the house, now searching the purse's main compartment, digging around her wallet. "I know they're in here someplace." She gave the pouch a shake. "I can hear them."

When she pulled the two keys on a ring with a distinctive Ashworth House keychain free, they slipped from her fingers, falling not only to the ground but into the bushes on the right side of the walk. Peg knelt to retrieve them.

The door opened. An abrupt shuffle and panicked sidestepping of feet told her someone had nearly tripped over her.

"I beg your pardon." Peg heard in the most distinguished British accent, but she did not look up. "Do you require some assistance?" he asked in that upper-class to-die-for pronunciation.

Still looking at the ground, with her keys in hand, Peg saw an amazingly shiny pair of black cap-toe shoes.

As she began to rise, Peg spied the deep crease running down a pair of legs clad in gray slacks. Straightening even further, she saw the man's striped tie with a coordinating pocket square tucked into the breast pocket of his jacket.

Now standing, Peg stared into his face.

His patrician nose was perfectly straight, and his light hazel eyes sparkled with intrigue, adding to his already handsome face. His medium brown hair had been cut and styled into absolute perfection.

"No, it's all right. I got 'em." Peg held up her keys for the English gentleman, the extremely *good-looking* English gentleman, to see.

His cool stare bore straight into her eyes an instant before proclaiming, "Well-done, you. I'll bid good day to you then, ladies." He made an ever-so-slight incline of his head and continued on his way.

Katie peered at him from behind the tall pile in her arms. Peg moved toward Katie on the sidewalk and they both watched him walk to a gleaming, dark green car parked on the street, hop in, and drive off.

"Wow," was all Katie said.

"You can say that again," Peg returned.

"*Wow*."

When the car turned the corner, Peg rose out of her daze, gave Katie a nudge, and held the front door open.

"That was a pleasant and unexpected English sight," Katie said, passing Peg with her armful of their shopping spoils. "*Wow*."

Katie headed straight for the front desk. She rested her arms on the counter, leaned forward and said, "Excuse me, Mrs Taggart."

The hotel manager set aside the ledger and turned toward the reception desk.

"Who was that—um, very distinguished, handsome gentleman that just left here?"

Mrs Taggart proceeded with a very knowing smile. "That was the owner of Ashworth House, Viscount Alison."

"Is he related to Lady Margaret's Viscount Alison?"

"A direct descendant," Mrs Taggart stated with pride. "He's that Lord Alison's great-great-great-great grandson."

It's too bad the current viscount didn't resemble the sixth viscount. Not to say the current viscount wasn't attractive, because he was. Peg just had a thing for the sixth one, that's all.

Perhaps the present viscount took after Lady Margaret's side of the family, and how many other families as the generations went on? The family resemblance on the paternal side had been lost. Lord Alison's dark eyes and blond hair were such a striking contrast. A feature Peg would have liked to have seen close-up and personal.

Mrs Taggart set a small, paper-wrapped parcel tied with string on the counter.

"Margaret." Mrs Taggart lightly tapped two fingers on the parcel, giving Peg an odd sort of look. "Lord Alison left this for ye." Mrs Taggart slid the package toward Peg. Katie's eyes went wide and her mouth dropped open.

"For me?" Peg felt as surprised as Katie looked.

"I thought you said you didn't know anyone here, Margaret?"

"I don't." Peg eyed the package, still confused by its presence. "Are you sure this is for me?"

"He was quite specific. I'm surprised he didn't say somethin' to ye on his way out."

"But he doesn't know me." Peg took the package, sliding. "I don't know him either."

"Aren't you going to open it?" Katie urged. Mrs Taggart looked on with a wide, encouraging smile.

Peg looked from Katie to Mrs Taggart. By the expectant expressions, both were dying to know what was inside.

"I think I'll wait until I get to my room." Peg gathered her shopping bags while holding the parcel securely in her hand. She heard the quiet, but audible, harrumphs that told her the others were not happy with her decision.

Why Peg didn't toss her purchases on the bed and immediately rip open the package the second she closed the door to her room, she didn't know. Was she scared? Or was the mystery so delicious she wanted the anticipation to last? To be honest, she was a bit frightened.

Peg laid the parcel on the table and set her shopping bags next to the sofa.

It looked like something one would see in a museum. The brownish color of the wrapping paper was not its original coloring. She knew it must have been almost white, but had yellowed with age. Nearing for a closer look, she felt the edges of the package and ran her finger along the string.

It was brittle and dry.

From the way the package was bound, it was all too apparent someone wanted to make sure the parcel remained undisturbed.

It looked old.

Really old.

The paper, it was rigid and cracked in places. Well, it wasn't exactly paper, the wrapping was thicker. More like old-fashioned parchment. She could make out what she thought was the spine of a book and the sharp corners at the edges of a hard book cover.

Pulling the string to unravel the bow. Even that was stiff with age. The strands that crossed and rounded the edges had to be pried off. It had solidified into position as if it had been there for centuries.

But of course, this couldn't have been that old.

Peg freed the book from its confines. It was in beautiful condition. The leather on the book was soft, surprisingly so. She turned the spine right-side-up to read the title:

Childe Harold's Pilgrimage
Lord Byron

Peg turned to the inside cover, there was an inscription.

To my dear Lady Margaret,
À tout moment.
Yrs B

Lady Margaret?

Could this have been signed by Lord Byron himself? That sounded crazy. Maybe the original Lord Alison was somehow the mysterious B? With the name of Brandon, Billy, or Bertram.

But why would this book be given to Peg? And why on earth would a twenty-first century English aristocrat bother delivering it to an American tourist? This didn't make any sense. The only reason he noticed her was that he almost tripped over her when he left the house.

She felt the urge to run downstairs and show the book to Mrs Taggart. Maybe she could clear this up. Maybe the owner, *his lordship*, had an odd sense of humor. Maybe this was all a practical joke?

Eyeing the pristine first edition, Peg decided it would have been a very expensive practical joke.

She wanted to tell Katie. Certainly, she could come up with a psychological answer, or a snappy response at least. But Peg knew she would just have to wait. All the guests would be making their last-minute preparations before the re-creation ball. It was an evening that was promised to be the be-all and end-all of their Regency tour, lasting well into the wee hours of the morning just as balls did more than two centuries ago. Byron's book and all the questions that came with it would just have to wait until later.

Peg set the book aside when she changed into the cotton chemise she had adapted as sleepwear since coming to England.

Moving to the window to draw the curtains, Peg thought it odd that while it was still full daylight, it seemed a bit early for what she thought was fog. Would it be chilly this evening? Maybe she would need to bring a wrap.

Peg took up the book, held it close and slipped into bed to rest. She didn't think she could fall asleep, not with all the unanswered questions roiling around in her head.

Why did Lord Alison bring her this book? And what did the book mean? Who was the mysterious B? And why, because she was not tired, did she have a problem keeping her eyes open?

She moved her fingertips back and forth, feeling the softness of the cover.

Only a few minutes passed before a desperate last, waking thought plagued her as she slipped from the conscious world into one of dreams.

She should not fall asleep.

"Lady Margaret, it is time to wake." There was the sound of heavy cloth rustling.

Lady Margaret? Peg lifted her head, roused from a deep sleep. Who was in her room? She could barely pry her eyelids open.

"It's only Betsy, your ladyship." With the drapes thrown aside, late afternoon sunlight softly illuminated the room.

Betsy? Peg didn't know anyone named Betsy.

"Did not mean to frighten you, ma'am." The stranger was dressed in a brown serge dress with a small white apron and matching mob cap.

No jeans, tee shirts, or Sketchers.

But Betsy, in her role as a maid, said no more and continued to move about the room. Sitting up in bed, Peg realized this must have been part of her Regency era experience, part of her tour.

She heard the sound of clinking porcelain coming from the

other side of the room before the maid brought a cup. This was unbelievable. These people really knew how to give a real Regency feel to the guests' experiences.

This all felt awkward but Peg was willing to go along with the play-acting. Attending a London ball was something she'd always dreamt. She rubbed her eyes and smiled.

All this was truly amazing. Peg set the book on the nightstand and accepted the cup of tea. "This is so wonderful, thank you," she replied, savoring the experience.

Betsy stepped back wide-eyed, staring hard at Peg. "Are you feeling all right, ma'am?"

Peg blew on the tea, knowing it was too hot to drink. "Quite well. Why do you ask?"

"Your voice," she whispered, covering her own throat, looking frightened.

"Is there something wrong with my—" Peg mimicked the maid's gesture, bringing her hand to her neck.

"It sounds strange, if you don't mind me sayin', my lady."

Peg knew it was her accent. The American accent didn't fit in with the Lady Margaret persona. And Peg knew exactly how to remedy that. It was ever so simple for her to slip into the alter ego of *Lady Margaret* she assumed for formal Regency functions at home. With a slight rise in the pitch of her voice, she rounded her vowels and took on an aristocratic air.

"Am I improved?" she asked.

"Yes, ma'am," the maid replied and smiled, looking greatly relieved. "Nora will be in with your dress soon."

Peg nodded. Nora must be acting as a lady's maid, for there was no other reason for her to have Peg's costume for this evening.

There was a scratch on the door before Nora entered, carrying an armful of what looked like cotton candy.

The look on Peg's face must have alarmed the lady's maid.

"Yesterday you said you were to wear your new pink crepe frock with the gold buttons, my lady."

Peg didn't know what Nora was talking about but went along with the play-acting. "Then that it will be," she agreed.

Peg had never experienced such detailed role-playing and had no idea it would start before the assembly. The London chapter was hosting the ball that evening and if they wanted to try something different this year, she'd play along.

Nora laid the dress out on the counterpane. It was clearly a better design, material, and color than the dress Peg had brought from home to wear. Still, she wondered what had become of her own costume.

Peg fingered the dress, admiring it. Sliding her fingers under the bodice, she discovered the gown was nearly transparent.

"The slip, my lady." Nora laid the equally thin undergarment next to the dress.

"Where are the pantalets?"

"You do not own any, ma'am." Nora looked startled and exchanged an alarmed look with the maid.

She's got to be kidding.

"I'm not going out in public without..." Peg trailed off. Underwear, knickers, or what the Brits called pants, is what she thought. She slid out of bed and strode to the free-standing wardrobe. The edges of the scrolls and carvings looked deep and sharp, making the antique look like new furniture.

Peg pulled open the door and stared inside. Not only were her bikini briefs missing, but all her clothes had disappeared, replaced by other linen and folded garments.

What had happened to her clothes? It must have been some kind of optical illusion, some trick of the light or...she didn't know what. Peg wasn't about to miss the ball, but showing up without wearing anything under this dress'...no.

"Are there not any drawers?"

"I have a pair," Nora confessed, her voice timid.

"May I borrow them?" Peg asked.

"Yes, ma'am, if you insist." Nora and the maid exchanged nervous glances again. "But they are woolen, not at all fine or fashionable."

"I don't care. They will do."

Nora bobbed a curtsy and left the room, following Betsy who had made a hasty, quiet exit first.

Peg took this moment alone to slip across the hall to the bathroom. Stepping out into the empty hallway, she drew open the door to the W.C. and gasped.

In a room where she would have sworn up-to-date plumbing facilities once stood now lay a room half the size she remembered, filled with different types of bed linens and household supplies.

CHAPTER 3

What happened to the bathroom?

"Are you in need of something, ma'am?"

The loo, Peg thought, feeling nearly crossed-eyed with confusion. She swung around to face Nora who had the woolen drawers draped over her arm.

"Christine did not forget to replace your chamber pot again, did she?"

Chamber pot? Then Peg remembered this evening's event, the re-creation ball. This all must be a part of the re-enactment. Of course, the management and staff of Ashworth House would cooperate in any way they could. But hiding her clothes and sealing up the bathrooms was going a bit too far.

Nora entered Peg's room and knelt, retrieving a large, flowered-porcelain bowl from under the bed.

It was a chamber pot.

Nora offered it to Peg. Did Nora really expect her to use this thing?

"I don't think so." She held up her hand, keeping the device at a distance, attempting a smile and felt the sides of her mouth twitch upward. They certainly took their re-enactment seriously in England.

Nora handed Peg a thin silk slip. Peg stepped out of her chemise, slid on the slip and stepped into the woolen drawers. Next came a pair of pale pink stockings. Peg pulled them on her legs and fastened the garters above each knee.

A pair of pink satin slippers were set before her. Nora held each in place for Peg to step into before going through another elaborate procedure to fasten them.

Was everything such a ritual?

"Shall we put sausage curls on the sides tonight?" Nora asked, preparing the nasty looking curling tongs next to the dressing table.

Peg knew her straight hair never held the slightest curl even a blow dryer, hot rollers, or electric curling iron. Good luck, Peg thought and sat at the dressing table, watching Nora go to work.

The uncomfortable tugging and the heat of the tongs reminded Peg to sit very still. She hoped that Nora knew what she was doing. One false move and it would be a singe, smoke, then a burned spot on her scalp.

"Here we are," Nora announced. "Ready in no time at all."

Ten minutes later, Peg saw the first strand of hair spring into the curliest of ringlets she had ever seen.

It took a good full hour for Nora to wield the old-fashioned curling irons, turning Peg's once straight hair into a mass of curls then another half hour to style it into a breathtaking master-piece. Her hair had never looked better.

When Nora had finished, she helped Peg into her dress and fastened the strings tightly under her arms and used several straight pins for a better fit. It felt snug, but not so uncomfort-able she couldn't bear it for an evening.

Peg had seen many pictures of Regency dresses and

authentic ones at various museums and even modeled a few, but those had been old and their material thin.

This was exquisite. The dress was new. Its thinness was a characteristic of its material rather than being worn from age.

It wasn't until Peg don the dress did she realize the low cut of the décolletage. Peg wanted to be tactful. "This neckline," she pointed out to Nora.

"Yes, my lady?"

"It's so... so...low." Nonexistent is what Peg really thought. Nora seemed unconcerned about the decency of the dress.

"It is one of your more conservative gowns."

"It is?" Peg blinked, clutching at the nearly non-existent neckline. She felt the dress pull taut across her breasts when Nora fastened the back.

"Very fine golden buttons, ma'am. It's going to take an hour just to do all these up." Nora giggled. "Lor, if this don't make a gent stare. You'll have your pick of 'em tonight for sure."

❦

Peg descended the stairs dressed as a perfect Regency lady. There was nothing she wanted more than to compare herself to the real Lady Margaret. As if she could compare herself to someone who died two centuries ago. Tonight she felt every bit of a lady as her rival. The urge to face the portrait this evening was strong and she headed for the front parlor.

Walking down the hall, she noticed the indoor lighting seemed dimmer. Not darker, but softer. It was strange, she thought, she hadn't run into a single person. She had expected to see other guests waiting about in similar dress to leave for the ball. Where were they? Peg entered the parlor and stopped in her tracks, staring in shock at the painting.

It was a portrait of Lady Margaret...of *only* Lady Margaret.

They...someone had changed it, but why?

What happened to the painting with Viscount Alison? She looked around. It was nowhere in sight.

A woman's shriek of laughter filled the air, followed by the low rumble of man's raucous chuckle. Peg ran down the hall, following the sounds and came to a stop in the doorway of the dining room.

A man, for Peg could plainly see he was no *gentleman*, had one of the kitchen maids cradled on his lap. The robust, blonde maid giggled with delight, kicking up her skirts.

"Dor-rie," he rolled the 'r' in his throat, in a display of pleasure, and proceeded to bury his face in her ample cleavage.

"Lady Margaret!" Dorrie panicked, managing to struggle free, leaping from the man's lap, and slapping his hands away. He yelped and laughed.

Peg could do nothing more than stand there and stare.

Dorrie hurried back to the kitchen, doing her best to curb her delight by masking it with a half-hearted look of shame Peg found unconvincing.

The man rocked his head back and laughed again. He took up his teacup from its saucer and drained it in a single swallow.

He was revolting. He acted just like her brother Jerry, lecherous and juvenile. He probably thought he was God's gift to women, just as her own brother did.

"Please, do spare me." He held up a hand. "I know, I know, you feel as Gerald Ashworth, Viscount Sinclair" —he placed his hand to his heart, showing appropriate humility— "I should show more decency than to degrade myself by groping the help. I know how heartily you disapprove, I simply can't help myself." Gerald lifted a newspaper and leafed through the pages.

If he was supposed to be Gerald Ashworth that would make him Lady Margaret's brother. This *Gerald* was not one of the guests taking on the role. Peg had never seen him before.

Perhaps he was an actor, just as she had assumed the role of Lady Margaret.

With that mountain of hair, those sideburns and with his face smothered behind the multiple folds of his cravat, who could tell what he really looked like. From what she could remember reading from the family information display, Lady Margaret's brother Gerald had died in a duel. The way this guest portrayed the late Gerald Ashworth, Peg could imagine the duel might have taken place with some lady's jealous husband.

But Peg wasn't about to ruin the fun for everyone just because of this one person. She would play along. And she would not allow his bad behavior to bother her evening's enjoyment.

"I take it, you're finally ready?" he said in a not-so-kind-tone. Gerald allowed the top half of the paper to fall back, folding the paper in half.

"I am," she returned with equal intensity.

"I never could understand why you need to *make an entrance*." Gerald stood, dropped the paper on the table and pulled firmly down on his waistcoat, removing the wrinkles. He left the room, brushing right by Peg without a further word.

Peg glanced down at the paper.

The London Gazette
July 5, 1813

It was the details down to the dated newspaper that made the play-acting all the more real.

She followed him, *her brother*, to the foyer.

"Lady Margaret, your cape." A butler, who never hinted he was anything but a butler, held the garment. There hadn't been a butler yesterday, nor this morning. Peg moved down the hallway toward him and tried not to stare but gave him a fast once over. Must have been another actor, the butler was a very convincing Jeeves type.

She turned her back to him and faced what should have been the front desk, hidden behind wood paneling, looking as seamless as always when closed. Peg felt the weight of the cape settled neatly on her shoulders.

The sound of the door opening drew her attention. The butler stood stationary, waiting for Peg to exit. Stepping outside, she expected to see some sort of car or van, something other than what was there: a crested, horse-drawn carriage.

This was, much, too much detail. Almost to the point of overwhelming her.

A footman in dark green and black livery opened the carriage door and handed her up. Peg felt like Cinderella going to the Prince's ball.

That dream-balloon quickly deflated when she spotted Gerald inside. In the story of Cinderella, Peg thought the rat drove, not rode. She took the opposite bench and the door slammed closed behind her.

"Are we the last two?" she wondered aloud.

"I wouldn't doubt it for a minute," came the unexpected answer.

Peg could have kicked herself for speaking out loud. She didn't want to start a conversation. She felt too... Well, something didn't feel quite right about all this. Peg kept to her corner.

Actor or not, guest or not, Peg would keep her eye on this... *Gerald.* She hoped whoever he was would remember he was supposed to be her brother and keep his hands to himself.

Gerald tapped on the roof, signaling the coach to depart. He crossed his legs at the knee and placed his outstretched arm across the back of the seat, looking comfortable, as if this mode of travel were an everyday occurrence.

Peg remained still, waiting to see what he would do next. Would he just sit there and stare at her with that smirk on his face? Or would he try and start a conversation? Peg preferred to pass the time in silence, icy as it was.

Gerald uncrossed his legs and leaned in her direction. His hand reached out, nearing her face. "I hope you don't mind."

Peg pressed back into the squabs, held her breath and readied herself to scream. She'd bite his hand off before she would let him touch her.

Except his hand kept on going, avoiding her face and took hold of the shade near the window and drew it down next to her. By the time he had closed all the shades on her side, Peg chided herself for being so silly.

What did she think he would do to her?

As convincing a performance as he had given at Ashworth House of an aristocratic rogue, this man was an actor and not really Lady Margaret's brother Gerald.

It wasn't until the carriage rolled to a stop that she realized all modern sounds, along with the sights, must have been closed off with the shades shut. The only sounds she remembered hearing were the clip-clops of the horses' hooves, drawing the transport to their destination.

When the door opened, Gerald leaped out first and dashed off, leaving one of the liveried footmen to help Peg down. She couldn't see much in the inadequate outdoor lighting and followed the few remaining, last-minute guests into the building before her. It was a grand house, that much she could see.

Peg's first impression was this must have been a museum and not some assembly hall rental. As she took in her setting and noted the details around her, the word *extravagant* surfaced over and over in her mind. The highly polished marble tiles in the foyer, the elaborately carved columns that flanked the archway leading to the main part of the house and the high-quality antiques decorating every room. Here they were generously applied with wide brush strokes slathered on in rich, obvious detail.

Re-enactment parties at home were simple, being held in a large public room with a piano and perhaps a violin or a harp for music for dancing. Small details were set into place to imply the flavor of the Regency period. There were no ornate decorations and definitely no liveried footmen.

Bathed in light from a thousand candles, the guests and embellishments of this room sparkled with a magical glow. With the wide, smooth wood floor allowing guests plenty of room to dance there was no mistaking this was a ballroom. A twenty-piece orchestra, outfitted in period costume, played at the farthest end of the room, the sounds of their music coursed through the air. Peg could have easily have thought this all was real. But as she well knew, this was only a re-enactment.

"There you are!" Katie said with her pseudo-English accent perfectly in place.

It was a pseudo-accent, wasn't it?

"I thought you would never arrive." Katie drew Peg off to one side. "Now tell me before some dashing young Gallant steals you away. What was in that package?"

"Package?" Peg repeated, studying Katie a bit closer. This was Katie, wasn't it? Somehow, she looked different. Peg couldn't tell if it was a new hairstyle or the period dress that had so drastically altered her friend's appearance but there was something about her that didn't seem quite right.

"You know very well what package to which I am referring. I was with you this afternoon when it arrived."

"Oh, *the package*," Peg remembered. Had it been just this afternoon? It seemed as if it had happened ages ago. "It was a book."

"A book?" The answer did not seem to please Katie.

"*Childe Harold's Pilgrimage.*"

"Really?" Katie's original look of disappointment blossomed into one of acute interest. "I thought it was Desmond you fancied."

Desmond?

Gazing across the room, Katie drew open her fan and moved it with a smooth, deliberate motion, fanning her face. "I understand. You are waiting to see what each has to offer, are you not?"

"Katie!" Peg snapped, feeling a bit short-tempered by her unusual, unexpected surroundings. It was becoming all too much. "You haven't said one single word that's made any sense."

"Do not concern yourself any further" —Katie looked across the room, making a pretense of ignoring Peg— "I am only your closest of friends, why should you confide in me?"

Peg did not have a chance to respond. An extremely handsome, exquisitely dressed gentleman approached. Katie sighed as if her fondest wish had just come true.

"Excuse me, I do hate to interrupt you lovely ladies." He gave a low, magnificent bow. "Lady Catherine, I wish to claim my dance."

"And so you shall." She gave him a dazzling smile and offered her hand. "*Au revoir*, dear," she said, leaving Peg.

Au revoir, *indeed*.

Peg watched the couple step onto the dance floor. Dressed in early nineteenth century finery and in these magnificent authentic surroundings, the guests seemed to be standing straighter, gliding with more fluid movements, and looking more splendid than in any other re-creation event she had attended at home.

Did an English upbringing really have such a diverse effect? That couldn't have been the answer, as not all the guests were English. It was amazing how much more gracefully the ladies moved. The men carried themselves altogether more regally.

Peg watched the concentration on the faces of the dancing couples. They had entirely focused on their partner, never looking away. There were no amateurs in attendance here.

And more strange, Peg thought, she didn't seem to recognize anyone. Surely some other people than Katie from her tour group were around.

Then she saw a man heading in her direction. A very handsome gentleman with a pronounced limp. His dark profusion of loose curls cascaded over his wide forehead.

"Lady Margaret," he greeted her. Peg had never heard a voice like his. It was low with an intriguing lure. The sides of his wide mouth turned down at the corners. His full lips compensated for the morose look by the promise of a smile that might appear at any moment. "Since I am unable to dance, would you do me the honor of conversing with me?"

Peg resisted the urge to look down at his feet. After all, she had noticed he was limping. Before she could answer, he laced her arm through his, trapping her hand in the crook of his elbow. He showed no intention of surrendering his hold and led her away from the dancing couples.

"I must know," he continued, speaking just above a whisper. "Have you received the parcel I sent?"

His parcel? This was just one more uncertainty among the many that she had come across today. He was certainly not the one who had delivered her the Lord Byron book.

Byron? Peg realized that she did recognize him.

Well, of course, he wasn't the real Byron. A second look at the gentleman told Peg he bore a resemblance, a very convincing one, to the late poet. He must be a celebrity impersonator. Of course, they must have them in England just as they had in the US.

He stopped and placed his pale, almost delicate hand over his heart. "It is only the smallest of tokens. I had hoped it would please you."

The book was signed with the initial 'B'. Then the 'B' must have stood for—

The name 'Lord Byron' shrieked through the air.

An elderly woman with three enormous white ostrich plumes waving high over her head approached. Almost immediately the surrounding guests resume their previous activity after being interrupted by this lady's entrance.

"Lady Melbourne, my immense pleasure as always," he greeted her and bowed.

"I do feel I should warn you," she said in a hushed tone, drawing near to him for a few confidential words.

"Warn me? Of what, my lady?" he said, remaining on the whole, entirely unconcerned.

"Caro, she is here. I imagine probably watching you this very moment."

Caro? Caroline? This Lady Melbourne could not possibly mean Lady Caroline Lamb.

Lady Caroline? Lord Byron?

What was happening? This was unbelievable.

"Lady Caroline is no longer any concern of mine. As you can see" —he cast a smoldering look at Peg— "my *interest* lies elsewhere."

The dinner gong sounded in the background.

"She may do something rash," Lady Melbourne insisted.

"Please, if she cares to enact the thespian arts, so much the more this ball will be remembered. Now if you will excuse me," he said, keeping a firm hold of Peg's arm and he led her aside to whisper. "I do not wish to be rude. As much as I would care to remain with you, I have promised I would escort Lady Ossulston into dinner."

"I understand completely." Peg gave her most gracious smile and felt relieved when he released his hold of her.

"Shall we say later?" His suggestion sounded more like a proposition.

"Of course," she agreed, praying all this was an act.

"If you will permit it, I should love to read some select passages to you," he whispered.

Peg could feel his intensity, his dark eyes staring deeply into hers.

"Later we shall make arrangements to meet tonight then." With a nod of his head, he left, never giving Peg a chance to answer.

She drew in a labored breath.

He was very, very convincing. That was the most realistic impersonation she had ever seen. Down to his eyes and, dare she say it, his magnetic manner.

A few minutes later, *Byron* escorted a lady, presumably Lady Ossulston, to the supper room.

A young lady with a knife in hand came out of the room in a rush. A collective gasp followed by a hushed, 'Caroline' echoed throughout the room.

"Byron!" the young woman with the knife shouted. "I mean to use this!"

"Against me, I presume," Byron replied amused. He said something more, but Peg could not make it out.

The young lady burst into tears and ran out of the ballroom. No one followed her.

Peg heard glass shatter and a woman scream. A few minutes later a blood-stained, sobbing Lady Caroline appeared with Lady Melbourne and two other women dragging her by the elbows through the parting crowd.

"Was all that real?" Peg said mostly to herself.

"I imagine so," Katie answered, now standing by Peg. "Caroline is Mistress of the Dramatic, but even she could not feign such a convincing performance."

"That's what I thought." Peg felt a wave of nausea hit. She pressed her fingers to her lips. Something told her this was no act. It all seemed too real.

"Do not think you can fool me by saying Caro was jealous of Lady Ossulston."

"I wouldn't dream of it," Peg threw out.

"I had heard it was you she saw with Byron." Katie inched closer. "Is he to be the *next*?"

Byron? The next? Peg couldn't think.

The people. The place. The time.

The time? And all this should have been a re-creation but it was too real...everything was becoming a jumble. This was her own time, wasn't it? It was growing increasingly warm and becoming harder to breathe by the minute.

"Please, I need some air." Peg left Katie and shouldered through the crowd to the terrace.

She leaned against the railing. Her knuckles whitened, gripping the edge of the balustrade to keep her balance. She closed her eyes and inhaled the cool, moist English air.

After several minutes had passed, Peg thought she should have been hearing police or ambulance sirens blaring towards them by now, not the sound of music. Moving toward the doorway, she peered into the room.

The last of the guests were leaving for the dining room. The only hurry was to be seated for dinner.

No one had dialed 9-1-1 or the British equivalent 9-9-9, and all of a sudden she knew why. She could not ignore the strangeness around her. It was all too strange. Unbelievable.

There was no phone.

There was no electricity.
There was no indoor plumbing.
There was no way this was the twenty-first century.

CHAPTER 4

This wasn't happening.

Things like this were only possible in the movies and in novels, works of fiction, not to real people.

Maybe Peg really had flipped out.

Is this what happened when one went crazy? The mind creates a safe haven and retreats from the real world. In her case, it would be Regency England...and here she was.

She'd always felt better suited to life in the nineteenth century than in her own. She secretly craved a life with Society rules and strict propriety. But to go back in time and live that life...that was impossible.

It was impossible, wasn't it?

Peg rubbed her eyes. What was she thinking?

This couldn't be real, it had to be a dream.

Only a dream.

Oh, please let this be a dream. She closed her eyes, hoping when she opened them she'd be lying in bed, waking from her afternoon's nap.

Lifting the frothy pink hem off the ground, Peg looked at the pink satin dancing slippers on her feet. They were none like she had ever owned. They must belong to Lady Margaret.

Somehow, Peg had literally stepped into Lady Margaret's shoes, into Lady Margaret's dress, and into Lady Margaret's life.

Peg began to feel a trifle dizzy. She stumbled back to sit on the bench and bent forward, placing her head between her knees.

Slow deep breaths, she repeated to herself. Drawing in careful, measured portions, she took care not to hyperventilate.

How? How could this have happened?

With her nausea and dizziness subsiding, Peg sat up. She closed her eyes and focused on sounds. The sounds she should hear in modern day London.

Cars? Airplanes? Traffic? Nothing.

She heard nothing but the music from a twenty-piece orchestra, voices, and laughter from guests attending a party inside. Once she would have given anything to be here, back when she thought it impossible.

She looked into the house. This wasn't a re-enactment, this was the real thing.

She was here. And this was all real. It must be 1813 just as she saw printed in the newspaper.

Her eyes fluttered shut. The next moment brought a second wave of dizziness. Again, down went her head between her knees, and she inhaled, slowly and deeply.

"I beg your pardon. Are you in need of some assistance?"

Peg barely heard the question through her mental mist of confusion. She tilted her head and saw a pair of men's black silk evening pumps.

Directing her eyes higher, Peg discerned a pair of shapely calves and well-toned thighs encased in a pair of evening breeches. He wore a black evening coat, and an intricately tied, snow-white cravat.

His face, she could not see. A blazing torch behind the man haloed his head in golden light, shadows obliterating the features of his face.

"Have you lost something?"

Besides my mind? "I... I..." Peg blinked and with his assistance rose to her feet.

Recognition lit his eyes. "Lady Margaret..."

He stepped to her side and the light that had blinded her now revealed her companion's face. Her breath caught in her throat when she recognized him. Viscount Alison, the man from the portrait.

"It's you, isn't it?" she whispered.

An incredible smile crossed his lips. "Why, yes it is," he replied modestly, making a minute adjustment to his cravat.

He was here.

Alive.

Flesh and blood.

Peg looked at him again and she knew she must have been staring. She could hardly believe it. For some mixed-up, crazy reason, destiny had meant for them to be together. Lady Margaret and Viscount Alison. Maybe there were some good points being Lady Margaret.

It was a glorious feeling. All the way to her weak knees that were going out from under her again. Peg began to sway. Her eyelids were growing heavy and she found it impossible to keep them open any longer.

"Hold on there, my dear." He caught hold of her hand. His other arm stole around her waist to steady her on her descent. He helped her onto the bench and settled next to her, remaining very close.

"Ouch!" Peg jerked upright. It was one of those accursed straight pins in her bodice, jabbing her.

"Are you feeling unwell? Perhaps I should see you home?"

By the way the one side of his mouth turned up and the tone of his voice, he made the offer sound a bit salacious.

"Go home?" Peg whispered, echoing a sentiment she could barely comprehend and with no hope of achieving. Then everything went black.

PEG AWOKE THE NEXT MORNING. Her memory of the party she attended last night seemed muddled and somehow had intertwined itself into her dreams, making it all impossibly confusing.

It was hard to separate the reality from the fiction. She remembered that the ball, although she did not dance, had been incredible. The dream had been, in contrast, very strange.

Something about going back in time to the nineteenth century. Something about meeting Lord Byron. And, oh yes, meeting Viscount Alison. From what she could remember, he was not the swain she had expected. As far as dreams went, she'd classify him as a bit of a disappointment.

Peg lifted her hands over her head, stretching, and smiled to herself. Wouldn't it be fun if it were really possible? It would be just like in the movie *Somewhere in Time*, in which Christopher Reeve traveled back to meet Jane Seymour.

Peg would have loved to meet the real Lord Alison. As if such things were possible. Except he'd be more inviting and charming than he had been in her dream. More like the Byron impersonator had been.

Still lingering in her wistful mood, Peg rolled out of bed and stretched again. She slipped on her wrapper, tied it at the waist, and shuffled to the bathroom across the hall.

No waiting line this morning. She'd almost welcome one. It would be a chance to hear about everyone's experiences without having to wait until she got down to the breakfast table.

She opened the bathroom door.

And screamed.

In the dimly lit, small room there was a man and a woman intertwined in passion. At first, it appeared Peg's outburst went unnoticed by them and before she could step back and close the door, the man's eyes opened, then he winked at Peg.

The man was Gerald.

Lady Margaret's brother, Gerald. How utterly, utterly horrible.

Which meant she was in the nineteenth century.

The nineteenth century. Still.

Peg slammed the door, ran back to her room. Her dream wasn't a dream. It had been real.

Real.

Then it hit her. She had really gone back in time.

Things like this didn't happen to people. But then again, wasn't this what she had wished for most of her life? This was turning out to be more of a trip than she had bargained for.

And how was she to get home?

What if she never went back?

What if she never saw her friends or family again? She'd even miss her obnoxious brother Jerry.

Peg couldn't dwell on that. She had to believe all this was temporary, like a vacation. All this might only last a couple of days, maybe even a little longer, and then she'd be back home. That would suit her for now.

She couldn't stay locked in her room until she returned to where she belonged. She'd miss the opportunity of a lifetime. If Peg was really stuck here, she'd make the best of it.

After several minutes, her anxiety subsided and Peg felt about as ready as she would ever be to start her new life and rang for Nora. She had remembered, in her dream that wasn't a dream, that several maids inhabited Lady Margaret's life.

As Lady Margaret, Peg was the daughter of an earl and had a viscount for a brother, as loathsome as he was. Peg knew the man she was to marry, even if Viscount Alison hadn't a clue.

It was a delicious secret.

For now, she could strike up a temporary friendship with Lady Catherine, who may have resembled Katie but did not behave at all like her friend. And Gerald... she could have happily done without him in her life.

After what he'd done, after what she'd seen him do, how could she ever face him?

DRESSED in a delightful green sprig muslin, Peg descended the stairs and made her usual turn about the parlor, for a portrait check, before heading to the breakfast room.

She stopped just inside the portal to the front parlor and stared at the painting. Aside from having brown hair, not even the same shade of brown, she didn't see any resemblance between her and Lady Margaret. She wondered why no one else had noticed. Peg looked the same when she looked into the mirror, but everyone seemed to think she appeared as if she were Lady Margaret.

Leaving the front parlor, she headed toward the breakfast room. Her steps slowed the closer she neared. She dreaded entering.

He would be in there. Gerald.

If they could just get past discussing this morning's horrendous encounter, he would surely prove to be a wealth of information.

Peg stepped into the room, trying to act as if nothing out of the ordinary had happened. As far as Gerald was concerned, she hated to think, perhaps nothing out of the ordinary had happened. Maybe that was how he started every day.

He sat at the breakfast table and the newspaper hid his face.

"Good morning, Gerald." Peg tried her utmost to be pleasant.

Gerald looked over the top of his paper. "Margaret," he replied, in a belittling tone. His eyebrows rose and almost touched together. He dropped the paper onto the table and burst out laughing. "You should have seen the look on your face!"

Peg felt a warm flush wash up onto her cheeks at the mere mention of the incident. She stepped to the sideboard in the pretense of pouring herself a cup of tea, but it was mostly to hide the heightened color on her cheeks.

"It was as if you'd never seen or ever done the like yourself! You'll see little sister, your time will come as well." He sounded just like a brother.

Her? As if *that* would ever happen to her.

Across the table from Gerald stood a pile of invitations. They were addressed to 'Lady Margaret White' and clearly meant for her.

White? That was odd. If she remembered correctly, Gerald's surname was Ashworth, his title, Sinclair. Their father was the Earl of Westchester.

"You're the one who's married, not I," he drawled, giving her the answer she needed.

She was already married? Peg knew Lady Margaret was to be married to Lord Alison. Obviously, she did not know the whole story. Now Peg understood why she had lacked a chaperone. Lady Margaret was a married woman with an absentee husband and perhaps questionable morals.

"This isn't your house, you know." Gerald shook his finger at her. "It's father's and someday it'll be mine, so don't be looking down your nose at me.

"At least I'm discreet about my carrying-ons. Why, you" — he grimaced— "You flaunt your affairs in front of the whole bloody country."

"Me?" Peg was shocked to learn this about herself. Correction, about Lady Margaret. She needed more information from Gerald. She was never good at manipulating people. What could she say to him?

"Everyone knows, you never make it secret. And why not? You are freed by the bonds of your unhappy arranged marriage. Your husband would do best to take the back of his hand to you. I'd not stop him. It would most probably send the old man into one of his fits." Gerald swiveled in his chair no longer facing her. "You have what you want."

So Lady Margaret's husband was old. How old?

"You have your own money, you've maintained your social position, and you've gained your freedom to do whatever you want with whomever you want. The only thing left for him to do for you is to make you a widow."

That was a nasty thing to say. There was one thing that Peg felt certain. If she now led the life of Lady Margaret, Lady Margaret was about to become a changed woman.

The butler arrived, stopping just inside the breakfast room and announced, "Your ladyship, Lady Catherine Holloway has called and awaits you in the front parlor as usual."

Not Katie but Catherine. "I shall be there momentarily," she answered.

The butler bowed and left.

"If you will excuse me, I have a visitor waiting." Peg stood and headed out of the breakfast room.

Gerald chuckled. It almost sounded evil. "Give my best to Princess Kate."

Without thinking, Peg returned, "That's the Princess of Wales." She stilled, recalling that in this century the Princess of Wales was not Catherine Middleton, but Prince George's estranged wife Caroline of Brunswick.

Peg quickly stepped out of the room. Gerald was just as infuriating as her own brother. Not even the passage of centuries could alter the combative interaction between siblings.

Some things just never changed.

She needed to take more care. She couldn't allow an automatic response to take over again. It might put her in a difficult position of having to explain herself. And an explanation, the truth, she would not tell to anyone.

Peg told herself she could pull this off. She could. She could convincingly portray a Regency Lady without getting caught. Not that she thought she was better or smarter than the people here. At least she could comprehend what had happened to her and how her actions now might have consequences for the future.

The differences in common knowledge between the nineteenth and the twenty-first centuries were many and she was no expert by any means.

She could do this. Definitely. Mentally setting herself, Peg headed out to greet her visitor.

"What a performance!" Katie exclaimed when Peg entered the front parlor. But this *Lady Catherine* was not quite the *Katie* she knew. Then Peg recalled that Gerald had called her 'Kate'.

"Do you mean Lady Caroline's?" The whole Caroline Lamb/Lord Byron incident was surreal, completely Oscar-worthy.

"Heavens no, yours." Kate made herself at home on the sofa.

"Mine?" As exciting as last night was, to Peg last night was still pretty much an indefinable blur with missing pieces. Big missing pieces.

"Be a love and have Herbert send for tea, would you? I came over as soon as I woke. I'm afraid I haven't had a bite."

"Why not come to the breakfast room and have something to eat?" Peg offered.

Kate took to her feet, ready to venture forth. "Gerald has gone, I take it."

"No, he's still here."

Kate settled back onto the sofa, planted her reticule in the middle of her lap and sighed. She looked as if she were planning to stay a while. "I believe I have lost my appetite."

So Kate did not care for Gerald. At least her new friend showed good taste. "I'll send for tea. Herbert," Peg used the name she had heard Kate call the butler. "Would you have a tray brought in please?"

Kate paid an inordinate amount of attention to the simple task of removing her gloves. "I saw you with him last night." It didn't seem *this* Kate was subtle about anything.

"Byron?"

"Not Byron, Desmond."

Desmond? Didn't Kate mean Lord Alison? Perhaps Desmond was Viscount Alison's first name.

"Are you going to tell me what happened or not?"

"What happened? When?"

Kate rolled her eyes. "With Desmond, of course." She set her gloves and reticule to one side, inching closer. "Did you, or did you not succumb?"

After a lengthy silence, Peg answered. "I did succumb." And she'd never fainted in her life.

"To Desmond?"

"To the vapors!" Peg corrected. Kate seemed a bit disappointed. "I'm afraid I swooned on the terrace. I cannot say for sure what followed. Everything went dark after that."

"I can tell you."

Peg could see that Kate was only too happy to volunteer. Her explanation was interrupted by the arrival of their tea. Kate waved Dorrie away and poured the tea herself.

"Desmond carried you through the empty ballroom while the rest of us sat at supper."

"How do *you* know?" Peg asked.

"I kept my eye on you." Kate brought the teacup to her lips, testing the temperature. She set the cup back on the saucer. "Besides, you and Desmond were the only two missing from the table. It was quite obvious to everyone the two of you must have been together." With raised eyebrows and a knowing smile, she intimated something lewd. "And we could well imagine what you two were doing."

Kate was wrong. They were all wrong.

They couldn't have guessed if they tried.

Not in a million years.

A strange, dreamy look came over Kate. She stared upward with a silly half-smile plastered on her lips and gave several deep emotional filled sighs.

"To be pressed up against that formidable chest of his...just thinking about those broad shoulders." She gave another, deeper sigh. "He must have a body of a Greek God."

Peg hated to tell Kate she was wrong. Not about Desmond's body being like that of a God's, but about how much, or how little, went on between them. Nothing.

"And he brought you home, you say?" Kate asked when she had quite recovered. Peg knew people with vivid imaginations, but Kate was something else.

"I have no idea. When I woke this morning I was in my own bed."

Kate leaned forward. "And then what?"

"And then, I suppose, I went back to sleep."

"Were you alone?" Kate sounded more angry than shocked.

"Of course I was alone." Peg did remember hearing Nora's sad voice contemplating the loss of one of the gold buttons from her pink dress that she had worn that evening.

"You never would have let such a ripe opportunity pass. That's not like you at all." Kate must have expected a more titillating version than the one Peg gave. "Who *are* you after then, Margaret? Byron?"

Byron, of all people. From what Peg knew of him, he was a poet, a bulimic, and a bisexual. She had no intention of getting close to him. In reality, the poet's attention did not flatter her, it scared her.

Kate gave a disheartened sigh. "I was hoping when we came for the Season's festivities you would stop mourning."

"Mourning?" Mourning for whom? Peg knew it was not her husband nor her father.

"I know how attached you were to him." There was a solemnness to Kate's voice that displayed some sympathy for her friend.

Him? Now who was she talking about?

"*He* wasn't your husband, so there's no need to don widow's weeds and observe an official mourning period. I had expected once we returned to London you would find someone else," Kate's voice lowered to a confidential whisper.

Someone else as in a significant other? A lover?

"I thought that someone might be Desmond." Kate stared at Peg for a reaction. "You cannot tell me you are not interested. I've seen the way you look at him."

Peg had no intention of confirming her feelings nor admitting her simple crush on a man in a painting into a proclamation of love.

"Alison's death was months ago. You can't still think you are responsible?"

Alison? Desmond? Katie spoke about them as if they were two different people.

"It was a hunting accident for heaven's sake. An accident. You were nowhere near." Kate dropped her tea set on the table with a clatter. "I gave up my new inamorato months ago to console you during your dark period. But Margaret, here we are and the Season is nearly at an end. The long, cold winter approaches. I do not wish to be without...companionship. I insist you end this foolishness. I plan to attend the Covington soiree tonight. You are as well, are you not? You promised!"

"If I promised, then, of course, I shall attend." Peg had no idea what Lady Margaret had or had not promised, but at the moment, it seemed safe enough to go along with Kate.

Kate pulled her gloves on. "It is to begin at nine o'clock, so be there by ten." She took up her reticule.

With a *tout à l'heure*, Kate left.

Kate must have passed Desmond in the front walk on her way out. Without introduction, not two minutes later, he stood where Kate had in the front parlor.

CHAPTER 5

"Pierce Desmond, at your service, my lady." Desmond's bow was low, deep and like the man, impressive. He had not appeared this charming to her last night.

"Pray, what are you doing here," —she did not know if he was a mister or a lord and kept her address to him simple— "sir?"

"It is customary to pay a call after making an acquaintance the night before," came the gentle reminder.

"But we did not dance." Peg had to draw in a deep breath and somehow appear that his presence had no effect on her.

"No. However, I do recall bringing you home. I came to see if you have recovered." His gaze swept over her, studying her from head to toe.

"I have," she responded, trying to show the manners she expected one to display at such times as this.

"And how are you feeling today?" he asked.

"I am feeling quite well. And you?" she returned, but she could see he looked to be doing nicely using nineteenth or twenty-first century standards.

"My day has improved since sharing your company." Then he smiled.

Peg wasn't sure how, but in a matter of moments, she was sitting next to him on the sofa. Actually, *he* was sitting next to *her*. Very *next* to her.

She knew she shouldn't be alone with him on the much too spacious sofa in the front parlor with the doors closed. And he looked at her as if he expected... expected something she did not want to share.

"Shall I send for a fresh tray?" she interjected before he could make an alternate suggestion of how they should pass the time.

"Only if you wish it. I have no need for tea." Desmond took one of her hands and used it to hold her near.

"Actually, I believe I am in need of some air." She launched off the sofa and out of Desmond's reach.

With his arm still draped across the sofa back, Desmond asked, "Are you going to succumb?"

"Of course not!" Was he talking about succumbing to him or the vapors? It didn't matter, she had no intention of submitting to either.

"Would you care to take the air in my curricle?"

Peg agreed, deciding she would not need to be so concerned with his hands if they were busy with the ribbons and his attention turned to his horses. While Peg collected her hat, Spencer, and reticule she wondered why she felt the need to be close to him. Would she not have fared better if she had just sent him away?

A good twenty minutes later Desmond helped her up then climbed in after her. As they drove down the street, she chanced a glance at him. He was more handsome than she remembered last night. Perhaps she thought that now because she had a better look at him in the daylight.

Peg had to remember that he was not Viscount Alison as she first thought. His name was Pierce Desmond. It might be a few years before he would come into the title and how that would happen, Peg did not know. She wasn't about to go poking around for answers just yet. After all, Peg had just met the man. And she imagined she was already half in love with him. And he was really here, sitting next to her, taking her on a drive in a tasteful dark blue curricle with a white pinstripe.

The fashionable place to go would have been Hyde Park but that was not where they were headed. They had passed the front gates a half-hour ago. The curricle rounded a corner and rolled onto a cobblestone street. They approached a small twin-gabled thatched cottage with small diamond-paned windows set in thick stone walls. It looked as if it had stood for centuries, and could easily stand for several more.

It seemed like the type of place that would rent rooms by the hour. Peg sincerely hoped that was not why she was here. The discrete sign read: *The Poached Pheasant.*

Desmond must have read the fear written on her face. "We're here for tea, you understand," he said. "I know this place is somewhat on the unusual side. However, they have a cook, Monsieur Anton, he makes the most delectable creations. Frenchies come here for that very reason."

"Is that so?" She hadn't heard about this place, maybe it no longer stood in the twenty-first century. Maybe it had been replaced by a Tesco or Sainsbury.

"This place is not exactly known for its spotless reputation."

"Exactly what does that mean?" Peg hated to speculate on such matters.

"Well, the 'poached' in the inn's name does not refer to the preparation method. It refers to how the fowl they use was obtained."

"Oh." So what he meant was illegally-procured game. That

was different. It's no wonder that they might have lost their business license in her time.

"Several hundred years ago, this was a small establishment outside the King's hunting grounds. But the word of their delicious fare has spread and it has managed to turn a nice little profit over the years." Desmond stopped the curricle in front of the cottage. "They don't do that anymore, of course. It's a pity they cannot seem to rid themselves of their bad reputation."

Once inside Peg followed Desmond through the nearly full dining room toward an empty table. The conversation sounded strange until she realized the other guests were speaking French. It was a French spoken over two hundred years earlier than she had learned, leaving the four years of high school and college foreign language education woefully out of date.

Arriving at the table, Desmond sat next to her instead of sitting across from her, well within arm's distance, which made her feel uneasy. There were no menus, and Desmond did not appear to need one.

"A selection of biscuits and cakes and a bottle of your finest claret. And, I almost forgot, we'll have the" —he snapped his fingers a few times to help him remember— "Rice mould."

Peg wondered if it was something made out of rice or something that grew on it.

Desmond gave that disarming smile that easily won her over. "You'll have to trust me on this."

Trust him? With a smile like that he could probably have anything he wanted.

The wine and two glasses arrived. "Do you imbibe?" He held up a small decanter.

It was just red wine. She could handle that.

"Yes, of course." He poured out a glass and handed it to her.

Peg took her first sip. Not bad. She relaxed, leaning against the back of the chair and took a second sip.

Seated to the table next to them there was a woman who wore a bit of lace under her fully exposed breasts out in public!

Peg choked and spit out her wine, sending it spraying across the table.

"Are you quite all right?" Desmond leaned toward her.

Peg nodded. He glanced over his shoulder looking for what had caused her reaction. When he saw the woman, he did not find it as alarming as she had. Nor did he even seem to notice. How could he not notice?

"Would you dare to adapt the fashion?" He smiled, lifting his eyebrows in concurrence.

"No," —she dabbed at her mouth with her napkin— "I do not believe so." Okay, so she was wrong. He did notice, but he certainly did not make a big deal about it.

Desmond stared more at Peg than he did at the topless patron. But didn't he think that was totally indecent?

Apparently not.

When Peg glanced around her, the other gentlemen seated in the area were busy with conversation and drink, ignoring the half-naked woman.

It was obvious Peg was the only one in the place who thought there was something wrong with the way she dressed. And what did that say about the kind of people who patronized this place?

***

SEVERAL HOURS LATER, Peg sat at her dressing table, digging through Lady Margaret's jewelry box. After what she saw this afternoon, Peg realized her wardrobe could have been much less conservative than it was. She made a silent promise to herself that she would never complain about Lady Margaret's necklines again.

Tonight she would be wearing a Pomona green silk frock with a profusion of lace, cascading down the sides of her over-skirt. Pearls would look nice. Simple yet elegant. It may not have been Lady Margaret's style but it was Peg's.

It appeared Sarah would tend to Peg's hair this evening. The maid tinkered with the curling irons, carrying them to the dressing table to begin work.

Desmond. Although he had not mentioned it earlier, Kate said he'd be there.

And she'd see him again.

"Ouch!" Peg moved out of the chair and away from the hot tongs. Sarah leaped back. The smell of burnt hair filled the room. The curling irons tumbled to the ground, scorching a spot on the rug.

"Please don't hit me again," Sarah begged, shielding her face in a gesture of protection.

"Of course not," Peg replied. She would never hit the girl. Then it dawned on Peg that perhaps Lady Margaret had.

Sarah retrieved the irons and rubbed the burned carpet with the edge of her apron.

"Do take more care," Peg hesitated to scold the girl with any more than a few cautionary words.

"Yes, my lady." Sarah stood, replacing the irons on its stand. Peg could see the maid's hands were still shaking. She really didn't want the maid-in-training close to her with those things.

Then a miracle happened. Well, almost. Nora came in, perhaps she would take over. She set a small bowl of violet-scented water on the dressing table.

"What's that for?" Peg asked.

"Will you not dampen down your chemise this evening?"

"No, I will not!" Peg refused the water, shocked at the very idea.

A look of surprise flashed across Nora's face before she took the bowl away and returned with a lace handkerchief. The lace matched that of Peg's dress exactly.

Peg took the handkerchief from Nora and eyed it. There was a small embroidered 'M' on the corner. It was not so much a handkerchief as it was a doily, nearly all tatted edging. Peg tucked it into her glove just under the button at her wrist, allowing it to trail.

To Peg's great relief, Nora took possession of the curling irons and finished her hair without further incident.

❧

PIERCE DESMOND's valet gave the back of his employer's coat a final brush, eliminating any lint that might have settled.

"Please, Rodney, that's enough! If you don't stop, you'll brush the bloody coat right off my back."

Rodney withdrew. Another five minutes with the brush would have removed the dissatisfied expression from the valet's face. But tonight Desmond could not tolerate someone flustering about him.

Inspecting himself in the glass, he smiled, satisfied with the results. Tonight, he was anxious to attend Covington's soiree. It would be where the women put on a display of their wares, and the men encouraged them.

There were women, and there were ladies. After running into Lady Margaret last night she was something far more than just a lady. There was something decidedly different about her. An elusive quality that he could not identify. He found her intriguing.

It was odd he had not taken more interest in her before now. He had known of Lady Margaret for years. Her father, the Earl of Westchester, her brother, Viscount Sinclair, her husband, the old, rich Squire White, and her last lover, Viscount Alison.

If Desmond had a say in the matter, he would be the next to fall into her bed.

In the library, he poured himself a brandy and waited until it was time to leave.

"Here you are." Chance stopped short and made a sharp right turn into the library.

"Is your room comfortable?" Desmond asked.

"Splendid. Simply splendid. You're a deuced good sport to put up with me like this."

"I'm glad for the company. It's only a few days of inconvenience." Desmond joked. "We'll be off soon."

"Weekending at a solicitor's." Chance shook his head. "I cannot think it agreeable. It's like consorting with a merchant."

"It's only once a year. Makes for good working relations," Desmond explained.

"For what we pay him, he should put us up for a month's stay in Brighton."

"Does it cost all that much?"

"You'd be surprised, Pierce. Those wretched solicitors. Not a good one in the lot. Mark my words, someday we'll discover he's up to some shady business."

"Come now, Chance. Bevans is a stout fellow. He's given me no reason to complain. In fact, there's been a substantial increase in my last quarter's earnings."

"I know, I know. Financially, he's done well for us. Perhaps too well."

"Care for some brandy?"

"Absolutely," Chance replied, looking near desperate for a drink.

Desmond retrieved a second glass of the spirit. "Can one do too well? Are you complaining that you're *too* rich? You might add *too* good looking."

"Speaking of good looking, have a look at these breeches. Bang-up to the mark, say what?"

Desmond leveled an inspecting eye at his friend. "A bit on the snug side, don't you think?" A distinctive bulge disrupted the smooth fabric across the front of his hips.

"The ladies like 'em that way. Lets them see a man's prime piece." Chance pointed to his nether regions. "The Admiral likes to show off. Sometimes just thinking of the ladies makes him stand at attention."

"Are you sure you won't scare them off?" Desmond gestured with his glass.

"Nonsense!" Chance exclaimed and chuckled.

Desmond did his best to suppress a smile. He handed Chance his brandy before easing into one of the leather, wing-backed chairs, motioning for his friend to take the other.

Chance pulled his coat tails forward and started to sit. He halted his descent mid-way, unable to continue.

"Will you be able to manage in those tonight?" On closer examination, the side seams showed minute signs of strain. "I'm not even certain they're acceptable for eveningwear."

"It ain't Almack's, you know." Chance ran his palm over the taut doeskin and straightened. "I'll be fine. They'll loosen up after a while." He made a quarter turn and struck a pose. "I'll have you know, these are my calves. No padding there." He indicated his lower limbs. "I hope Bevans has invited some extra ladies. It'd be dashed-dull without females, don't you know." He lounged against the hearth, crossing his ankles in a casual manner.

"Ah yes, the fairer sex." Desmond felt that a subject worthy of his attention.

"There's no use involving you in business matters, Pierce, is there?"

"Especially when it is nothing with which I need concern

myself. Our man of business has everything well under control. And there are so many other aspects of life to be enjoyed."

"Missed the Melbourne's do last night. Read about it in the paper, though. Lady Caroline and Lord Byron having a row over his attentions to another woman." He whistled. "You were there, weren't you?"

"As always," Desmond replied.

"Do you know who the mysterious lady was?"

"I'll ask you to keep your distance from her, if you please," Desmond warned.

"Ahh," Chance intoned. "Not only do you know who she is, you're interested in her as well I see. How goes the battle? Is she partial to you or Byron?"

"Hard to say. She doesn't seem to be particularly taken by either of us."

"And what, may I ask, is her name?" Chance inquired.

"If you behave yourself, I'll introduce you." Desmond took a deep drink from his glass, pondering silent, delicious thoughts of said lady.

᪑

PROMPTLY AT TEN, Gerald escorted Peg to the Covington residence. After greeting the hostess upon entering, he led Peg farther inside. Looking about the room, she thought the music and dancing was everything a perfect Regency evening should be and hoped she would be able to enjoy it all before the night was done.

Gerald leaned closer, brushing Peg's arm with his sleeve. "Look, there's Sir William Carlisle," he whispered.

Was she supposed to know who Sir William Carlisle was? Let alone pick him out of the crowd?

"He'd kill to have you back, you know." That would imply

she and Sir William had once been together. Gerald's tone suggested more than just a casual acquaintance. The comment sent a shiver down her spine.

Peg wished Gerald would just leave her as he did the night before. And it couldn't happen too soon for her.

Eventually, the voices, music, and laughter of Gerald's friends, or so Peg thought them to be, caught his attention and he went off to join them.

Once she was alone, Peg expected Kate would show herself. But she didn't. Then Peg began her search in the great parlor in a clockwise direction.

"Lady Margaret," a dark-haired gentleman called. He performed an exquisite leg. The way he looked at her, Peg could tell she was not a stranger to him.

Was this Sir William Carlisle?

"It has been a very long time, has it not?"

"Yes, it has," she agreed.

What does one say to a supposed ex-lover one doesn't remember? The way he looked at her made her think he wanted to reignite those lover-like feelings. She had no intention of encouraging him.

"And you are even more lovely than last I saw you."

Peg didn't care to know what he knew. She just wanted to get away from him, which was growing more difficult by the moment. Sir William closed in on her and she stepped back to avoid him. Within the moments of their short conversation and without her realizing he had very cleverly steered her into a secluded cove.

The way he looked at her body made her feel as if she wasn't wearing a stitch of clothing. The familiarity in his eyes frightened her.

"Meg, not even a peck on the cheek for an old love?"

Peg tried to dash by him, but he grabbed a hold of her and trapped her in the corner.

"Come on, Meg. Stop playing around." Sir William's voice changed from a comfortable civil tone to a firm and coaxing one.

Peg tried to dissuade him. "Please let me go. I am not who you think I am."

"Are you the scullery maid and I, the stable boy? Or perhaps we shall play the highwayman and the tavern wench? Oh, my dear sweet Meg, how I have missed you." Sir William smiled at her in a wicked way. He was quick to grab her by the waist and pulled her against him. "I'll do whatever you want. Now that Alison's gone, I am very interested in renewing our acquaintance."

All of a sudden, his hold changed ever-so-subtle from holding her to him to holding her against him. Sir William had managed to push her against a wall and worked one of his legs between hers.

His hot, moist mouth kissed and tasted her flesh, traveling down and around her neck to her décolletage. Peg knew the delicate material could not withstand the assault of his over-amorous hands.

She struggled to free herself. "Let me go!" But he had a tight hold of her.

"Do fight me, Meg. You know I like it rough." Sir William's mouth came down on hers in a hard, unrelenting kiss. His tongue threatened to invade her mouth and pushed against her clenched teeth.

I'll give you rough.

She jerked her knee up, catching him in the groin. Sir William's grip on her was instantly released and he folded onto the floor, curling into a fetal position with his eyes shut tight.

He had asked for it, and she had given it to him.

Peg took one last look over her shoulder at Sir William,

sucking in his colorless cheeks and looking not at all well before stepping into public view. Nothing looked amiss. None of the guests, even those standing a few feet away, had noticed anything out of the ordinary.

Not her abduction. Not the not-so-silent disposal of Sir William.

She passed behind a trio of ladies deep in juicy gossip and resumed her search for Kate. It was hard to see anyone through the mass of people. Peg decided a higher vantage point might help and headed for the staircase.

She caught sight of the dark, curly-haired Byron entering the great parlor and her heart began to pound. She didn't want to bump into him again. Now that she knew who he really was, she would do her best to avoid him. Peg slipped out through a nearby door, hoping to make a successful escape.

Finding Kate would just have to wait.

Peg shuffled down the corridor with only a whisper of her skirts sweeping the floor. Hopefully, she had escaped unnoticed by the poet and could find a place to hide until she could decide what to do next.

She stopped at the last door and took care to open and close the latch without a sound. The sole illumination inside the room was a moderate fire glowing in the hearth, casting soft shadows on the walls.

Turning around on tiptoe, Peg saw a shocking, but not a totally unfamiliar sight.

That rascal Gerald had wrapped himself around the hostess.

This time Peg had the mind not to scream and averted her eyes. This morning Gerald had his way with one of the servant girls. Now he was having his way with the hostess.

Peg thought it very bad form, especially in Lord Covington's study, on Lord Covington's desk, with Lord Covington's wife.

CHAPTER 6

She doubted Gerald or Lady Covington had noticed her presence. Peg eased out of the room as quietly as she had entered, quietly exhaling when she reached the other side of the closed door. She wanted to get away. Now—if not sooner.

In her haste, Peg's foot got tangled with the hem of her gown. She reached out to steady herself and headed down the hall back into the parlor, only to run straight into a wall.

Oof! Not a wall. It was a chest.

"I'm sorry," she apologized before she could really see who it was.

"On the contrary, I am finding this quite enjoyable," Desmond said and smiled at the mishap. He took advantage of the situation and stole his arm around her. "I can't tell you how relieved I am to see you tonight." He leaned forward and looked closely into her face. "Although, I believe you do look a bit on the pale side. Would you care to sit?"

"I feel fine, really." Peg struggled out of his arms. She didn't want to go into detail about what caused her to feel so unsettled. There was no way she would ever get used to seeing Gerald like *that*.

"Our exit from Lady Melbourne's party is one of the latest *on-dit*." When Peg did not respond, Desmond continued. "I thought it might vex you that our names have been linked."

"Why should you suppose that would upset me?" What did concern her was how physically close he seemed to be.

Desmond smiled and leaned even closer, taking up her hand. "How very happy I am to hear you say that."

"As long as you and I know there is not a shred of truth in what they say, what does it matter?"

"But I do so wish it was true," he said, his eyes sparkling. He tightened his grip, assuring she could not pull away.

As strong as her feelings were, Peg knew that would mean a deeper involvement. And she shouldn't. She might have fancied herself in love with him but acting on that impulse was another matter.

"If you do not care for me, I can always leave you to your other suitor." Desmond glanced over his shoulder. "You do know Byron is watching you like a hawk."

Circling like a vulture was more like it.

If that man was indeed the real Lord Byron, she would do best to stay clear of him. The moment Desmond stepped away, Byron's clubfoot notwithstanding, the poet would be there to take his place.

"Shall I leave, or would you like me to stay by your side?"

The casual question sounded more like a threat. His ultimatum was for her to choose the less detrimental of the two. Desmond was not at all dangerous nor loathsome, just formidable.

"I think I should warn you, he will not relent in his pursuit."

"Is he as persistent as you?" she asked, thinking perhaps she should reconsider Desmond as her safer choice. Peg would never use the word safe in regard to him either.

"I would say so. I should add that he don't treat a lady nearly as well as I."

"Such a conceited remark and from someone as humble as yourself," she replied with the lift of her brows for poignancy.

"Just a truthful one. If you should ask me to stay, I shall be the pattern card of escorts. The most attentive of *cicisbeo*."

Not a wishful lover? Because she had no intention of ever going that far. "Then yes, I prefer that you stay. But it is only to show the pretense of affection between us."

The look on Desmond's face was one of triumph. She knew he wanted to hear her say those words. It wouldn't mean he'd won.

"You would do this for me?" she asked. "Why?"

"I don't know." It appeared his answer had shocked him more than it had her. "Perhaps I feel no lady should be exposed to his unusual tastes."

It wasn't sounding good. Even Desmond must have been aware of Byron's sexual proclivities.

"As you say, it is only a pretense," he said, turning on his charm. "I fervently hope after all this that you change your mind and realize we should set aside this pretense nonsense and get on with things."

§

OVER THE NEXT FEW HOURS, Desmond kept close to Peg's side. He was attentive, considerate, and fiercely protective, robbing Byron of any opportunity to approach. And it gave her a chance to study Desmond.

If he left her breathless as an image in a portrait, in person he was magnificent. It wouldn't be too hard getting used to having him around. Already Peg felt that standing by his side was as natural and necessary as breathing.

His light flirtations with other ladies proved his popularity with the fairer sex, but he ultimately returned to Peg, demonstrating his devotion to her. She could easily get used to that.

When Peg and Desmond moved from Lady Wilcox and her circle of friends, Peg noticed two men heading in her direction.

Both men stood about the same height. One man had been poured into his breeches. The other was of a slender, almost delicate build. They nodded to Desmond, evidently well known to him and fairly scraped the floor, bowing and uttering a courteous 'my lady', in unison.

"Pierce, will you do the introductions? I must know who this enchantress is," the man in the snug breeches urged. Considering the tightness of his pants, Peg expected his voice to be at least an octave higher. "Well?"

Desmond hesitated and gave the impression he might refuse the request. When the man in the tight breeches gave him a hard stare, Desmond broke into laughter.

"All right, all right." Desmond waved to his friend and turned to Peg. "Lady Margaret, these are...dare I say it, my friends." The men laughed. "May I introduce to you Mr Chauncey Waite and Mr Carroll Sumner?" They bowed respectfully in turn. "Lady Margaret White."

"Gentlemen," Peg replied, with a shallow curtsy.

"It is my very great pleasure," Mr Waite said, taking up her hand.

"It is nice to see you again," Mr Sumner replied. "It has been quite a while. Just before Alison's death, I believe."

At the mention of Alison's name, Peg stiffened. A swift, dark look from Desmond chastised Mr Sumner for bringing up the late viscount.

"My apologies," Mr Sumner uttered in soft tones and slid his delicate hand down his waistcoat. "It was a poor choice of words on my part."

"Think nothing of it," Peg replied.

It was not the thought of the late Lord Alison that really bothered her. What really concerned Peg was how well did Sumner know Lady Margaret? Could he expose Peg for the imposter she was? She thought it would be best if she kept her distance from him.

❦

AFTER CIRCULATING in the room for most of the evening, throwing angry looks in Desmond's direction, Lord Byron left the soiree in a huff.

"There he goes," Peg said, watching Byron's final retreat. "I believe you have given him the disgust of you."

"I thank you for the compliment," Desmond remarked. It may have stung, but it appeared he was not truly injured.

"I am sorry. I did not mean to sound dismissive." Peg laid a hand upon his arm. "You have been most kind to come to my aid. I am pleased to inform you that you are free to do as you wish."

Desmond gave her a devilish grin and his voice softened into one of intimacy. "Then we should not be standing in a crowded room."

"What I mean is, there is no need for you to remain by my side." And there was no need for him to waste any more of his evening as her escort.

"Are you casting me aside?"

"You do not need to state it so bluntly, but yes, I am."

"Wounded to the core, ma'am." As if an arrow had pierced his chest, he clutched his heart, squeezing his eyes closed in severe pain. He made an expeditious recovery. "Alas, if you have no further use for me, I have no choice but to join the men and drown my sorrows." Desmond kissed her hand. "I shall see you later then."

"Will you?" She wondered if he suspected what Peg knew to be true, that they were destined to be together. Perhaps some inner sense also told him the same.

Desmond bent to whisper in her ear. "For appearance sake, it is expected that we should arrange for our tryst."

Peg leaned closer to return his whisper. "Then let them believe it. I would not wish you to misunderstand and unnecessarily raise your hopes."

"It is not my raised *hopes* I fear will be disappointed," he returned in an arch tone. "Until we meet again," Desmond announced. It was done a little too loud and too obvious for Peg but she understood his reasons for doing so.

She watched him cross the room and before moving out of her line of sight, he bowed. Only then did Peg notice every guest had stopped to watch what had transpired between them. Everyone had noticed, and it shocked Peg that they clearly were interested in Lady Margaret's personal affairs.

DESMOND REMOVED to the library where the other men had gathered. Most were seated. Some were blowing clouds or took snuff while enjoying their drinks. Some had already managed to have quite a bit to drink and were deep in their cups.

Desmond spotted his friends Chance and Monty seated across the room and moved toward them.

"There you are." Chance waved for him to join them and pulled the chair out next to him.

"Managed to break those in, I see." Desmond referred to the once overly-restrictive breeches and sunk into the proffered chair. "Monty, how goes it?" he said to the man on his right.

"From what I hear, not as well as it does for you, Pierce." From Monty's intonation, Desmond knew Chance had filled Monty in on all the details he'd discovered about Lady Margaret.

Knowing Chance as well as he did, Desmond could well-imagine his friend had also added his own embellishments to give the story some added flavor. Who knew how far Desmond's dalliance with Lady Margaret had grown. Chance had the unique ability for stretching the tale until it was nearly beyond recognition. The truth would prove a dull story indeed if anyone else had known Desmond had yet to kiss the lady.

Monty waved to a footman for a refill and motioned for another glass for Desmond. He flipped open his snuff box and applied a pinch to each nostril before snapping the red enameled box closed.

"Nasty." Chance grimaced. "Won't do at all. Ladies find it such a filthy habit." To hear Chance speak, he sounded as if he were the authority on women. In reality, he was more adept at weaving women's fiction.

"Can't be worse than making a glutton of yourself," Monty returned, attacking Chance's adoration of food.

"Ladies like to see a man with a healthy appetite, denotes sexual prowess." Chance slid his hand down the silver shot waistcoat, reassuring himself that regardless of his frequent tendency to overindulge at the table, that his torso remained slender. "I enjoy my repast as I do my women."

Monty was quick to respond. "In haste and as often as possible." A round of ribald laughter punctuated the air.

"You are entitled to your own opinion and I shall adhere to mine." Chance did his best to ignore Monty and directed his conversation to Desmond. "I've got my snares ready for this weekend."

"Snares? What are you intending?" Desmond asked.

"He's lowered himself to trapping women so they won't take flight when he makes his approach," Monty interjected with a long, multi-modulated chuckle.

"Rabbits!" Chance snapped. "They run rampant at Saffron Hall. And the cook, François, he is a master at preparing them. Rabbit in mustard sauce, roasted rabbit with chestnuts, smothered rabbit, and rabbit in Julia sauce. I've a mind to have one every day, twice a day if all works out well. If I am to suffer in that God-forsaken lodge, let me at least have my fill." Chance lifted his glass for a toast.

"Isn't that what we all pray for? Eh, Pierce?" Monty meant something entirely different than rabbits.

Desmond lifted his glass, joining Chance. "Ah yes, to Lady Margaret."

Monty's glass clinked with the other two. "To the generous lady who bids me welcome into her portals of pleasure, whoever she may be."

"Here, here," they chorused and drank.

WITH BYRON GONE and Desmond off with his friends, Peg did not need to wait long in the ballroom to wonder what had happened to Kate. When Kate finally arrived, she appeared to be glowing. Positively radiant.

"There you are," Peg scolded. "I've been looking all over for you. You told me to be here by ten and it's past twelve now. Where have you been?"

As soon as she had asked the question, she'd regretted it. Peg was afraid to guess what Kate must have been up to.

"Oh, you know... I've been occupied," Kate announced in euphoric tones. The heightened color on her cheeks nearly matched the crimson of her dress. She smoothed one of her stray hairs and tucked into her chignon, which already looked less than perfect.

"If I am any judge of your demeanor," Peg started. "It looks as if you have discovered someone to keep you warm this winter."

"Not necessarily," she cooed. "I've just had my fire stoked a bit."

"Don't you have any respect for yourself?"

"What has respect have to do with it?" Kate asked.

"You fall into bed with every man who comes along."

"Not *every* man," Kate amended.

Peg's jaw dropped open and she knew her eyes were bugging out in disbelief. "Kate, you're the queen of denial."

"Thank you."

"That is not a comparison to Cleopatra, I'll have you know," Peg clarified.

A complacent smile crossed Kate's face. "And it's not always in a bed."

"You're impossible," Peg added. "Is there a man in existence you can say 'no' to?"

"I am sure there is...somewhere." Kate's eyes became fixed, staring straight ahead. "But it shan't be this fair Adonis."

Peg saw the approaching blade who had captured Kate's attention.

"Lord Nolan." Kate offered her hand before moving closer.

Lord Nolan was as handsome as they came. And he was just Kate's type. Male.

Without much trouble, he could probably charm the panties off Kate. Knowing Kate, she probably didn't wear any.

From the range of telling expressions that passed between them, Peg thought he might have already found that little fact out for himself.

What happened to Peg's idea of a prim and proper Regency era?

Kate wasn't the only one who behaved like that. It was all of them. The worst part of it all was from hearing them talk, they expected her to act like that too.

۶

THE SOIREE HAD BEEN everything Peg had ever imagined. Throughout the evening she spoke the Regency talk and danced through the Regency dance steps. She even participated in some gossip. All on the receiving end since she didn't know a soul.

By the end of the evening, she had heard much more than she ever expected or wanted to learn. Nestled safely inside her carriage with her ivory Tyrolese cape pulled tight around her, Peg settled back onto the squabs and waited to be on her way home.

She was very happy not to share the coach. Gerald would be off doing 'Gerald things' that she didn't even care to think about.

Moments after the coach moved forward, it came to an abrupt halt.

Why had they stopped? She tried to look out the window but the surrounding darkness made that impossible to see anything. Peg startled when the door swung open. She could only stare when a disheveled Desmond rolled onto the floor of the coach, groaning when he landed at her feet.

"I beg your pardon, Mr Desmond," she said, not sure if she had his attention or was even if he was conscious at this point. "Mr Desmond?"

He lay still and his eyes fluttered at the mention of his name as if he were trying to respond.

"I believe you are in the wrong carriage."

Desmond fumbled for a hold of the bench. His arms slid

onto the seat and he pulled himself into a sitting position. His gaze made a sweep of the interior before settling on her.

"I'm not if you're here," he said, displaying a wry smile. He clambered onto the bench next to her and continued to move closer. "The footmen are helping us with our romantic liaison. Why else would I be here?"

Why else, indeed.

When Desmond moved about, Peg caught the scent of cigar smoke and the smell of strong liquor. "You're drunk!"

"I may be deep in my cups, but I can assure you, I shall not disappoint. My *hopes* remain high." He gave a coarse laugh.

Desmond moved toward her. Peg moved away but could not escape him in the small confines of the coach. He drew her to him by her lace handkerchief firmly tucked into the wrist of her glove and kissed the palm of her hand. He leaned heavily against her and ran his lips along her cheeks and down her neck and she was afraid he would not hesitate to go beyond to where her cape lay open.

"You know you want me," he whispered, his breathing turned ragged.

Peg was finding it difficult to breathe. To her own surprise, she found him attractive, even in this disgusting condition. His tousled hair and his roughened, dark-whiskered chin gave him a rakish quality and now she understood why so many heroines had fallen for a Regency bad boy's charms. The way Desmond looked at her, the way he made her feel, the way he could have probably have had his way with her if she didn't do something to stop him.

"I know nothing of the kind," she lied. "Please stop." With a half-hearted attempt, she pushed him back and moved to the opposite bench, leaving an empty space and Desmond to fall across the seat.

He landed on his face. Desmond pushed himself upright,

his chin rested on his chest, his hair fell forward, hanging in front of his eyes.

"Why do you continue to deny me, Margaret?"

"It is Lady Margaret to you, sir."

"Ah," he crooned. "I see that I must remain patient a while longer. I shall do as I am bid for I am only your ever-humble servant."

Soon the coach slowed to a stop and moments later a footman opened the door.

"What does my lady wish of me?" Desmond groveled, dropping once again, to his knees before her. He clutched at her legs with his uncooperative arms. "I am only too happy to obey."

Peg made for the opening, stopping only long enough to make sure she wasn't being followed. She pushed on Desmond's chest, sending him flat on his back. "What I wish is for you to go home!" She shut the door herself and called out to the driver. "See this *gentleman* to his residence."

"Aye, my lady," the driver answered. The horses lurched forward, drawing the coach away.

How could she have thought herself in love with that drunken man? All she saw was his devilishly handsome looks and had imbued him with every good quality a hero should have. The one thing she didn't imagine or could escape was the piercing look in his eyes. It was the same as in the painting. The memory of it took her breath away.

It wasn't the painter who had put it there, it was there.

She had seen it for herself and heaven help her.

AFTER MARGARET LEFT, Desmond didn't bother to reseat himself and endured the bumpy ride on the hard floor of the coach, rocking him from side to side. For some deuced reason she was toying with him. Under normal circumstances, he would never have tolerated such treatment from any female.

He found it strange that he had never given her a second look before. Something about Margaret made him notice her at Lady Melbourne's party. Desmond couldn't quite figure out what it was but would do as he always did and trusted his instinct. His instincts about women were never wrong.

Margaret would be well worth the chase—he sensed some excitement about her, a worthwhile adventure if he could classify a dalliance with a married woman to have such qualities. Married ladies were usually safe.

She'd be worth the wait. And again he would prove himself, his instinct, correct. But what if he were—wrong? Him? Perish the thought.

Rounding the corner of Curzon Street he called out to the driver. "Pull up here, John Groom." The carriage stopped, a footman opened the door and Desmond poured out of the transport. Before he could stand, the footman, coach and all, had gone, abandoning him.

Enveloped in darkness, Desmond took the well-known path to the rear of his house. The faint sound of horse hooves and the jingle of harnesses resonated not far off. It came as a surprise to him when he recognized his own carriage. In his inebriated state, Desmond could not quite follow the subsequent events taking place around him.

"This's a robbery, Guv." A voice called out from the dark.

Desmond stopped. In the insufficient illumination of the tree-filtered moonlight, he caught sight of a ne'er-do-well with a pistol in hand.

"It's not your riches I'm after, it's your bloody life." The footpad lifted his weapon, aiming it at his target.

Desmond reacted before thinking and hurled himself at the scoundrel. A shot exploded, echoing through the quiet night.

The footpad scrambled to his feet and ran down the street, escaping through a side alley into the darkness.

The lights in Desmond's house came up. The rear door to the house opened and the butler appeared.

A shaft of light fell where Desmond lay. He pushed himself upright with one arm and lifted the other. His hand glistened in the light. Covered with something thick and sticky, blood ran off his arm and had soaked his coat sleeve to the elbow.

"Maypink..." Desmond called out with a groan. "Send for the surgeon."

PEG COULD TELL the household was not prepared for any of its occupants to wake before the hour of nine. She couldn't help it if she woke at seven. For her, life in the nineteenth century was still new and exciting.

Betsy scampered about, rushing a morning tray upstairs before Nora arrived to help Peg dress.

Inspecting the final results of her morning toilette, Peg gave a last look in the glass when Kate came bursting into the bedchamber.

"Oh Margaret, I'm glad to see you up so early." Kate was breathless and looked as if she had pulled her hat over her untamed curls and thrown a cloak over her nightrail.

"What is it?" Peg couldn't imagine what could have caused her friend to charge in at this hour, looking as she did, unannounced.

"I've heard the most horrible news." Kate stopped for a breath. "It's Desmond."

"Has something happened to him?" Peg had the most awful feeling. A twinge of guilt shot through her. Perhaps by some freak chance whatever happened to him might have been her fault.

"He was attacked by footpads when he returned home last night."

Peg felt a shot of adrenaline. "You did say attacked, not killed. Is he all right?"

"I don't really know," Kate replied. "I didn't want you to hear about another lost lover from anyone but me."

This was not the time to argue whether Desmond was or was not Peg's lover. All Peg wanted to know is if he was alive.

"I must go to see him at once." Peg bolted out of the room.

"I'll go with you." Kate followed. "You might need me."

CHAPTER 7

THE COACHMAN, the same one who had driven last night, brought Peg and Kate to Desmond's residence. When they approached the townhouse, Peg noticed the drapes had not been drawn nor were there any swag of black cloth framing the doorway that would announce a death.

The butler answered the door.

Peg grasped the lapels of the servant's jacket. "You must tell me how he is."

The butler's face remained impassive. "I believe the master enjoys good health."

"He's not dead?"

"Not that I am aware of, my lady," came the equally uninformative answer.

Peg saw the ridiculous position in which she had put herself. Loosening her grip of the butler's garments, she straightened her shoulders, raised her chin, and tried her best to regain some composure.

"Do you wish me to inform Mr Desmond of your arrival, ladies?"

"Yes, thank you." Peg had forgotten that Kate stood nearby.

"I believe he would wish you to wait in his library."

"The library," Peg repeated, still trying to get a hold on her racing anxiety. Desmond was all right. He was all right.

"This way, if you please." The butler pulled the front door wide to admit them.

Kate snagged Peg by the elbow. "What on earth has possessed you?"

"I'm sorry... I suppose I just had to know." She had to admit it, Peg was losing her mind. Just hearing that Desmond had been attacked was too much for her.

"Manhandling the butler is certainly not the way to go about it. And you chide me for my behavior."

Peg shrugged. What could she say?

Kate gave a nudge, urging her friend forward, and nodded toward the tolerant butler. Peg, followed by Kate, trailed after him into the library. When she turned to thank him, he was gone.

Facing into the room once again, Peg took in its elements and decided that this was definitely a man's space. It was a small world within a world. Peg, descending into a whimsical mood, ran her finger along the top of the polished inlaid Mahogany desk.

Wood paneling surrounded her and two walls were lined with books. The abundant morning light poured in from the window, illuminating the room. She inhaled the subtle mingled scent of leather and wood. A small leather sofa set back, centered between two leather wing-backed chairs flanking the hearth.

"Isn't this lovely?" Peg said mostly to herself.

"Thank you, that will be all, Maypink." Came a familiar voice from the doorway.

Peg pulled her hand away from the desk and spun around.

There stood Desmond. The mixture of relief that he was

alive and fear of his unexpected presence rushed through her. Tears filled her eyes and she blinked them back, hoping he wouldn't notice.

"Is it a habit of yours to visit a bachelor's residence alone?" He closed the door, trapping her in the room with him.

"Alone?" Peg glanced around. Where had Kate gone? "Lady Catherine accompanied me. We were concerned about your welfare."

"*We* were, were *we*?" He sounded more hopeful than skeptical of her interest in him.

Peg looked around, thinking she might have overlooked her friend the first time. Kate might have been standing in a corner but she wasn't.

"Pray tell, where is your companion?" he asked, showing polite interest.

"I cannot imagine." At the moment, Peg was growing more concerned about her well-being than for her friend's. It had to be a man. Kate had probably followed some testosterone trail to a willing male somewhere in the house.

Desmond took Peg's hands in his. "So concerned, you've forgotten your gloves, I see."

She hadn't realized. Peg had run out of the house so fast, she had forgotten. She tried to pull her hands away, but he had a firm hold of her. The feel of his hands was warm, his touch gentle. The feel of his skin, heavenly.

After a few moments, he allowed her to pull free. "I am quite touched by your concern," he remarked, clearly pleased with her presence. "I, however, am not the unfortunate, injured party. It was Chance."

Chance?

"My friend, Mr Chauncey Waite. You met last night." Grazing the smile on his lips with his fingers, Desmond headed for the window. "He is the one who has been injured. I think I might call him Luck from now on. He might have been killed if I had come along any later."

Chance? An unusual name. Yet, it sounded familiar. Where had she heard that name before?

"Had it been a few minutes sooner, it might have been me who caught the ball."

Chance. It came back to her now. Chance was the name of one of the Tontine members.

Peg remembered Mrs Andrews at Saffron Hall telling the story of his father giving his son that name, hoping to bring his son luck.

Chance would not win. He might have been killed last night if it were not for Desmond's intervention and Peg wondered if perhaps he was meant to die then. She studied Desmond's handsome profile while he stood in a contemplative, quiet moment, staring out the window.

Why hadn't she paid more attention when Mrs Andrews explained the details of the Tontine? Peg had been feeling those odd sensations and hadn't heard more than a few words here and there.

She did recall hearing about the last three deaths. They had happened within the same week of July. Maybe Chance's death was the first to occur.

If so, it had not happened.

Was Peg's presence in this time somehow have changed history? It was always a possibility. Maybe her being here had changed the outcome. Could that mean Desmond might not survive as he should?

Now that Chance was alive, perhaps he would win instead of Desmond. Peg had to help him, warn him of the danger to come.

There wasn't time for bandying about words or tactful strategies. She needed answers now. "Tell me, are you in line to inherit a title?"

He pivoted to face her, wearing a quizzical expression. "Now that is very odd you should ask."

"I'm just wondering, that's all." She feigned idle curiosity and shrugged as if his answer meant nothing.

"Does it matter as long as you find me desirable and willing?"

Peg felt her face grow warm. She had not intended her question to solicit his affection. She knew very well how he felt and didn't want to encourage him further.

She should keep her distance but fate, in her strange way, dictated they would be together. Peg didn't know how long she could fight her growing attraction to him.

"Are you not feeling off after all that drinking last night?"

"Not at all." He smiled that devilish smile of his. "As I told you I can handle my liquor."

She ignored his base remark. "Well, as I said, I only came here to see that you were well." Peg clutched her reticule in front of her, placing it between them as an ineffective barrier. But it was a barrier nonetheless. "I can see you are unharmed and now I can be on my way. Tell Mr Waite I am sorry to hear of his accident and I wish him a swift recovery."

Peg tried to walk past Desmond, but he blocked her way, causing her to bump up against him. His gentle hands went to her sides, holding her close. Capturing one of her hands, Desmond drew it along his smooth cheek and kissed it.

"I really must go," she insisted, forcing his hands away as she rushed to leave.

His tone changed from playful to serious. "Margaret?"

Peg stopped and faced him after opening the door.

"If we are to have a dalliance, shall we not waste any more time and have one?"

Feeling the comfort of the open door, Peg could make a

quick escape if it was necessary. She found her haughty tone and responded, "Whoever said we were to have one?"

"I know your reticence must be due to Alison's passing and you need to mourn him. But you do realize, it is only a matter of time until we become lovers."

The question wasn't if they would become lovers or not. The real question was, did Desmond have the time to wait? He did not know that he might be on death's door.

Stepping into the foyer, she heard soft, muffled steps and the rustle of skirts descending the stairs. With the glazed-over look of haze, a bright flush washed over her cheeks, Kate looked to be quite out of breath.

Peg had seen that expression on her friend's face before. Only one question remained. Was it the butler or a footman?

"Are you quite finished?" Peg could hardly believe Kate's... behavior.

"For the present." Kate pulled the shoulder of her cape over the small, white puffed sleeve, sliding off her arm.

The butler, Maypink, stood ramrod straight, not a hair out of place and opened the front door.

Not the butler, Peg thought, definitely not the butler.

Peg tried her best to hide her bare hands behind her reticule and in the folds of her pelisse. Why did she even try to conceal her lapse in customary fashion from the butler?

After her semi-scandalous attendance at the party with Desmond last night, and now paying a call on an unmarried man's residence, Peg expected both tidbits should spread around the servants' grapevine by late afternoon. She was really making a name for herself here.

"Perhaps I shall return, and lend some comfort to Mr Waite later." Kate did not wait for Peg and sailed out the door.

Not that Peg needed to know, but it wasn't the footman either.

RETURNING TO ASHWORTH HOUSE, Peg and Kate took tea in the drawing room, sitting at opposite ends of the sofa. With teacups in hand, they sipped in silence with only the occasional delicate clink of china cups against saucers. As Kate recovered from her mid-morning escapade, Peg pondered her dilemma of the future.

How was she to know that last night's attempt was meant for Desmond and not Chance? After all, the attack did take place outside Desmond's house.

If Chance had died, that would have meant over the next seven days the other two would have followed, and the Tontine would come to an end. And somehow during that time, Desmond would be declared the winner.

He had won... Would win ... Or would he?

How was she to know? Hadn't someone once said that history could not be changed? Hadn't someone else said history doesn't repeat itself?

What was she to do?

"My God, I cannot believe my eyes." Gerald came in, glancing from Peg to Kate and back again. "The both of you are quiet. I never thought the day would come." Kate huffed in annoyance and turned her back to him. He chuckled and handed an envelope to Peg. "The footman is waiting for your reply."

In keeping with his self-imposed, lowly messenger status, Gerald backed out of the room, bowing the entire way. Once he had left, his boisterous laughter echoed in from the hallway.

Kate swung around. "What is it?"

Peg was in no mood and opened the letter before handing it to her friend to read. Kate placed her teacup down on the tray and focused her full attention on the paper.

"It's an invitation...for both of us." Judging by the trill in her voice, she could not have been more delighted. "Saffron Hall!"

Peg should have known, should have expected it, really.

"The weekend party! How simply wonderful!" Kate cried. "Desmond will be there you know." She announced in alluring tones as if the news would tempt Peg. "Chance told me all about it. It should be deliciously dull there. Plenty of time for all sorts of fabulous flirtations and delicious dalliances, I should think."

"What are you talking about? I don't think we'll know anyone there."

"Perhaps, perhaps not. It is to be the clients of Mr Samuel Bevans and only a few chosen others." Kate leveled a smoky gaze and a hazy smile at Peg. "You know how quickly I can make friends."

Only after two days of knowing *this* Kate, Peg knew how well. She had a definite talent for it.

It should also prove to be the perfect opportunity for another attempt on Desmond's life. Under no circumstances would she allow that to happen. He was meant to live. Peg wanted to do anything she could to make that happen, up to and including attending this weekend's party.

"It's exactly what you need, some fun for a change." Kate worked on one of her gloves. "You've been so dull and boring ever since Alison's death."

Dull and boring? Peg might have been offended but she had no idea of the real Lady Margaret's character and tried not to take Kate's words as a personal slur.

"You and Desmond need to become better acquainted, that's all." Kate took the letter in hand after she'd finished donning her second glove. "I'll accept on your behalf." She stood and headed for the door. "I must dash home and begin packing immediately."

Peg stood and trailed her friend to the foyer.

Kate motioned to the waiting footman. "Please relay our acceptance to Mr Bevans."

"Yes, my lady." He bowed and went on his way past the butler to relay the reply.

Before departing Kate turned to Peg. "I'll expect your coach at one tomorrow afternoon," and she swept out the open door.

That was subtle.

Backtracking into the hallway, Peg turned to the left into the parlor instead of right returning into the drawing room. It brought her to face with Lady Margaret's portrait.

"You know this is all your fault," she said in fierce tones the painting. "Why have you done this to me? Can't you see I don't belong here?" She paused, waiting for... Peg didn't know what response she could realistically expect from a painting. "Why don't you say something? Give me some sort of sign."

Gerald appeared at the open door, hesitating to enter. "I say, Margaret." He glanced about the room. "Are you talking to someone?"

"Only to myself." She glared at the painting. Her heated stare should have set the canvas on fire.

"Oh, I see." He regarded her with tolerant amusement, no doubt humoring her. "I just want you to know I've already made my acceptance."

"To the Bevans' house party? Are you to attend as well?" This was unbelievable. Could things get much worse?

"Little sister," he approached and laid a protective hand on her shoulder, which she promptly tried to shrug off. "You know that I am to lend an air of respectability to the whole situation." He waggled his eyebrows in a most disgusting way. "You and Desmond, what? However, I shall contrive. Dashed-inconvenient these last-minute affairs, don't you think?"

Peg let out a sigh. She was afraid he'd do exactly that.

Gerald would *contrive* with the maids, *contrive* with the guests, and heaven forbid, *contrive* with the hostess.

What a mess! As if she needed him to save her.

Peg said a silent prayer, hoping if anyone was on her side, they would grant her the simple wish that he would travel separately.

THERE WAS NO SUCH LUCK.

Precisely at one-ten the following afternoon, the journey had begun. There was dreadful, icy silence for most of the journey. Kate sat opposite Peg and stared out the window. At least there would be no need for her to look at Gerald while he sat next to her.

Gerald crossed his booted feet on the bench opposite and shot Peg a glance every now and again. No doubt he enjoyed causing the two females as much discomfort as possible.

The combination of the restricted interior of the coach, snug-fitting clothes, and overhanging brim of her bonnet dangling before her eyes only added to Peg's claustrophobic feeling.

With her two ill-tempered traveling companions, Peg didn't know how long she could stand the confinement. The atmosphere felt thick with its unbearable, silent tension.

As unbelievable as it might be, Gerald must have been the only man who held no interest for Kate. And it was understood that there wasn't a female in existence who could say No to Gerald. So why was it these two could not stand one another?

As MUCH AS it disappointed him, Chance was given approval by his surgeon to travel. While Chance mumbled his grievances, Desmond gave his personal assurance that the patient would not overdo.

On arriving at Saffron Hall, Desmond and Chance were shown to the Great Saloon to join the other guests all recovering from their journey.

Chance refused a helping hand from Desmond, did not wish to appear weak in the eyes of the ladies. He hated to be seen using a cane but did so since it allowed him to manage alone. His perception changed when the women, in seeing his injury, flocked around him, coming to his aid.

The ladies saw to his every comfort. While one fetched him a drink, several helped him settle into a chair and two others helped elevate his wounded leg while Mrs Bevans tucked a plump cushion under his foot.

Seeing his friend was well looked after, Desmond left Chance and stood with Monty. "He's finally found a ploy that works." Desmond retrieved a glass off a passing tray.

"I'm sure if he knew he'd gain all this attention from the ladies, he'd have shot himself in the leg years ago." Monty tossed back his drink.

Perusing the occupants of the room, Desmond quickly spotted the familiar faces. Lord and Lady Holster, Mr and Mrs Trevor Brown, and Sir Quincy and Lady Payne attended the function year after year. Although his friends Sumner, Chance and Monty were here, this wasn't the company Desmond usually kept.

There were a few new faces that appeared every year. Merchants, military men, and various titled sorts with one thing in common: wealth.

Monty nudged Desmond with his elbow and gestured to the door. "Your lady has arrived."

Desmond could not describe the feeling that surged through him when he gazed upon her...*my* Margaret. He felt a hand upon his arm.

"I do beg your pardon," a Pink of the *Ton* interrupted.

He was tall, elegant, and impeccably dressed. As a dandy should be, Desmond noted in silence.

"I am Sir Cornelius Poole. I know we have not been properly introduced, but I am under the distinct impression Mr Bevans is also your solicitor."

"Yes, that's right," Desmond replied. "I am Pierce Desmond and this is Sir Julian Montgomery."

Monty responded with a shallow bow, displaying his reluctance at this sort of informality which he thoroughly despised.

Sir Cornelius continued, "I noticed the two of you observing those lovely ladies as they entered."

This tulip was referring to Lady Margaret and Lady Catherine.

"Do you happen to be known to either of them?"

"Why, yes," Monty was quick to answer.

Desmond wasn't sure he wanted this Sir Cornelius to have the pleasure of Margaret's acquaintance. What exactly did he have in mind?

"Please," Sir Cornelius' claw-like hand grasped Monty's shoulder. "You must tell me the name of that goddess!"

Didn't he know Margaret was his? Desmond wanted to punish this upstart for his impudence.

"She moves with the grace of a feather floating ever so gently along with the breeze. Her eyes are twinkling stars plucked from the heavens above. Her golden hair—"

Golden hair? Margaret had dark hair. Desmond's gaze swung to Margaret and her friend. Lady Catherine's hair was light, he might even go so far as to describe it as golden. Sir

Cornelius was not infatuated with Margaret as Desmond had first dreaded but with her friend.

"Ah, Lady Catherine," Monty clarified.

"You must do me the honor of an introduction to her," Sir Cornelius pleaded.

"I'll do what I can." Monty lifted one side of his mouth in a half-smile and took Sir Cornelius by the arm and started in the ladies' direction.

※

OTHER THAN A MORE RURAL FEELING, Peg decided Saffron Hall had not changed all that much. Stepping into the house, she felt more at ease than she had on her previous visit.

It was a little confusing, now that she thought about it, as her first visit happened more than two hundred years after the second.

Forget it. This time travel really could be confusing.

The under-butler led the way. Kate and Peg followed while Gerald seemed to have gone. Probably to keep as far away from Kate as he could.

Peg recognized the white and gold of the Grand Saloon. She spotted Chauncey Waite in one corner surrounded by women, in another Gerald, who had wasted no time, flirting with a young lady and somewhere ensconced in the middle she saw Carroll Sumner, whom she had met the previous evening, and Pierce Desmond, standing with a third man.

"Sir Julian, how nice to see you again." Kate held out her hand.

Again? If Kate knew Sir Julian there was a good chance Lady Margaret had made his acquaintance as well.

"Lady Margaret, how do you do?" Sir Julian asked.

"Quite well," Peg replied. "Thank you."

"Lady Margaret, I wish to introduce Sir Cornelius Poole. Sir Cornelius, may I present Lady Margaret White."

"*Paul?*" Peg gasped. He was a dead ringer for Paul from her Regency tour group from her time.

"That's *Poole*, my lady," he corrected over-enunciating his surname. "Sir Cornelius..." He looked directly at Kate, into Kate's eyes. "...Poole."

"Lady Catherine Holloway." Kate offered Sir Cornelius her hand.

Sir Cornelius took Kate's hand, instead of kissing it he held it and drew closer to her. The two seemed to be quite taken with one another.

"If you will please excuse me." Peg tried to slip in before making her exit. She headed for Desmond, he turned to face her as she approached.

"I am so very delighted to see you," he said, raising her hand to his lips. He fingered her glove, noting their presence this time and lifted one side of his mouth with amusement. "I had no idea you had been invited."

"I believe it was done as a favor to Mr Waite for additional guests to keep him entertained because of his condition."

"Lady Margaret," Mr Sumner acknowledged. "A pleasure as always."

Peg bowed her head.

"Let me introduce you, Lady Margaret." Desmond turned to the impeccably dressed solicitor next to him. "Our host, Mr Samuel Bevans, may I present Lady Margaret White."

"How do you do?" Mr Bevans swept a bow. "I am entirely charmed, I assure you."

"And I, you," she returned. So this was the keeper of the secret, Samuel Bevans. There was no way this lawyer could have known that she knew about the tontine.

"I hope you will enjoy yourself this weekend. If you are in

need of anything, do not hesitate to inform me or one of the staff."

"How very kind of you. Thank you very much." Margaret gave a tug on Desmond's sleeve.

Sumner leaned toward Desmond and whispered, "Lady Margaret seems most insistent. She is quite beautiful. I wish I had such luck."

"That remains to be seen. If you will excuse us," Desmond said to Bevans and Sumner. Desmond stepped to one side at Margaret's urging.

"I must see you alone," she sounded most insistent.

"How I have wanted to hear you say that." Desmond's pulse quickened. He wanted to show more tact than dragging her off to the first vacant room. He pressed a kiss upon her fingers and forced the words through gritted teeth, "I shall come to your bedchamber tonight."

"No." Is all she managed sounding rather breathless. "Now."

"Now?" How she must burn for him. The thought of her desire for him flamed his lust. His gaze ran over the subtle shifting features of her face.

"Come out into the garden with me."

"Now? In the garden?" He might have sounded like a young, inexperienced buck on his first *al fresco* abandon, which he was certainly not. Somehow he imagined Lady Margaret was more of the boudoir-type and not the adventurous-type.

Margaret pulled the glass from his hand, waking him from his daydream. She led him from the room and down the corridor.

My, she *was* anxious.

CHAPTER 8

THERE CERTAINLY WAS no stopping Margaret when she decided what she wanted. And Desmond had no intention of disappointing her.

Margaret had hold of Desmond by the hand and was literally dragging him to the back door. He was certain she never been here before, but she seemed to know her way around quite well.

He had not dared to imagine making love with her before this moment. She would be a fine tumble between the sheets or leaves, for that matter. Then they would lie in one another's arms until he felt ready for a second go-round. Or if so inclined, she might encourage him to give a repeat performance. He had no doubt she might just try it; she was a saucy little thing.

What Desmond had not foreseen was Margaret seeking public but out-of-the-way places to inflame their passions. To mingle the sin of adultery and the risk of discovery was beyond what he could imagine excited her.

The possibilities were endless. From one moment to the next, his mind weighed each fleeting thought, lingering on certain arousing aspects that he might want to attempt first.

He could see her brown hair spread across the manicured green blades of the lawn. Her white thighs spread atop the low branches of the trees. Perhaps she cared to grip onto the gazebo post to hold her upright while her legs wrapped around his waist.

It had been a long time since he had had a tryst out-of-doors in broad daylight. Knowing he might need to bare his backside in the midst of the garden, Desmond gave a silent prayer that the rose bushes had been pruned.

Margaret climbed the steps and into the gazebo. "No one can approach without being seen here," she said, glancing around as though concerned about potential onlookers.

Desmond could have cared less who saw them and pulled Margaret into his arms, holding her firmly against him. With his arms wrapped tight around her warm body, he felt her soft, full breasts press against him.

"Other than dancing, do you realize this is the first time I've had you in my arms?" His fingers grazed her cheek, feeling its smoothness. He looked deep into her eyes and imagined an equal passion to his own. Desmond bent his head and claimed her lips.

It was a very strange kiss.

Margaret's unresponsive lips together with her rigid posture surprised him. She was no innocent. Why in heaven's name did she behave like one?

With a firm hand on his chest, she pushed him away.

"There's no time for that now."

"As you wish." He shrugged. "If I must get to the crux of the matter, I shall do as you bid."

Desmond preferred more playful frolic before the actual coupling but he was more than willing to proceed if it pleased her. He reached to unbutton his breeches.

"What are you doing? No!" she screamed. "Stop that!"

It should have brought the entire house full of guests to her aid, except he suspected they all knew what was going on and would never think to interfere.

"Did you not bring me out here for a tryst?"

"No, I did not!" Margaret said in a firm, adamant tone. "I asked you to come out here because I need to speak to you—in private."

How had he misunderstood?

"You are in great danger," she said. "I fear someone is trying to kill you."

He ran his hand down his face, hoping to draw some of the frustration he felt from showing in his expression. "Driving me mad, I would more likely believe."

"I'm serious."

"So am I," he returned, having difficulty fastening the single button he had managed to fumble open. Desmond gave a quick exhale.

"Have you ever questioned where your money comes from?"

He was filled with desire and she was going on about money. Desmond lifted an eyebrow, becoming indignant. "As if it is any of your business, my solicitor handles my finances. He did so for my father as well, and his father for my grandfather."

"I know."

Desmond chuckled. "How could you know? And what does it matter?"

Margaret ignored his question. "Did you not notice how your portion increased after Alison's death?"

Good God, Alison again!

"I had not related the two." He paused. "I do not really see what one has to do with the other."

"For your information, he has—*had* the same solicitor as you."

"That may well be, but I still don't see what that has to do with me."

Peg closed her eyes and squeezed them tight.

How could she explain without telling him everything? It was impossible. She would have to tell him. What choice did she have?

"Your father enrolled you in a tontine when you were born," she blurted out.

"A tontine?" The tone of amusement in his voice told her he didn't believe her. "Oh, I see. What you're driving at is someone killed Alison to eliminate him from this archaic arrangement. And that is why my portion grew."

"Precisely." At least he knew what a tontine was. A ray of hope filled Peg. He did understand and he would heed her warning. "Just as your life is in danger now."

"Ah, we come back to that, I see. I knew you must have had some reason that made sense." Desmond chuckled. "You must forgive me." His laughter grew and he covered his mouth, attempting to restrain himself.

Angered, Peg spun away and headed straight for the house. He might be laughing now but he wouldn't be laughing for long. All the remaining tontine members were present at this party. She didn't know who they were, but she knew this would be the weekend when all but one would die.

❧

PEG SLAMMED THE WARDROBE DOOR. No underwear. "What do you mean they're not dry?"

Nora quaked at Peg's raised voice. "I beg your pardon, Lady Margaret, you told me to wash the pantalets you wore yesterday and they've been left in the airing cupboard at the house to dry."

"I suppose you are not to blame." Peg should have remembered this was the age before the invention of the clothes dryer. "I'll have to go without." She had no choice.

Nora clapped the curling irons, readying them for use. Peg sank into the chair at the dressing table and faced the glass. She watched Nora fold a thin square of paper around the base of her hair, drawing the strand through the hot irons.

All Peg could do was sit there, watch, and think. She didn't want to think about that foolish scene this afternoon in the gazebo with Desmond. She didn't want to think about Desmond at all. She wasn't sure she wanted to think about him...ever.

He made her so mad. Why couldn't he just believe her?

Peg focused on Nora's ministration to keep her mind occupied. Nora had rolled a strand of Peg's hair around the iron, then pinned it in its circular position and pulled the iron free. She repeated the exercise twenty-two times before Peg gave up counting.

Desmond eased his way into her thoughts again. Peg didn't appreciate him laughing at her that afternoon. She had merely voiced a warning and had done it for his own good. Why couldn't he have listened to her? And why couldn't he just stay out of her mind?

Peg was determined to concentrate on the gold-edged blue ribbon, matching her gold-shot blue sarsnet gown. She followed it as Nora picked it up and tied it into her styled hair.

Nora helped Peg draw off her wrapper and step into her evening gown. The heavy, gold-colored fringed hem gave the skirt a languorous motion when she moved and swayed with every step she took.

In a fleeting thought, she wondered if Desmond would like it. Desmond! She changed her mind, telling herself she didn't care if he liked it or not.

Peg wriggled uncomfortably in her dress. The flattened silver wires at the back that comprised the hook and eye closures scratched. Why couldn't this dress have some nice buttons? Her pink frock had too many, this one had none.

Better yet, when were they going to invent the zipper?

❦

DESMOND WATCHED Margaret enter the front parlor. Her attitude this afternoon had bothered him more than her words. He could have sworn her alarm was genuine, but that story about a tontine—that was ridiculous. And the thought of someone trying to kill him was preposterous.

Margaret need not have spun a lie to gain his attention. Desmond had already noticed her, and she had more than caught his fancy.

But no one was trying to kill him.

Then again, Margaret knew about his recent quarterly increase. How could she have learned of it? A lucky guess perhaps? Her claims could not be true, could they?

His solicitor Samuel Bevans had handled his finances for years, and more than satisfactorily without Desmond's intervention. Why should he have questions now?

Perhaps a word with Mr Bevans might allay his...not fears, but any *concerns* about the matter of a tontine. If any such thing really existed. Desmond had his doubts.

A tontine? Hadn't those things gone out with the last century?

But then again, perhaps it was not so unlikely. His father and his wealthy friends were a bit eccentric in their day. Could they have participated in such a capricious scheme?

Why on earth was Desmond even considering such a far-fetched tale? Did he really believe there was any truth in Margaret's allegation?

Of course, no one was trying to kill him. It was nonsense.

Perhaps that wasn't the way to go about getting answers. What Desmond needed was proof. Irrefutable proof. And what better place to find such than at the solicitor's own home.

Once proven, there would be no denying the arrangement. And if none were to be found... well, he would deal with that once placed in that uncomfortable position. How better than to address a madcap notion than by a madcap solution. He would search for proof himself.

He couldn't really believe in the existence of a tontine. He couldn't believe his solicitor was dishonest. And he couldn't believe that he was in love with a madwoman.

Fifteen minutes after the dinner gong had sounded, Peg entered the Front Parlor, joining the other guests for drinks before the evening meal.

"Margaret!" a voice called to her. "Margaret!"

Although she would have liked to, Peg couldn't ignore Gerald, eager for her to join him, waving at her.

"Over here, Margaret. Will you please..."

What did he want?

Peg headed over to Gerald, who held out his hand to her.

"Margaret, may I present our hostess, Mrs Bevans."

With a slow nod and a polite smile, Peg acknowledged the petite woman in an elegant apricot gown. "How do you do? I am pleased to make your acquaintance."

"Mrs Bevans, this is my sister, Mrs White."

Peg glared at Gerald. The smirk on his face told her he knew exactly how much Margaret had hated the common name.

What a rat. Was there no decency about him at all? No

redeeming characteristic? No part of him resembling a kind human being? Probably not.

"How do you do? I am very happy to make your sister's acquaintance, Lord Sinclair," Mrs Bevans replied.

Lord Sinclair? This was the first time Peg had heard Gerald called by his title. Lord Sinclair sounded so regal, so respectable, so *un*-Gerald. Peg thought *Lord Sin* would have been more apt.

"I believe you are acquainted with Mr Waite, are you not?" Mrs Bevans asked Peg. "Do you happen to know how he was injured?"

"I believe he was shot during a robbery."

It wasn't Mrs Bevans' expression as much as the tone of her voice that told Peg of the hostess' empathy for Chance. "He was *so* brave."

So lucky was more like it.

"We are very glad he could join us. He has such a pleasurable nature and what a delightful wit." She gave a sigh of adoration and glanced in his direction. "And to think we were nearly deprived of his charming company."

Oh, that would have been a shame. And it also might have kept him alive. Margaret did not dare tell her the truth of his injury.

"If you will excuse me" —Mrs Bevans was flagged by her husband— "I see that I am needed." She left and headed for the crowd in the center of the room.

"You may release me now." Peg pried her hand out of Gerald's.

"Terribly sorry, you know how I love the touch of a female."

Gerald's slimy words were wasted on her. She shook her hand like a cat with a wet paw, trying to remove the unpleasantness.

Rising from the crowd, the tip of a closed fan circled in the air caught Peg's attention.

"I believe it is Princess Kate." Gerald pointed out. It seemed the gesture didn't go unnoticed by him either. "Her Highness requests your presence."

With a huff Peg left. She crossed the room, stepping around a couple and past three men in a heated conversation, keeping her steps small and mincing. It felt weird knowing one was naked except for a barrier of thin material. She had to admit it did wonders for her deportment.

She snagged two glasses from a passing footman before arriving at Kate's side.

"Your favorite, champagne." Peg seated herself in the chair facing the sofa where Kate sat and handed her one glass. "Have you seen Desmond?"

Seen him, no. Nor did she really wish to. Peg hated to act petty. It really wasn't her. She took a sip of champagne. How could she blame him for his reaction? She had to admit that she couldn't.

"I think I must have a word with him." Peg was thinking along the lines of an apology. She glanced around the room. "Have you happened upon him, Kate? Kate…"

Kate had not heard a single word Peg had said, but was focused on something or someone over Peg's left shoulder. Had she been eavesdropping on the couple seated behind them in private conversation? No.

Kate's breathing became heavy and her chest began to heave. Her gaze was fixed to the right of the couple. Shifting to her left and lifting her head higher for a better view, Peg caught sight of Gerald.

No, not him.

Gerald leaned languidly against the hearth. His left elbow rested casually over the marble chimneypiece. He held a glass of wine from which he took occasional sips. With his other hand, he caressed the marble woman's breast.

An audible moan escaped from Kate.

Clearly, Kate was not the intended audience, but who was it? Peg followed Gerald's stare toward the windows on the opposite side of the room. There sat a wide-eyed, pale Mrs Bevans, whose gaze was riveted on Gerald.

Not the hostess again.

By her reaction, Mrs Bevans was not used to this type of overt seduction.

If he had to seduce someone, Peg wished Gerald would restrict himself to the guests, only if they were willing.

Glancing about for a less distasteful distraction, Peg spotted Desmond standing with a military man. Unless she missed her guess, Chance would be seated nearby.

Desmond's gaze met hers, and a faint smile touched his lips.

Peg took a sizeable swallow from her glass and felt her anger melt away. How could she ever help him and keep her feelings from becoming involved? Involved? She was half in love with him before she met him.

And that was another secret she had to keep.

The best thing would be to stay away from him. But he needed her, whether she liked it or not. She had to save him, whether she liked it or not. And deny it all she might, Peg cared for him, whether she liked it or not.

Before she approached Desmond, Peg steeled herself against the onslaught of his devastating charm and willed herself to keep from fidgeting, uncomfortable with the knowledge of feeling naked. She told herself he couldn't know she hadn't a thing on under her skirts. He always looked at her like that; as if he were ready to devour her. She finished her drink and set her glass on a table.

The military man had left Desmond's side when Peg arrived.

"So he has a promotion now, does he?" Chance's query took

on an envious tone. "Sir Quincy Payne has made his mark I see."

Peg looked from Chance to Desmond and decided she was coming into the middle of a touchy topic.

"Do be a good fellow and lend a hand, will you?" Chance waved his arm about, waiting for Desmond to come to his aid. Desmond helped his friend to his feet.

"Enchanted to see you again, Lady Margaret." Chance groaned, placing weight on his injured leg. He must have seen the confused expression on Peg's face and explained. "The recently knighted, Sir Quincy Payne, has since advanced to the rank of major."

"Oh, I see. Major. Sir Quincy is Major Payne?" Peg snickered, unable to stop herself from laughing at the silly, bad joke. It must have been the champagne on an empty stomach. "I can see why he was knighted," she mumbled, which she thought was under her breath.

"His knighthood had nothing to do with his service to the country."

Oh yeah, right.

"I shall leave you two to your en *quête d'amour* and will attempt to find my own entertainment."

"I thought you were injured beyond endurance," Desmond argued playfully.

"There are some activities a man cannot put off," Chance blustered, puffing himself up. "Until later," he excused himself and limped off leaning on his cane. He gathered cries of sympathy and the company of several females who insisted they aid him to his destination.

Desmond cleared his throat, drawing Peg's attention. "Are we still speaking?"

Peg gazed into his dark brown eyes and the hostility she felt toward him thawed. "We are." Then just as quickly, she justified to herself that she couldn't remain angry with him if she wanted to stay near him. "I would like to apologize for my behavior this afternoon." She waited for his reaction. From the next room, the dinner gong sounded.

"Yes, well... We could speak of that at a later time."

There wasn't a hint of emotion on Desmond's face. Was he still angry with her? Had he forgotten what had happened? Not likely.

Carroll and Juliana Sumner passed by on their way to the dining room, followed by ailing Chauncey Waite who was aided by Penelope Blake and Sophia Whitford.

A practiced smile slid over Desmond's face. "In any event, I do believe it is time we went in for supper. May I escort you?"

Desmond placed his arm under her hand and led her into the dining room. After locating her seat, he held her chair, then strolled around to the opposite side, taking his place across from her.

After laying the cloth napkin in her lap, Peg removed her gloves for dinner. She spotted Kate on the opposite side two down from Desmond, toward the head of the table.

Peg glanced at the nameplates on either side of her place setting. She would be keeping company with Sir Cornelius Poole, lucky her, and Mr Thomas Rowlandson.

Thomas Rowlandson the artist?

Peg remembered seeing a sketch of him in the Print Room of the National Portrait Gallery. He drew caricatures of funny, plump people from all walks of life, several of them a bit more than risqué. If he hung out in this crowd that would certainly explain where he got his ideas.

A portly, balding gentleman stopped on Peg's right. "Ah! Here I am."

Peg recognized the artist.

He took his seat next to her. "I don't believe we've been

introduced." His eyes twinkled with delight, he thrust out his hand, making it obvious that he was eager to become better acquainted.

Peg couldn't help but feel a little awed and flattered by the artist's attention. "No, I don't believe I've had the pleasure."

"And I can't tell you how disappointed I would be to deny you any pleasure." His eyebrows rose and his eyes grew large. He brought her bare hand to his wide, smiling lips.

"I am..." she began to introduce herself.

"An earthbound angel," he interrupted. "Here to tempt the mortals who cannot endure the many charms of your divine presence? How may I refer to you?"

"Ah... Lady... Margaret... White." Peg's awe turned to embarrassment. Was he putting her on? Rowlandson looked to be at least sixty, Peg figured and fairly harmless, getting his jollies from a little flirting. He was old enough to be her grandfather.

A giggle slipped out. She couldn't believe it. The champagne had unfettered her inhibitions. Then another giggle. For Pete's sake, she had to stop.

A wide, open-mouthed grin lit up the man's face. "How fortunate that we are seated next to one another. The heavens are indeed smiling down upon us today. I am Thomas Rowlandson, a poor but honest artist."

The fact that he was here told Peg he wasn't poor. And as for being honest, if she wasn't mistaken, didn't he earn his money by selling his own knock-off sketches under an alias? She wasn't sure.

On top of that, he had a Dr. Jekyll and Mr Hyde personality. One moment Rowlandson was all kind words and smiles the next, he bellowed at the wine steward filling the guests' glasses.

"I'll have none of that bubbling grape piss! Fetch me the claret!"

"But sir, the soup will be served with a remove of fish. They are to be served with champagne."

"Claret—I said!"

"Yes, sir, at once." The servant bowed, gesturing to a footman to retrieve the requested drink.

The wine steward filled Peg's glass next. More champagne. Good thing food was on the horizon. She'd feel more than a little light-headed after another.

The first course of turtle soup arrived only moments after the claret splashed into Rowlandson's glass.

Mr Bevans raised his glass for a toast. "To my esteemed colleagues, invited guests, and honored clients, I welcome you all. May the coming years hold as much promise and be as lucrative as the last."

A chorus of 'here, here' and raised glasses came from every person at the table. Peg made the pretense of drinking. If she had anymore, she'd be at the dancing-on-the-table-with-a-lampshade-on-her head stage.

Those around Peg partook in the meal with zest, proving to her, she wasn't the only hungry one. Peg took up her spoon and hesitated. She had never had turtle soup before but wasn't about to let that keep her from digging in. She brought it to her lips. The aroma made her hesitate.

Tastes like chicken broth, she tried to convince herself and took a little of it in her mouth.

She tried again and lifted a second spoonful to her lips. It wasn't working. It didn't taste like chicken broth. It tasted like rotting fish, and it smelled worse. No wonder she had difficulty eating it. She laid the spoon in the bowl and dabbed the edges of her mouth with a linen napkin.

Peg glanced down both sides of the table. She wasn't the only one finished. Chance hadn't touched a spot, while Desmond made only a modest sampling.

From her seat, Peg couldn't see Gerald but caught Kate having a grand ole time flirting with Mr Sumner as poor Sir Cornelius pined away for her in silence.

It felt as if two hours had passed before the 'turtle soup' was removed when in reality Peg knew it couldn't have been more than one.

The servants carried in a platter with several braces of some kind of poultry and set it near the head of the table. They looked very tasty.

Lesser dishes of small game birds, puddings, and vegetables were placed in strategic locations. All, Peg thought ruefully were just out of her reach. If she knew any better, she would have thought it was some sort of nefarious plot against her to access anything edible.

She caught a whiff of what looked like a good-sized ham that a footman marched past her and placed at the far end of the table. Peg's mouth began to water. She couldn't wait to get started.

A massive platter was placed in front of Peg. It held a large fish, scales and all. Its head lolling over one side and its tail over the other, resting on the table. The fish was staring at her.

Too much champagne, she thought. Or insanity taking over.

With another swallow, Peg wondered what new delights were in store for the next course.

CHAPTER 9

Unfortunately, Peg's portion of the fish included a lateral fin —as if she needed a reminder of where it came from. She liked fish but didn't think she could eat it while it watched itself being devoured.

Deep masculine chuckles, feminine titter, and subdued conversation filled the period between the courses. Once the food arrived, the voices silenced as if on cue. Why couldn't she have been seated nearer to the end of the table? Either end. Clearly, the closer one sat to the host or hostess, the better the dishes. Small game birds—quail, grouse, or pigeons—at the head, she should have known—lobster.

Peg sipped at the champagne. By now, it was very warm and mostly flat. The buzz in her head told her she had had enough and she pushed the wine glass away.

Boy, did Kate luck out.

Peg thought she spotted some new platters containing filleted fish, fruit tarts, and puddings.

"I believe you are to carve, sir," Rowlandson leaned forward and pushed the serving platter toward Desmond. He took up Peg's plate and held it alongside his in line for the meat.

"Is she not lovely?" Of course Sir Cornelius w as referring to Kate. Kate held a fork in one hand and gestured with the lobster claw she held in the other.

What a delightful picture that made. As long as table manners weren't up there on the list of desirable qualities, how could Sir Cornelius resist? Hunger had made Peg not fit to be with other people, she could barely keep the churlish thoughts to herself.

Desmond placed the first slice on Peg's dish and glanced at her. If there was a meaning in that look, it was lost.

Peg eyed the meat on the dinner plate in front of her suspiciously. If she couldn't identify it, she didn't think she could eat it. On her right, Rowlandson cut into the meat, the lace of the ruffled edges of his cuffs brushed against the platter, absorbing the *au jus*. He didn't allow the entree's mysterious identity to stop his enjoyment and ate it heartily.

Sir Cornelius took his time to cut his meat into bite-sized pieces. He chewed his food between deep heartfelt sighs and languishing looks toward Kate's end of the table. *What a shame he couldn't sit next to the one he adored*, Peg fumed, unable to control her *ha-anger*. If anyone was hopelessly and transparently in love, it was he.

When the meat joint was removed, small stemmed, wide-mouthed goblets were placed on the table. The clear water looked very inviting. Peg couldn't wait to have a sip. She knew ice cubes were too much to ask for and only hoped it was somewhat cool. Peg grasped the goblet by the stem before she could draw it near, Rowlandson's food covered fingers plunged into the clear liquid and wriggled his fingers about, removing bits of gristle, meat, and fish scales. The dried brown sauce staining the tips of his fingers melted away, discoloring the water.

She pulled her hand away. She had planned to drink that. Not anymore.

It didn't stop Rowlandson. He grasped the stem and tossed back the contents, orts and all.

With her eyes closed tight, Peg pressed her napkin to her mouth, trying to erase the sickening image. When she found the courage to open her eyes, Peg saw the other guests follow Rowlandson's example, alternating between taking sips from the water and washing their fingertips.

She thought table manners in the 1800s were a bit more advanced than they apparently were. Peg sat quietly waiting for her stomach to settle. Her stomach vacillated between ravenous hunger and complete repulsion.

"Are we in consensus, Lady Margaret?" Rowlandson asked, catching her off guard. Apparently, he had been deep in conversation with Mrs Sumner who sat on his right. Peg hadn't realized...had she been included?

She had better say something. "Of course," she threw out without knowing what the two were talking about.

"I told you." The artist shrugged, returning to the discussion on his right. "It is a very common notion."

"Alas, she is married but if you will, Lady Margaret" —this came from Peg's left— "Please tell me, does she have a...lover?"

Lover? Singular? As in only one? No.

"It is not for me to say," Peg replied. Talk about sticky situations. She didn't want near that subject. "Although I can with all confidence tell you, she would not be averse to your attention."

"Do...I...dare?" Sir Cornelius' yearning could not have been more obvious.

"I think you may," Peg encouraged. Maybe that would convince him to turn his talk into action.

What Sir Cornelius did was to take up the carving utensils and focused his attention from Kate to the platter in front of him which, there was no mistaking, was tongue.

Peg wasn't going to eat a dish that could taste her back.

A dish down at the end of the table caught her attention. "What's that?"

"Calf's head, hashed," Sir Cornelius replied.

"I'm not eating that tripe."

"Lady Margaret requests the white dish," Sir Cornelius relayed to the footman.

Alongside the tongue, Peg could have crowed with delight when she saw a plateful of asparagus. Plain asparagus.

"Would you please be so kind as to put some asparagus on my plate?" Peg handed her plate to Rowlandson.

"You crave the nourishment of the elongated spear?" He sorted through the various widths of stems with a fork. "Do you care for the thick or the more delicately built taper?"

"I don't have a preference really." She'd have eaten it raw if it came down to it.

"Bless you, you're a woman after my own heart."

Sir Cornelius spooned out a generous portion of something slimy onto Peg's plate.

"How did you manage that?" Rowlandson jabbed at her plate with his food covered index finger, pointing at the white honeycombed slime moving dangerously close to two spears of asparagus remaining on her plate.

"The sweetbread is down at the far end. Sent a footman 'round when I wasn't looking, did you?" Rowlandson's greasy lips parted in a wide smile. A chunk of meat dropped from the finger he shook at her. "Would have known you'd have your way," the artist teased Peg with an all-knowing tone. "Don't she always, Desmond?" He gave a suggestive wink.

"Yes, Pierce, do own up. She does, don't she?" Chance, seated two down from his friend, joined in.

Desmond's gaze slid from Rowlandson to Chance to Peg. "She most certainly does."

"I knew it!" Rowlandson declared in triumph. "I would care for some myself," he mumbled, trying to catch the attention of one of the busy footmen to make the trek down to the end of the table. "Can't catch their..." Moving his head from side to side, Rowlandson did not seem successful. "Damn them all! The blackguards only take notice of the ladies."

"Allow me to oblige you." Peg tilted her plate, allowing the tripe to slide off her plate onto Rowlandson's dish.

"How very kind of you," the artist remarked.

"May I have more asparagus please?"

"Seconds?" He said with a peculiar tone.

Peg almost leaped out of her chair. The lecher had his hand on her knee. Under the pretense of a caress, he was inching up her thigh.

"Seconds?" The artist roared with laughter. "I would venture to say it would do me more good than you. Zounds, you must have an insatiable appetite." It was a comment meant for Peg's ear clearly had crossed to the other side of the table.

"That, sir," Desmond confessed, "is something I cannot confirm."

AFTER A PERFUNCTORY LOOK around the table after the final course, Mrs Bevans announced, "I believe the ladies have finished. We shall leave the men to their port." She laid her neatly folded napkin beside her plate. The other ladies followed her example, stood and followed the hostess out the door.

Sumner leaped from his seat and rushed to the sideboard. "Didn't think they'd ever leave." He retrieved the stowed chamber pot and relieved himself with a groan. "Made it just in time."

"Send a footman to alert the King," drawled Monty, taking the seat between Chance and Desmond.

"I do not know if I shall survive until I set eyes on her again," Sir Cornelius declared.

No doubt the remaining gentlemen would soon be subjected to a barrage of divine qualities, extolling the loveliness of Lady Catherine. Sir Cornelius began his soliloquy. Desmond wished, for once, he would be proved wrong.

"She moves as lightly as a cloud through the windswept sky. Her breasts are orbs that should take their place in the heavens above out of man's reach."

"Let's have the lovelies out so you can have a look at them, eh?" Chance suggested, followed by a hearty chuckle.

"I will not sit idle and allow a public slur on her character. Do not force me to call you out," Sir Cornelius warned through clenched teeth.

He behaved as if Catherine's breasts were holy relics.

Chance leaned toward Desmond and added, "The Admiral would love to be held captive between those mounds of creamy flesh."

"I heard that!" Sir Cornelius leaped to his feet. "I will not stand here while you continue your degrading remarks."

"Nothing to be fussed about. Chance can't possibly meet you on the field. He's got a queer pin, you know."

"Excuse me, gentlemen." The host, Samuel Bevans stood at the head of the table.

And just in time, Desmond thought.

"I ask you not to delay finishing your port so we might get started with this evening's entertainment."

"I do hope it includes some slap and tickle with the ladies," Monty said confidentially to Desmond before pushing away from the table. He followed Sir Cornelius who was the first to leave the dining room.

WITHOUT A DECENT MEAL, Peg felt impatient and jittery when all the women settled themselves in the Saloon. They sat in chairs congregated around the hearth. Peg sat on the sofa, close to one of the side doors and wondered if there was a way she could slip out unnoticed.

With the men tending to their port and the women occupied in gossip, this would be the perfect opportunity to search of Bevans' private study, more specifically the desk with the secret drawer. Would she find them here?

She'd have to risk it. What was the worst that could happen if she were caught? She could explain that she was on her way to pluck a rose and got lost. Believable story or not, she was going to stick with it.

When she stood, Peg moved as not to draw attention to herself and only got as far as two steps toward the door. She startled when the main double doors flung wide open. The gentlemen had arrived.

Her plans were now on hold. Peg didn't want to make a search at midnight, but she might not have any other choice. Lady Margaret...in the study...at midnight...it sounded like the Accusation in a *Clue* board game.

A minute later, Desmond stood by Peg's side. "The other gentlemen are hoping to begin the evening with a little *distraction in the dark.*"

Peg tilted her head, puzzled.

"Do you wish to be distracted? I would be more than willing to oblige you."

Ain't that the truth. And Peg didn't doubt for a moment that he'd do more than an adequate job. Distraction, that is. She had to keep focused. His safety came before any of her or his fantasies.

"The mate to this is what you seek." Mr Bevans held up a white satin slipper then passed it to one of the guests to examine. "I wish you all happy hunting! We begin in fifteen minutes."

Hunting?

"Need he use that word?" Peg felt sick to her stomach.

"Do you still insist I am in danger?" Desmond whispered.

"You just won't believe it, will you?"

"It is difficult to lend credence to such a claim."

"Don't worry," Peg assured him. "I plan to find you your proof." As soon as everyone split up for the slipper search, she would head for the solicitor's study.

Chance limped over, interrupting their coze. "Bloody bad luck, Pierce," he grumbled. "I couldn't fetch the blasted slipper. It would need to be set in front of me on a silk cushion."

Desmond clapped his arm around his friend's shoulders. "But think of the fun you'll have discovering its whereabouts."

"Damned waste of time, I say."

Desmond's brows furrowed. "That's not at all like you, to turn down an opportunity to dally with the ladies."

Chance wriggled out from under Desmond's arm and walked away, leaning heavily on his cane accompanied by disgruntled sounds. With a confused look on his face, Desmond turned from his friend to Peg. "This is an evening full of abnormalities. I couldn't help but notice you barely touched a thing at supper."

Who made him food monitor?

"I wasn't very hungry." She lied. He didn't need to know she was starving. "I couldn't help but notice your friend, Mr Waite, he hardly took a bite either."

"No matter how odd his behavior appears now, I can assure you, his appetite is quite normal. *Mr Waite* had partaken of a rabbit, in Julia sauce I believe, and two mugs of ale only hours before the dinner gong sounded," Desmond explained. "I hardly think he would care to indulge further."

Peg glanced at Chance. So he ate before he sat down to dinner. *Smart man.*

"Now tell me, where shall we conduct our search?" Desmond's voice softened, growing more intimate.

"*We* are not searching anywhere. I have plans of my own." Peg couldn't imagine a more perfect opportunity.

"Is that so? Anyone I need concern myself with?" He arched an eyebrow and the muscles in his jaw tightened.

Peg smiled. Desmond looked good jealous. Too bad she hadn't the time to enjoy it.

"Not at all," she replied. "You make your search and I'll make mine."

"Good luck to you, then." Desmond left Peg and strode over to Sir Julian. With his friend's help, Desmond shrugged out of his dress coat. His eyes turned dark and his face had hardened. He looked quite dangerous.

I wouldn't want to run into him in a dark alley.

"It is time!" Samuel Bevans pocketed his watch. "I wish you all luck finding what you seek."

The guests filed out of the room spouting rousing spirits and encouraging cheers. Besides the host and hostess, Desmond, Peg, and Kate were left. Peg held Kate by the arm, preventing her friend's departure and watched Desmond march out of the room and off to the right.

"Come on." Peg headed to the left.

"But Desmond went that way." Kate pointed off to the right.

"It doesn't matter which way he went. I want to find Mr Bevans' private study, the one next to his bedroom. And you're coming with me."

Peg didn't allow Kate to protest. She needed Kate to stand lookout while she searched the solicitor's desk for the secret compartment. That was where the tontine papers were kept. If she could get them and show them to Desmond, he would have to believe her. Then she could just replace them and no one would be the wiser.

Peg and Kate slipped down the hall, around the corner, and into the private library. Light from the fire and several sconces gave the room a warm glow. Enough for her to make her search.

"You stand here and keep watch." Peg turned Kate by the shoulders and positioned her at the slightly open door. "Let me know if you see anyone. I'm going to check his desk."

"I'm sure the slipper isn't hidden in there," Kate said.

"I'm not looking for the slipper."

"Then why are you doing this?"

"Just stand by the door and keep watch!" Peg ordered.

"Very well." Kate hustled into place. "I'm warning you, Margaret, if I do not meet up with Sir Cornelius I shall be quite vexed."

Peg ignored Kate. Sir Cornelius could wait. All Kate's men could wait.

Once inside the study, Peg moved to the desk. As far as she could tell it looked to be the same as the one in the museum. She pulled out the chair and lowered herself. She started her search at the top left-hand drawer.

Nothing. Peg looked in the other drawers. She searched for a catch, button, or some type of release that would open the secret compartment. It was somewhere in this desk, it had to be. She knew it was here, she'd seen it with her own eyes and it had to be here now.

"Someone's coming!" Kate pushed the door closed and headed into the room.

Peg leaped out of the chair and replaced it under the desk.

The footsteps became audible. Peg and Kate glanced at each other, exchanging horrified expressions.

"Hide!" Peg called out. With her skirts flying, she followed Kate who headed toward the window and darted behind the long drapery, arranging the bilious material in front of her. Not having the nineteenth century hide-and-go-seek experience, Peg mimicked her friend's action and hid behind the other.

Peg held her breath and waited. The soft sound of the well-oiled latch clicked open and *thunked* closed. Someone was in the room with them.

She detected the slight scent of sandalwood. It was a man. She could barely hear him breathing. She could feel his presence. After several moments in silence, Peg peeked out from behind her drape.

"Drat, it's Gerald." Peg couldn't believe it. "What's he doing here?"

"I don't know," Kate whispered back.

Peg cursed her ill-luck. This cloak and dagger stuff was complex. Far more complex than any Regency novel she'd ever read. Perhaps she would have been better off reading more Agatha Christie to hone her sleuthing skills.

Gerald paced about the room in a slow perusal, examining the fixtures as if they would spring to life. What had he expected to find?

"Come on out," he called. Gerald must have heard them. "I know you're here."

"Whatever are we going to do?" Kate whispered to her from across the window alcove.

"I don't know, but whatever it is, we should make it fast."

"Maybe he'll give up and go away."

"Darn his stubborn, pigheadedness," Peg swore. "Trust me, he never gives up."

"Is that you, Juliana?" he called out, almost singing her name. "Sophie?" he tried again. "Penny?" and yet again.

He waited expectantly. After a few moments when female companionship failed to materialize, he let out a sad, rueful sigh.

"Well," Kate's musical and dreamy voice sounded odd. "If he insists on staying, I do not see any reason we should disappoint him now, should we?"

A log in the hearth dropped and the light in the room flared for an instant when Peg caught Kate's strange expression. "What are you talking about?"

"Get out when you get the chance." Kate fingered the curls, feathering them soft around her face. She straightened the neckline of her dress, drawing it downward, displaying her cleavage. Lifting her chin and thrusting out her chest, she drew aside the curtain that had concealed her.

"Are you crazy? What do you think you're doing?" Peg just about gave herself away.

Kate sashayed into the room with a rustle of fabric. Gerald turned to face her.

"Who do we have here? Princess Kate," he crooned, in the usual pretentious tone he used for her. "You're just about the last person I expected to see."

"Was I?" she said in a coy voice Peg could hardly recognize as her friend's. Peg could only see Kate's back. Her head lolled to one side. Alternately, her shoulders swiveled to and fro and her hips swayed from side to side, as she advanced.

Gerald took Kate's proffered hand and brought it to his lips. "I always thought I disgusted you," he said, studying her face.

Kate returned his gaze with equal intensity. "Disgusted me?" She gave a trill of laughter. "You're so silly. Nothing could be further from the truth."

It seemed that Gerald didn't disgust Kate anymore. Kate ran her fingers through his hair, ruffling his once styled-to-perfection coif.

Oh no, this could not be happening. Not Kate and Gerald.

"On the contrary, I had hoped that someday our estrangement would end." Kate's voice grew husky and seductive. "I'm willing to span the gap between us if you are."

"How can I resist?" And he didn't even make the effort to try. Gerald launched toward Kate and pulled her into his arms. That was a sight Peg thought she'd never, ever see. They never even spoke. Although, they weren't speaking much now either.

Way to take one for the team, Kate.

Gerald slid his hands up her arms and ran his fingers along her neck. He jerked down on Kate's small puffed sleeves, baring her shoulders. The sound of strained fabric, then a gasp of pleasure rent the air when Gerald forced the front of Kate's bodice to her waist.

"Ah-hh, Gerald," Kate rasped in a hoarse whisper then laughed with pleasure. "Things might grow complicated, don't you think? Margaret is your sister and my best friend."

"Or it could make things very convenient," he said, offering an alternative perspective. "No searching for a warm, willing male when you feel the need. I'll be close at hand to satisfy your every whim."

They came together in a searing, open-mouthed, tongue-twisting kiss.

"Oh-hh, Ger-rald." She moaned.

"You see, I am always ready. At present, very willing and quite able to continue."

Kate rocked her head back, submitting in full to whatever his pleasure might be. Gerald ground his hips into her, pressing Kate against a piece of furniture. Their hands groped each other, exploring the other while the hearth blazed fully illuminating them. Gerald used one hand to sweep her skirts from her lower limbs. To no surprise to Peg, Kate wore nothing under her dress and he grabbed her...

"Oh-hh my...yes... Ger-ra-ald." There was more than a hint of a smile in her voice. Kate must have been well-pleased.

Peg did not want to see any more. She closed her eyes and turned away, trying to ignore the couple. But she couldn't shut out the sounds of their mounting passion.

Gerald growled.

Kate moaned.

Peg shuddered. There was no way she could occupy the same room with her brother and her best friend while they mended their fences or whatever they wanted to call it.

She had to get out. Now.

The only exits were through the door in which she had entered and the window behind her. The door was too risky. But as difficult as the window might be, Peg was sure they wouldn't hear any incidental noise she might make climbing out. Kate and Gerald were far too occupied.

Peg swung the window open and glanced down over the railing. She didn't have a fear of heights, but she did have a healthy respect for the distance between her and the ground below.

The couple's laughter, gasps, and moans urged Peg out onto the small balcony. She climbed onto the sill then stepped out onto the ledge. She hugged the building to keep her balance and shuffled along the narrow ledge, moving closer and closer to the next window.

She stepped over the railing of the adjacent room and opened the window that was slightly ajar. Luckily it was open. Peg looked inside. Good, it was dark. She hopped off the sill, stepped inside the room and closed the window. She waited, taking a moment to catch her breath and regain her balance.

Silence.

When she turned away from the window Peg came face to face with Pierce Desmond.

CHAPTER 10

"WHAT ARE YOU DOING IN HERE?" Margaret asked.

"A better question might be, what are you doing in here?" The single lit taper, providing the sole illumination, wavered between them in the room. Margaret's presence not so much surprised him as it amused him. Several ideas came to mind now that he was alone with her in a darkened bedchamber.

Margaret's tousled hair framed her slightly flushed face, making her look so very desirable.

Desmond's head jerked toward the door. Footsteps. "Quick, get on the bed," he instructed, hurrying her from the window into the room.

"On the bed?"

Desmond dove forward, catching Margaret with his arm, taking her with him. He wrenched his cravat askew and raked his hand through his hair, making it appear unruly.

After settling himself between her legs, Desmond drew her skirt up on the side with one hand, exposing her gartered leg to the hip. He cupped her bare bottom for those who entered to see, lending an authenticity to their staged drama.

Margaret groaned under his weight. Keeping a watch on the door, Desmond buried his head into her neck.

The door swung wide open and the light from the multi-branched candles reflected off her white thigh.

Desmond's head rose, facing the intruder when they entered. "Can't a man have some privacy around here?" he complained at the ill-timed interruption.

"Oh, I say, Desmond," Bevans replied casually. "This is my bedchamber."

Desmond looked around as if noticing where he was for the first time. "Is it?"

"Get off, you oaf," Margaret shoved Desmond, who obediently rolled to one side. "This isn't public entertainment." She stood, holding her skirts around her lower limbs and stalked past Bevans.

"Bloody hell," Desmond swore, sprawling across the rumpled counterpane. "I nearly had her."

"Sorry," Bevans said, not sounding the least bit sorry. "Perhaps next time you could plan on using your own bed."

Desmond stared from beneath his lowered lids and gave a lewd half-smile. "I don't ask questions when a lady is willing." He staggered out of the room after his flown ladybird.

PEG BOLTED OUT OF MR BEVANS' room, flew up the stairs, and promptly ran into Kate in the hallway.

"Where did you manage to get off to?" Kate asked, stopping Peg in the corridor.

"Where did I..." Peg uttered in disbelief. How could Kate bring herself to talk about what happened? She wasn't at all embarrassed or ashamed of what she did in the study with...

with... "You didn't expect me to stand there and...*stand there*, did you?"

"You were not discovered, and I—"

"I...I...can very well guess what happened to you. I...can't believe you'd...with...Gerald!"

Kate scanned the top of Peg's head. "And you've managed to lose your ribbon doing what I expect very similar," she pointed out, before turning on her heel and exiting down the hall.

Peg checked her hair. Her ribbon was gone. She could not deny it was Desmond's quick thinking that had saved them from discovery from someplace they ought not to have been. But to admit she lost her ribbon while playing toss and tumble with Desmond would have been embarrassing.

Peg marched straight to her room. Her dress was rumpled, her hair was one huge tangle, and her emotional state did not fare any better.

"I want to get ready for bed," she announced to Nora.

"Now?" Nora gasped. "But it is just eleven."

"I am well aware of the time, thank you." Peg sat at her dressing table, waiting for Nora to deal with the rat's nest that was once her hair. "If you please, Nora."

Peg requested Nora send for a pot of tea before starting. Which Nora did, then she sprang to work, removing the tangles and pins and brushing out the few remaining curls.

While Peg sat, she fumed at her bungled attempt to find the papers she needed to prove she was telling the truth. Gerald had ruined everything.

Gerald who came barging into the study.

Gerald who couldn't do without his hourly sex fix.

Gerald who had that fix with Kate, of all people.

Most of Peg's anger centered on Desmond. She couldn't discount he had also saved them from being discovered in a place they shouldn't have been but it was the way he did it. Tossing her onto the bed like a rag doll and exposing her naked body wouldn't have been her first choice in distracting their intruder.

Peg felt herself blush as she remembered the feel of his warm hand sliding up her thigh and cupping her— Well, he was loitering in an area that he hadn't any business near.

What did he think he was doing there in that dark room alone? Desmond might have been searching for a game female as Gerald had. But something inside Peg told her that wasn't true.

Normally Desmond's touch was magic, casting a spell keeping her motionless while his voice purred soft seductive words, and persuading her she wanted him as much as he wanted her. Tonight Desmond's mood had not seemed to be of an amorous nature.

He stared into her eyes to make sure his intentions were not misunderstood. She knew what he wanted...to see mutual regard in her eyes. She suspected that was the reason why he stopped. As they lay on the bed tonight, it was not her eyes he had watched, it was the door. He was waiting for the intruder, Bevans.

Peg had been in the study, while Desmond was in the solicitor's bedroom doing the same thing she did—searching for proof of the tontine.

Then he believed her.

It wasn't until the tea tray arrived that Peg wondered if he had found something. He really didn't have a chance to tell her before the interruption.

After Nora had left for the night, Peg sat at the writing table before heading to bed. She folded a sheet of paper and tore it in half, then in half again before writing a short note to Desmond.

She paused before signing her name. Not Peg.

Lady Margaret? Lady Margaret White?

With the quill poised in her hand, Peg signed: *Margaret*.

Affixing her name made it permanent. She wasn't Peg anymore. She was Margaret.

And from now on, she would think of herself only as Margaret.

By the time she had finished her second cup of tea, the ink had dried and she folded the note. This was not a task to be trusted to a maid, Margaret would deliver this message herself. She stepped outside her bedchamber, moved down the hall, and slid the note under Desmond's door.

❧

DESMOND WALKED into his room to retire for the night and stepped on a small, folded piece of paper.

Wait for me in your room tonight.
Margaret

No doubt she wanted to , or better yet berate him for his behavior earlier that evening. Even in the tense, rushed moments of panic he was fully conscious of her fragrance when he rubbed his face in the softness of her neck. He had not kissed or fondled her, he only did what was necessary to explain their presence in such an unlikely place, not for any pleasure. Although pleasure was had if only for a moment.

How much better it would feel if she had squirmed beneath him in passion instead of protest. Although protest was not so unpleasant.

He would wait until she gave herself to him. Love by consent was preferable to love by submission. And how she continued to tease him. Encouraging and eager for him one moment, cool and indifferent the next. How he wished she would stop all this nonsense.

She was taking up more and more of his waking thoughts. The same question he had continually fought to hide surfaced in his mind. Was she mad? He couldn't believe that. If she were, he might not be far behind.

It was three in the morning. An hour ago Margaret had heard the sounds of the guests retiring for the night. She donned her wrapper, getting ready to visit Desmond. She pressed her ear to the door and carefully cracked it open. The creaks and groans of the floorboards and muffled clicks of door latches from the nearby rooms caused her to pause. An acrid trace of burning candles wafted in from the hallway.

Margaret cracked open her door and peeked into the hall. She saw someone slip into Mrs Juliana Sumner's room next door. There were a few moments of silence before Sir Cornelius, carrying a light that illuminated his face, crept out of his room and slip into Kate's room. Margaret drew in her breath. She had just missed him.

Without the benefit of lighting, Margaret left her room and crossed to Desmond's. She didn't knock, he was expecting her. She opened the door and slipped inside, keeping her eye on the activity in the hallway.

"What is it?" Desmond drawled. He swirled his brandy and settled on a chair, crossing his legs on the footstool.

Her mouth dropped open in shock. "I just saw Sir Cornelius go into Kate's room."

"And, I fear" —he squeezed his eyes closed— "not for the

same reasons you are in mine." He took a long drink from his glass.

What was that supposed to mean? Margaret turned around and leaned against the door. She looked at Desmond, taking her time to study him.

He wore a dressing gown, the white linen of his shirt lay open at his neck, exposing the dark curly hair on his chest. The sleeves were rolled up displaying his sculpted forearms and his legs were bare to the knees.

"Do you have any idea how much I want to toss you in bed and crush you with my body." His voice was thick, filled with desire, looking at her from under hooded eyes. The shadows contoured his face gave him a stark, dramatic appearance.

He's probably had too much to drink.

"We've already done that earlier this evening, don't you remember? And what, by the way, do you think you were doing in there in the first place?"

Desmond sat up in the chair. "I was searching for proof of this tontine you say I am a part of. However" —He looked her from head to toe— "I managed to get sidetracked." His heavy-lidded gaze lingered on her. "Why can't you forget that silly notion and concentrate on more pressing matters?"

"Silly notion?" All he wanted to do was make love to her. "You are such a jerk!" slipped out in a burst of temper. "I'm trying to save your life and all you can think about is your raging hormones!"

Desmond stared at her as if she were more than just a little crazy. Maybe she shouldn't have said what she said. She was hungry, drunk from the champagne, or maybe hungover, and really tired.

Oopsy.

He remained calm. "By your tone, I imagine you were

insulting me. However, I find your choice of words strange." He looked at her, squinting. "To be honest, I never cause any whores to moan, because I have no need to frequent brothels." He paused for a moment. "And I believe your behavior to be somewhat peculiar."

"Peculiar?" She regretted her harsh words. What had she said? She couldn't even remember. "No, there's nothing peculiar." That came out more awkward than she would have liked. Margaret pretended everything was normal despite the lapse in her word choice. If he could only forget her outburst. At least she hoped he could. He had been drinking, after all.

"You know," he began, then stopped. Desmond pressed into the back of his chair, cupping his chin. He brought his index finger to his lip in contemplation and narrowed his eyes. Every second that he stared at her in silence made Margaret more and more uncomfortable. "The more I think on it, I find there is something rather unusual about you. Although I cannot name specifics."

"Unusual?" Margaret's voice rose, sounding odd to her own ears. "Whatever could you mean?"

"Just now for instance. You seemed shocked by Sir Cornelius entering into Lady Catherine's room."

"But it is the middle of the night," she added for credibility. "I understand that at house parties..."

"For a man to creep into a lady's room is not unexpected. On the other hand, a lady to come to a man's room is far more scandalous."

Margaret tried not to act self-conscious and said nothing.

"Not only do you come to my room, you find me in my undress, baring my legs and you do not appear in the least shocked."

"That's not at all true," Margaret countered. "I was. I mean

—I am. Very shocked." She was backpedaling as fast as she could. She displayed a delayed wide-eyed and open-mouthed gasp of horror that did nothing to convince him.

Apparently, he wasn't *that* drunk. Desmond wasn't buying her explanation.

"I had believed your unusual behavior was due to grief from Alison's death. But now, I think it is something else altogether."

Margaret knew exactly what Desmond meant. But he didn't know. How could he? She was out of place and he had felt it ever since she arrived. She hadn't fooled him one bit.

"I have a feeling if I were to shed my wrap it would not shock you in the least."

She swallowed hard during his contemplative pause. "It would, believe me, it would."

"But not like a *lady* with your experience would feign shock. For some reason, you can't pretend that. I don't think you are really Quality."

Margaret straightened and raised her chin to look down her nose at him, making a last-ditch effort to save herself. "I beg your pardon. I am the daughter of an earl. How dare you say I am not Quality."

He raised his glass in salute to her performance. "You've got the airs down, I'll give you that. But the subtlety escapes you."

It irritated Margaret to hear she couldn't pull off the Regency Miss act. Well, *he* was the real thing, of course, he would easily have been able to spot an impostor.

"There is another thing that strikes me as extremely peculiar. Before Lady Melbourne's party, I have never found you the slightest bit interesting. I can honestly say after that evening you interest me on the verge of obsession." Desmond took a deep drink of his brandy and studied her over the rim of his glass. "I cannot for the life of me imagine why. Given time, I believe I shall discover your secret." He smiled and winked. It appeared he took it as a personal challenge. "You present me with the most perplexing puzzle. I find it has made you most irresistible and I cannot wait to claim my prize." He gave a throaty laugh. "It may take some time but I will."

"It is far from a laughing matter," Margaret spoke in a grave tone, hoping he would take her just as seriously. "If I am not mistaken, it will not be only you who suffer. If I were you I would show some serious concern for your friend, Mr Waite. I'm afraid the first attempt on his life will not be the last."

With that, she left his room.

ۏ

THE NEXT MORNING, no one had acted as if any impropriety had occurred during the night. The sounds of guests returning to their own rooms around six woke her.

No wonder guests and house parties slept in until ten.

Not all the guests, Margaret thought. She shared the break-fast room with Chance, Mr Waite, who sat at the far end of the long table and he had erected a newspaper barrier between them.

He had been here before she arrived just after nine. Margaret heeded his body language that told her to keep her distance. She took a place at the opposite end of the table.

Not too much later, Sophia Blake and Penelope Whitford, wives of the other two law partners entered and greeted Margaret. As they strolled by Mr Waite and wished him the very same pleasant greeting, they were met with a most unhappy reply.

"It bloody-well is morning, and what's so good about it?"

The women faded back, moving toward Margaret's end of the table and settled with their morning tea in an empty section —far enough from the grumpy Mr Waite and just out of earshot from Margaret to conduct their conversation in private. From her end of the table, Margaret noticed how flushed his face was, and she imagined he had a right to feel embarrassed by the uncivil way he spoke to them.

"A man can't find peace and quiet around here! I could get more quiet at Pierce's Curzon townhouse in London. You cackling hens make this place an absolute hell!" He ruffled the paper, trying to arrange it into some desired shape.

He certainly got up on the wrong side of the bed. Maybe that was the problem. Getting up in his own bed and not some obliging female's.

Chance rubbed his eyes and cursed the print size of the paper. "I swear these blasted things get smaller by the week. Makes me think my eyesight's going when I full-well know I see like a hawk." Several deliberate blinks followed to clear his eyes before the newsprint barrier rose between them again.

"And how are you doing this morning, Margaret?" With an air of full-contentment, Kate took the seat next to Margaret.

"I'm afraid I did not sleep well. I couldn't quite get settled," Margaret admitted. She made a careful study of Kate. The palest shade of pink flushed over her cheeks. Her friend appeared absolutely radiant.

Kate gave a heavy, satisfied sigh.

At least with Kate's fickleness, she would have moved on after her momentary transgression with Gerald. "Who is he? Sir Cornelius?" Margaret had a momentary mental-flash of Sir Cornelius sneaking into Kate's room last night.

Kate did not respond.

"Is it Mr Waite?" Margaret whispered, her words barely audible. She glanced at Chance's newspaper then back to Kate.

Again, there was no reaction from her friend. Kate lifted her cup and sipped.

Margaret hated herself for being pulled into this but she

wanted to know who the mystery man that had so-captured Kate's attention. His identity really couldn't be all that much of a mystery. He had to be one of the guests.

"You never told me your brother was so charming, so attentive, so...accomplished."

"Gerald?" Margaret choked on her tea.

"Shhh." Kate glanced about the room. "No need to announce it to everyone."

Margaret leaned closer to Kate, settling her elbows on the table. "Gerald? You can't be serious."

"You never told me he was so... so..." Kate could barely contain her excitement. "But then again, I suppose you wouldn't know about that."

Margaret sat up, easing back into the chair. "Please, you'll put me off my breakfast."

"I hate to think what I've been missing these past years with our silly quarreling." Kate groaned. "Had I met Gerald earlier, I would not have bothered with Sir Seymour. Although, I doubt my husband would have appreciated his new bride spending her wedding night with another man."

"But what about— I saw—" Margaret stopped and lowered her volume. "If you're so taken with...Gerald, then why did you allow Sir Cornelius into your room?"

"Sir Cornelius means nothing."

"You mean to tell me you allow a man into your room in the middle of the night and do... whatever... and he means nothing?"

"Oh, pooh, Margaret. You cannot see more than one man at a time. You are so faithful."

Lady Margaret's husband, Mr White, might not see it that way.

"We can't all be as upstanding as you are." Kate took a sip of coffee then continued. "If you must know, I allowed Sir

SHIRLEY MARKS

Cornelius to spout his poetic words, kiss the arches of my feet, and then I sent him on his way." She leaned forward and whispered. "I knew your brother would soon arrive."

"He kissed your feet?" Her friend's words did not make a pretty picture; Margaret grimaced.

Kate laughed. "He's so grateful to have anything to do with me. I have been casting him loving glances since our arrival. He is an attractive man, don't you agree? It was time to move him on or lose him in the game."

"Love is not a game."

"I am not in love." Kate waved a hand at Margaret.

"Sir Cornelius is." How could a person treat another in that way?

"Oh, posh! He is playing the most complex game of all."

Margaret didn't understand what Kate was getting at.

"He recites his poetry until my ears are saturated with words of love. When I can hardly stand for him to utter another word, I bestow upon him a favor."

"Favor? What kind of favor?" Margaret was almost afraid to ask.

"Ours is a delicate balancing act." Kate chose her words with care. "I cannot allow him too much affection, too soon, else all is lost. I had captivated him with suggestive looks and kept him interested with stolen glances whilst I am occupied with other gentlemen."

"When you're with other men? How does he put up with that?"

"Put up with it? He expects it."

"Expects it? That's sick."

"You are so busy finding the perfect man that you don't have fun playing with the ones around you."

"Men are not toys," Margaret stated.

"That's rich, coming from you. You were the one who

taught me to play the game." Kate flipped the corner of her cloth napkin and broke out into a wicked smile. "But they can be very entertaining if you treat them correctly."

Lady Margaret! How could she? "At least I know you're not serious about Gerald."

"I don't know," Kate said with a tilt to her head, considering her options. "It might be worth divorce. Even murder perhaps."

Margaret stared. She couldn't believe Kate would even consider such a thing.

"A large dose of laudanum in Mr Holloway's brandy and no one would be the wiser."

"Kate!" Margaret gasped, outraged at the very mention of—

"It was only in jest." Kate chuckled. "Honestly Margaret, you're ever-so serious."

"Good morning, ladies." Mrs Bevans stopped at the empty chair on the other side of Kate.

"Good morning, Mrs Bevans," Kate returned.

"Are you feeling all right, Lady Margaret? You look a bit flushed," Mrs Bevans asked in apparent concern.

"Too hot," Margaret said. "The tea. I should have allowed it time to cool."

"One must take care, you wouldn't want to burn your mouth."

"Yes, it was careless of me." Margaret blew into her cup before taking another swallow. "I'm sure it'll be fine."

"Have all the men gone out hunting?" Kate asked and Mrs Bevans then flashed Margaret a sneaky side glance.

"Hunting?" Margaret nearly panicked, the idea of weapons terrified her. The prospect of another hunting accident wouldn't entirely be out of the question. After all, it had happened to the late Viscount Alison.

"No, dear," Mrs Bevans reassured her, laying her hand upon Margaret's arm. "The gentlemen merely went out for a morning ride. All the men have gone except for Mr Waite." The hostess gestured to the end of the table with a nod of her head.

A renewed smile settled over Kate's face, now she understood. "So Mr Waite really is alone?"

Margaret glanced toward the heavens. Without a doubt, if he were the only male around Kate would certainly amuse herself with him.

"His injury, you know. It prevents him from riding." Mrs Bevans rose and moved to the sideboard.

Kate smiled. "But it doesn't prevent him from being ridden," she added in a barely audible whisper meant for Margaret.

Mrs Bevans returned with toast and eggs on her plate. "He has managed to keep himself busy."

I'll just bet he has, Margaret thought.

Mrs Bevans chewed a dainty bite and swallowed. "He's caught three of them so far."

Three women? Is that what the hostess meant? Was it common for men to broadcast their conquests?

"I believe he's finishing the last one off this afternoon."

Margaret choked on her tea. "I beg your pardon!"

"Are you all right, Margaret?" Kate reached over to slap Margaret on the back.

She coughed, but managed, "It really isn't appropriate for the breakfast table."

"One would think in the dining room at supper, shared by all would prove to be the best," was Mrs Bevans suggestion.

"What?" Margaret must have misunderstood.

"And from what I hear there is plenty to go around." Mrs Bevans sat across from Kate and set her breakfast plate on the table.

Margaret just stared.

"Don't you care for rabbit, Lady Margaret?" The hostess paused, delicately holding her piece of toast.

"Rab-bit? We're talking about rabbits?" She uttered in a toneless staccato.

"Mr Waite has proved a real talent for snaring them," Mrs Bevans complimented. "As I said, the difficulty is he will not share them with anyone."

"And he is usually so good about sharing," Kate threw in.

CHAPTER 11

A WOMAN'S horrified cry rang through the halls of the mansion. Desmond had just entered the house, returning from his morning ride with the other gentlemen, and ran down the corridor to find Lady Payne in the library. She stood over the motionless body of Chauncy Waite.

"He's dead!" she cried. "Oh my God, he's dead!"

Desmond drew Lady Payne back, pulling her from the sight of the corpse. Carroll Sumner and Sir Quincy pushed through the gathering crowd at the door. Sir Quincy pulled his terrified wife into his arms, lending comfort.

"Good God, Desmond, what the bloody hell happened?" he demanded.

"It's Chance...he's..." Desmond could not comprehend what he now saw with his own eyes.

"I... I just...found him that way." Lady Payne sobbed uncontrollably between every few words. "He was...he was there...on the carpet. Just...just as you see...."

"There, there, Constance, let me take you away from here. Don't give this wretched business another thought." Sir Quincy gestured to Desmond that he and his wife were leaving.

Gerald, who stood at the door, allowed the couple to exit and barred any ladies from entering the room.

Monty knelt near the body, making a closer examination. Desmond looked down at their friend.

"He's dead," Desmond whispered. "She was right, he's been murdered."

"Murdered?" Sumner repeated, nearing Desmond.

"Margaret was right." Desmond couldn't believe it. "She said she *knew*..." He had to tell her. She'd told him Chance was next to die and it had happened.

Monty stood. "I daresay Chance had eaten himself to death. Death by gluttony," he eulogized.

"I think he must have been poisoned, Monty." Desmond assumed since he could not see any obvious marks of violence.

"Poisoned?" Monty repeated in a voice of mocking disbelief. "Except for those in the animal kingdom, he hasn't an enemy in the world. Who would ever kill *him*?"

"What's that you have there?" Desmond asked when he spied a small object in Monty's hand.

Monty had been swinging their recently deceased friend's lucky rabbit's foot by a finger. He handed it to Desmond. "A lot of good it did him." Monty pulled out his snuff box and chuckled.

"I think that's enough of your rapier wit," Desmond reprimanded, took the rabbit's foot, held it firmly in his hand, and continued out the door.

IN THE BREAKFAST ROOM, Kate gazed wide-eyed at the door at the same time Margaret heard heavy footsteps approach. She barely had time to turn around to see Desmond before he took her by the arm.

"Desmond, you smell like horse sweat and now you're acting like a horse's backside," Kate commented. "You might at least have the decency to have washed and changed your clothes unless you plan to play the stallion in search of a mare."

Without replying to Kate, Desmond ushered Margaret out of the room.

"What do you think you're—" she complained while he pushed her out the door.

"Do not say a word, do you understand me? Not one word."

Desmond kept moving forward and didn't bother to speak. Margaret took three to every one of his steps to keep up. In a serious calm, he repeated his warning to keep quiet and not to struggle all the way up the stairs to her room. Once inside he allowed her to wrench free.

"What the hell do you think you're doing?" she demanded.

"Chance is dead," Desmond said without preamble.

Margaret was too shocked to speak.

"Did you hear what I said? I said your premonition has come true. Chance is dead. When the authorities come around, what are you going to tell them?"

"What do you mean, what am I going to tell them?" He behaved as if she had done the deed. And no, she did not know who was responsible.

"You had prior knowledge of his death, did you not? And you have threatened me on several occasions, did you not?"

"Those were not threats, they were warnings," she clarified.

"You must tell me exactly how you knew lest be implicated in his murder."

"How could I be?" Margaret had known... Well, she knew *someone* was going to die. Actually, she knew several someones were going to die before this weekend was done. But she did not know any specifics.

"You may be implicated when the authorities ask questions."

"Me?" How could he repeat anything she told him in confidence? Margaret wanted to save his life. She didn't want— "You wouldn't."

"I fear I must. Whatever I feel for you, I cannot let a murderer go free. Even a beautiful one." He cupped her chin in his palm then drew away, lingering a finger down her jaw. "I cannot, in all honesty, think you guilty, but I must hear it from your own lips."

She wasn't guilty but she wasn't entirely innocent either because she knew that it—they would happen...the murder—the murders. But how could she tell him why she had known? This was impossible. Margaret turned away from him. He could misinterpret her indecision as some sort of admission of guilt. "I will tell you, but I doubt you will believe me."

"I cannot imagine an explanation so fantastic it would not be acceptable."

"All right then." Margaret took a breath and paused. She couldn't blame him for not understanding what had happened to her. This *had* happened to her and she had a hard time believing it. "I shall tell you everything."

Desmond pulled the chair from the writing desk and planted himself on the seat. He crossed his leg and with one foot on the fireguard he tilted the chair back, balancing on its back legs. He crossed his arms, stared at her, and drew in a breath.

"I am ready. You may begin at any time."

"I suppose I ought to start at the beginning." Margaret stood in front of him and clasped her hands together as if awaiting final sentencing. How could she explain and not sound insane? "I am from the future."

The leg balancing Desmond in his chair stiffened, sending him toppling backward, he landed in a sprawl on his back. "I beg your pardon. I'm not certain I heard you correctly." He disentangled himself from the chair and sat upright. His expression did not alter but his eyes stared back, dark and filled with distrust. "Did you say you were from the future?"

"You heard right. It's just not registering. Here." Margaret reached out to him. "Let me help you up."

He hesitated to take her hand and stared at her. Ultimately he managed to get to his feet on his own. "I'm not certain I know what that means." The wind had been knocked out of him and he may have even bumped his head on the floor. One thing was for sure, he had been shaken.

"I'm not even British." Margaret had maintained her accent for so long, she had to make a conscious effort to speak as she normally did. "America...I'm from America." Her voice sounded strange, even to her.

"America?" he echoed, sounding skeptical.

And he had every right to be. To top it off, she knew from here her explanation would only sound worse. Where to start... where to start... What could she possibly tell him that he'd believe?

"Although I may look like Lady Margaret to you—No...I can't speak in that voice anymore." She shook her head. "I am not really Lady Margaret."

"Then you are a fraud." Desmond righted the chair and sat.

That word made her sound as if she had done all this on purpose, acted with malicious intent as if she had meant to trick and deceive those around her. She hardly had a choice in the matter.

It wasn't her idea to travel back to 1813. It wasn't her idea to watch history play out in real time. And it certainly wasn't her idea to play guardian angel to Pierce Desmond.

"Fraud sounds so...dishonest. I didn't make all this happen."

"Really?" It didn't sound as if he believed her.

"My real name is Margaret... Margaret Swanson." She watched his face—the expression in his unbelieving eyes. "And I'm from over two hundred years in the future."

He broke out in laughter. Hysterical laughter. "Am I really to believe you're from the future? Based on what?"

What could she tell him? The existence of cars, planes, and smartphones would be too fantastic to believe. He didn't even know what a phone was. How could she even explain a computer? She'd stick to the immediate future and concepts she knew he could grasp.

"I know who will win the war, the Napoleonic War, and when Prinny takes the throne, and the queen who soon takes the throne after him."

"The Queen?"

Margaret covered her mouth, silencing a horrified gasp of realization. "I can't tell you. I can't tell you any of that. If I did, I might disturb past events, the way it's supposed to happen, more than I already have."

"What are you talking about?"

"If I am not careful what I tell you I might change the course of history."

"I see."

Margaret wasn't sure he did. But she had to tell him something. Weighing the facts that she wanted to reveal to him carefully, she took her time before speaking.

"In my time, history states you win the tontine. But when I heard you were attacked I thought you had been killed and that would have changed my past. I didn't know what my presence here meant at first. I don't know what I'm supposed to do. I think I'm here to ensure you win to make certain history has the outcome I remember. But I'm not sure."

"You will excuse me if I seem" —his fingers made a circular motion— "unimpressed...with your explanation. However, I

145

shall do my best to indulge you, if only for the moment. If you cannot tell me any specifics, can you tell me how all of this happened to you?"

"I'm not sure of that myself. It's not as if I stepped into a time machine, because we don't have those."

"A *ma-chine*?" he repeated carefully.

"Maybe some sort of odd vortex pulled me here." She sighed. "I'm not sure. I came to England with a tour group. That's where I met Kate."

Desmond leaned forward, his eyes widened. "Lady Catherine? Is she from the future as well?"

"Oh no, not Lady Catherine. You see, my friend, Katie and I were staying at Ashworth House. Except now, I mean, in the future, it will become a very posh boutique hotel." She sidestepped any mention of electricity and other modern renovations. "When I finally did come here, to the past, I hardly noticed until I tried to use the bathrooms because they were gone."

"*Bath*-rooms?"

Ugh, she did it again. "Indoor plumbing—" She hadn't wanted to go there. "Used in place of chamber pots. They'll come into fashion...soon-ish."

"Ah," he said as if he knew exactly what she was talking about. "And what exactly does the house have to do with your being in this time?"

"Don't you see? It's the perfect setting. It's fate playing a joke. Sending a Regency buff back in time? It's what I've always dreamed of. At least I did when I thought it was impossible."

"Have you encountered a problem with this era?"

"It's just that...that... It's not exactly how I imagined it would be. And to my horror, I suppose it's shown me I'm more of a twenty-first century person than I thought."

"But what specifically caused you to come here. And why now?"

"I'm not sure. The evening of Lady Melbourne's party was only hours after my arrival, I think. That afternoon I received a small package. It was really old."

"What was in it?"

"*Childe Harold's Pilgrimage.* The same book Byron had sent Lady Margaret in this century."

"Lord Byron sent you his book?" This was the first thing Desmond had no problem understanding. His words were tinged with jealousy.

"It was inscribed to Lady Margaret, not me. I believe that book might have been the catalyst." Margaret moved to her nightstand to retrieve the book and handed it to Desmond.

He opened the front cover, read the inscription, then flipped through the pages, as if to prove to himself it was only a book and no more.

She studied his face. Did he really believe her? She couldn't tell. At least he took the time to listen and didn't accuse her of being a raving lunatic.

Lost in thought, Desmond looked up and allowed the book to close slowly in his hand. "Then you really did know of Chance's death." His voice was calm, emotionless. "If you knew, why didn't you try and stop it?"

"Stop it? How could I have stopped it? I didn't know how or when he was to die. I only knew he would. Maybe he was supposed to die when he was shot in London. I don't know."

"Then to you, his life is only a page in a history book."

Margaret glanced down, half-ashamed and half-saddened by his words. Even though she had met him, she hadn't really known Chance, not like she knew Desmond.

"I came here to warn you. You must believe me." She gazed

at him waiting for an expression of acceptance. "I need you to believe me."

Desmond remained quiet in contemplation. He drew his fingernails up his neck to his jaw, scraping the stubble from his beard. His momentary silence would allow her to make one last plea. She had better make this good, he might never give her another opportunity. She *had* to convince him she wasn't a crazy person.

"In my time, this house, Samuel Bevans' house is a museum. That's where I first learned of the tontine. The information in the museum said they believed Bevans had kept the papers in a secret compartment in his desk. That desk was in an exhibit, opened, showing the back of the drawer that held the papers." She illustrated the construction with her hands as best she could. "Last night, I went to his study to look for that secret compartment."

Desmond arched his brow and peered at her with a widened eye. "I take it you did not find it."

"I didn't have enough time. Gerald interrupted my search and I was trapped in the room. I went out of the window and that's when I had the misfortune of running into you."

Desmond still did not speak, and only stared at her.

"I know it all sounds crazy. If it hadn't happened to me, I'm not so sure I'd believe it myself." Margaret finally found the courage to meet his stare. "You think I've lost my mind, don't you?"

"To be honest," he began. "That possibility has occurred to me."

❧

AFTER LEAVING MARGARET'S ROOM, Desmond headed to the library sideboard for brandy. He didn't usually start drinking this early in the day, but today he would make an exception.

From the future? What a load of gammon. Did she really expect him to believe she was from the future? What kind of fool did she take him for?

He poured himself a drink. A very large portion.

It was a ridiculous explanation. However, he could not deny that Margaret's *ridiculous explanation* explained exactly how she knew of Chance's death and made sense of her inconsistent behavior.

He would have to be mad to believe her outrageous story.

But he could not imagine she would lie to him. Why? He had no idea. He took a healthy swallow of brandy. What a fool he was. He believed her.

"Bit early for that, isn't it?" After pulling the door wide open, Monty strode into the room and considerately pulled the door shut behind him.

"I had the door closed for a reason." Desmond drained his glass and refilled it for the second or was it the third time?

"Do fetch me one of those, would you?" Monty sank into one of the overstuffed chairs.

Desmond poured a splash into a second glass, measuring out a much smaller quantity than his own.

"You're a lifesaver," Monty quipped when Desmond handed him the drink.

"I don't think I'm up to battling witticisms with you at the moment." Desmond sat on the sofa as far away from Monty as he could.

"Ah yes, Chance. Poor Chance." With an all-encompassing wave, a momentary disheartened look and a few seconds of silence, Monty paid his tribute.

"Are you quite finished?" Desmond snapped with impatience.

"I suppose. Although you seem to be taking his death quite hard."

Desmond glared in return. "He was my friend."

"Mine as well. But ruining our party won't bring him back." Monty sipped his drink.

"That's heartless, even for you." Desmond wiped his mouth with the back of his hand.

"Chance would be the first to admit he wouldn't want anything to interfere with our festivities." Monty smirked. "He would if he were with us, that is."

"Just be glad it wasn't you instead of him, then. We'd still be having fun. I shouldn't think I'd mind carrying on after your demise."

Monty leaned forward, taking an interest. "Do you mean you're having problems in the nether regions?"

"For God's sake, Monty, can't you be serious for even a minute?" Desmond's hand that held his drink stopped halfway to his lips. He set the glass down on the table and pushed it away. "Have you ever thought there was more to life than parties, gambling, and bedding women?"

"Is there?" Monty stifled a yawn and pulled out his red enamel snuff box. With one hand he flipped it open, took a pinch of snuff, and in a single motion snapped the lid closed.

"I can for once admit that there is," Desmond stated.

"You say that as if you are certain."

"I am. People matter. Family, loved ones, and friends. Even obstinate friends like you."

"I do, thank you." Monty smiled and gave a gracious bow from his seat.

Desmond could feel the effects of the liquor. It numbed his overwrought mind of the grief of Chance's death and softened the trauma of Margaret's confession. It helped him tolerate Monty's foul mouth.

"Did you ever stop to think it might have been you instead of Chance?" Desmond pointed out.

"Never occurred to me," Monty replied in his staid fashion. "Why do you ask?"

"Let me tell you, Monty. We're only mortal. Chance's death is a reminder of just how fragile life can be."

Monty sniffed. "Nonsense. I plan to live forever." Then Monty coughed. "Just to prove to you—" He seemed to have some difficulty catching his breath.

Desmond leapt from his seat to his friend's side.

Monty clutched at his throat, choking. He arched backward. Then he convulsed forward, falling to the floor. Desmond stepped away. Monty jackknifed back and forward again. And again.

Desmond could do nothing for his tortured friend. Lying on the floor in a stiffened state, Monty's eyes were wide open and the expression of horror frozen on his face.

"Monty..." Desmond stared down at his friend. There would be no reply. Just like Chance, now Monty he was... Desmond backed out of the room and closed the door behind him.

By the time he could see Margaret's bedchamber he was in an all-out run. "Margaret!" His fist hammered the door. "Let me in!"

Margaret was quick to answer. "What is it?"

"My God, Margaret—it's Monty, he's dead." Desmond was gasping for air. Not from the flight up the stairs, but from fright.

She had sense enough to pull Desmond into her room and draw him away from any passersby who were on their way down for dinner.

"Not Sir Julian?" She had just sent the maid away and glanced around, making sure they were truly alone. "Try and calm down. You're going to draw attention. The dinner gong has sounded. The guests will be gathering in the drawing room."

"And some in the library." If it was possible, Desmond looked more horrified. "We can't let the other guests stumble across him. Quick, come with me." He took up her hand and headed for the door.

Margaret lifted the hem of her dress and followed Desmond down the corridor then the steps. When they reached the ground floor he offered her his arm.

"Was Monty part of the tontine?"

"I don't know." The shock of his death and the profound effect it had on Desmond caused Margaret to realize all this was very real, not just some historic story she'd read. Real people were involved.

"It was frightful. So violent." Desmond must have been reliving the dreadful moments.

It must have been terrible for him. She could feel his arm shaking under her hand. Desmond glanced about, as she did, for guests. He led her toward the library.

"One minute we were sitting there reminiscing about Chance and the next—" Desmond stopped talking when he reached the library, he turned the knob and pushed the door open.

Margaret braced herself to see Sir Julian's body sprawled across the floor but once they arrived there was no one. Nothing. There was not a trace of the gruesome scene Desmond had described.

"I thought you said he was dead?" Margaret glanced around.

"He is. Well, rather, he was." Desmond's gaze swept the room. "I don't know about your century, but in mine, dead men do not walk away. Well, not without help anyway."

"Then someone must have helped him leave."

"I can assure you, he was here" —he pointed at the center of the carpet— "and in no condition to move." Desmond strode to the far window and struck each of the full-length, damask drapes, looking for a hidden body, alive or dead. "I cannot bloody believe it!" He moved to the next windows and repeated the action at the next set of curtains. "Another murder!"

Margaret shushed him. "Do you want to announce it to the entire household?"

Desmond drew a shaking hand down his face. His saddened, strained expression reflected the loss of a friend— now two. He moved to the sideboard and poured himself a drink and downed it in a single swallow.

"All right. I'm in danger. I bow to your future knowledge, my dear. I may well be the next to meet my maker. What am I to do now?"

"First of all, stop drinking so much." Margaret yanked the glass from his hand. "As much pain as you're feeling, you need to stay alert. The best offense is a good defense." The sport's aphorism seemed to fit the situation.

"Well said. We have a saying I think might apply, fore-warned is forearmed." Desmond settled into the sofa and stared at the carpet. Where Margaret supposed, he had last seen Sir Julian.

"You must be careful. Very careful," she cautioned. Don't let your guard down." How should one take it when next in line for elimination? Margaret settled by his side and laid a comforting hand on his arm. Had she done him a disservice by telling him?

"I'm so sorry you've lost your friends," she whispered, hoping her words would lend some comfort. "Would it have been better not to have known?"

"No. I do not begrudge you your honesty. I can imagine how

much courage it took to tell me your wild tales. I might have never spoken to you again."

"But you didn't do that," she reminded him. "You were very kind to listen to what I had to say, even if it did sound crazy."

They sat in silence for several minutes before he spoke again. "What kind of monster has done this?" Desmond could not have been more direct.

"I don't know. Presumably, one of the tontine members. Someone who hates to lose."

"Do you know who the other members are?"

"The only name I was certain of was *Chance*." Margaret stopped to think for a moment. "We could go over the guests staying in the house. Maybe I'll remember something more."

"I do not believe that is sufficient time to discover who the murderer is before we leave tomorrow."

"You might be right," she hated to admit. "But I think it's worth a try. Don't you?"

"I suppose some effort is better than none at all." Desmond stood and paced on one side of the room, away from the center of the carpet.

"I believe Mr Bevans and his wife can be ruled out," she said. "He's just waiting for the survivor."

"The same could be said about the law partners and their wives. None of them have anything to gain."

"How about Major Payne?"

"Sir Quincy? I think not," Desmond explained. "Since he's a military man, I imagine he'd sooner use a saber than poison."

"It's not his style, I guess."

The sound of passing footsteps alerted him. "The others are gathering for supper." He eyed Margaret's dress and nodded with approval. "You'd best join them in the parlor."

"And what about you?"

"I want to have a look outside. If Monty is not here, it only stands to reason that he's been moved. I'm quite certain it wasn't out the door and through the house. That leaves the window." Desmond pressed a kiss on her forehead and pointed her out of the room. "Off with you now." He departed in the opposite direction.

When Margaret entered the parlor, the atmosphere really didn't hold the aura of death. Most of the guests carried on their jovial conversation, drinking and laughing as if they had not a care in the world, and didn't even show concern for the recently dearly departed.

It seemed to her that no one realized they were sharing a house with a murderer.

CHAPTER 12

"You haven't been with Desmond all this time have you?" Kate asked Margaret in the most accusing tone.

"Why yes, I have." Margaret wondered what her friend was thinking and felt a bit guarded.

"And you think *my* actions are disgraceful."

"If I may have your attention, please." Mr Bevans stood in front of the hearth and the guests quieted, moving in closer to form a semicircle around the host.

Kate drew Margaret aside, keeping a vigilant eye on the others.

The host spoke. "Before we sit down for supper, I want to apologize for the unpleasant incident some of you were subjected to this afternoon. I'm afraid we've lost some of the gay members of our party. I'm sure we can understand Sir Quincy and his wife's necessity to leave. You may rest assured Sir Quincy is confident that with a few days rest Lady Payne will be quite recovered. I have also been informed that Sir Julian has forsaken our delightful gathering. He had some pressing matters that need his immediate attention."

Left the party? More like—left the living. This was a cover-up.

Mr Bevans stepped down and the murmurs in the room resumed.

Kate continued right where she left off, not offering a single comment on the host's announcement. "I am having such a time between your brother, Sir Cornelius, and—"

"Whatever are you up to now, Kate?"

"Up to?" Kate gave the most obviously phony, wide-eyed blink of innocence. "Whatever do you mean?"

"What do you expect when you're entertaining more than one man?" If anyone deserved to be at wit's end, it had to be Kate. It was impossible to feel sorry for her. She had brought it all on herself. "Don't come crying to me just because you have your hands full."

Kate gave an all-knowing smile. "If it were merely that, your brother needs no help in that quarter."

"Please, I don't care to know."

"Why should you?" Kate shrugged. "I know you're perfectly content with Desmond. I have noticed you two have been spending an inordinate amount of time together. More than I would think the polite society of London would find acceptable."

Since when had Kate become concerned with what the *Haute Ton* considered proper?

"I suppose I was a tad bit envious in the beginning," she confessed. "Not anymore. I have Gerald now." Kate cast an adoring glance across the room.

As if Margaret didn't have enough to put up with, she had to listen to Kate's drivel as well.

"Do look who's finally come to join us." Kate pointed toward the door.

Margaret's attention focused near the doorway. There stood

an anxious Desmond, scanning the crowd, Margaret assumed he was there waiting for her.

"If you will excuse me," Margaret said to Kate, before heading toward him.

"One would think he was an absolute machine," Kate mumbled. "Well, as I said, I do have Gerald."

❦

THE FIRST THING Margaret noticed about Desmond was his rumpled, dirty appearance, quite different from his usual immaculate dress. The cuffs of his shirt were stained, smudged with dirt or mud. His light-colored knee breeches and clocked stockings were stained from the knees down the length of his shins. It looked as if he had been crawling around on all fours.

"Desmond, move no closer, your clothes are filthy," Margaret whispered. She was terrified someone else would see him.

He glanced down at himself, apparently quite distracted and muttered, "What?"

"Your cuffs and breeches are covered in mud." She stood in front of him, doing her best to hide the state of his clothing from the other guests.

As if he had just realized the state of his appearance, he announced. "I need to change at once, then."

"Do get on with it, we're about to go in for dinner."

"I shall, right away, but you must come with me. I want to tell you what I've found."

Margaret tried her best to conceal Desmond's condition until they were out of the line of sight from the others. She followed him up the stairs to his room. He closed the door and begun to loosen his cravat.

"I checked outside, under the window. It seems the dirt

there had been disturbed, and very recently I believe. This is what I found." Desmond dropped a small red enamel box into Margaret's hand before disappearing into his dressing room.

The box had flowered ornamentation on the lid. Margaret turned it over in her hand to examine the minute details of the tiny scrolled, filigree gold feet. She vaguely remembered seeing this item or one very much like it in Sir Julian's possession.

"It's Monty's snuff box," he called out from the next room. "It must have fallen out of his pocket when he was taken away. But I didn't find him." There was a pause and a softly uttered oath. "Oh, I did do a bit of damage, didn't I? Rodney will ring a peal over my head for this. I haven't been this dirty since..." He trailed off, leaving an obvious silence. Maybe he thought better of what he should say and kept the incident to himself. Desmond walked in straightening a clean shirt before tucking the ends into his breeches.

Margaret made sure she stared at the enameled snuff box, making certain her attention did not stray anywhere where it shouldn't be for the next several moments until Desmond faced the mirror. He wrapped his neckcloth around his collar and worked on crafting the linen into a fashionable knot.

"Just before you entered, Mr Bevans announced that Sir Quincy, Lady Payne, and Sir Julian had all left. He made it sound as if Sir Julian had simply returned to London."

Desmond made a few last plucks to the cravat, narrowing his eyes. He stepped away from the glass and held out his hand, palm up to collect the last remnant of his friend. "I wonder how Bevans came to learn of Monty's departure?"

"He didn't say." Margaret placed the small red snuff box in the palm of his hand.

Desmond slipped it into his coat pocket. "Let us stop by Monty's room and see for ourselves how much of a hurry he was in."

Margaret followed Desmond from his room, across the landing, and down the hall. He stopped at the fourth door on the left and gave it three succinct raps.

Sir Julian's valet, Fredericks, answered. "Mr Desmond—"

Desmond stepped into the room. Margaret remained in the hall, standing just outside the open door.

"I've just heard Monty's left."

"Yes, Mr Desmond." Fredericks returned to the half-filled portmanteau lying open on the bed.

"Funny. He hadn't said a word about leaving to me."

"Sir Julian was in a great hurry."

"Was he? Back to London, wasn't it?" Desmond prompted.

"As I understand it, yes, sir."

"Exactly when was it he left? Did he leave any message for me?"

"He left sometime this afternoon, shortly after Mr Waite's demise, I believe. I did not speak to him directly, sir. A short while ago Mr Bevans informed me that I pack Sir Julian's belongings and return to Town."

"He departed just like that?" Desmond snapped his fingers. "And left you here? It seems very unusual for Monty to leave you stranded like this, without a word. I know how much he relies on you."

"I am at a loss for words myself, sir." Fredericks gave a great sigh. "I must agree, it is very unlike Sir Julian. Something of great importance must have occurred to require his immediate presence."

"You don't think Chance's death had anything to do with him leaving? Had he been thrust into an emotional turmoil?" Desmond observed the valet carefully. "Filled with a sense of overwhelming grief perhaps?"

"Grief?" Fredericks nearly choked, suppressing his reaction.

"I do not believe Sir Julian would have been affected in *that* manner by Mr Waite's death."

"No. I don't suppose he would." Desmond smiled. "We both know him much too well for that."

"Yes, sir," the valet returned.

"Well, I'll leave you to your packing, then."

"Yes, I'd best get busy. As you say, Sir Julian does depend on me. I must be off as soon as possible."

Desmond stepped into the hall and closed the door behind him.

Margaret, who had waited for him, said, "He wasn't much help."

WHEN DESMOND and Margaret finally reached the dining room, all eyes focused on them. Margaret knew she was blushing. She had never been comfortable with being the center of attention.

But Desmond was there to take her hand. It made her feel so much better, but when the gazes focused on that motion, she wondered if it only added to their so-called scandalous behavior.

He leaned towards her and whispered, "We must not make excuses for our lack or excess of our appetites, my dear." Desmond returned the stares with an unwarranted smile, then escorted Margaret to her seat for dinner.

AFTER DINNER, all the guests returned to the drawing room. Margaret and Desmond claimed the sofa on the west side of the room. Carroll Sumner, Thomas Rowlandson, Sir Cornelius, and Gerald began a game of cards. Mrs Bevans, Mrs Blake, Mrs

Whitfield, Lady Trumbull, Mrs Sumner, and Mrs Forbes-Bates sat together in two small groups, deep in conversation.

Huddled to one side, Kate sat with Regina, daughter of Mr and Mrs Whitfield. No doubt Kate was helping to corrupt the morals of Miss Whitfield while casting coy, flirtatious glances in Sir Cornelius' direction and lust-filled ones at Gerald. Now *that* was talent.

The three law partners sat isolated to one side, looking far more serious than any of the others. Were they discussing the matter of Chance's death and the tontine? Margaret could just imagine. What would they have done if they knew about Sir Julian? Did they know?

Margaret asked Desmond, "What do you suppose the ladies are talking about?"

Desmond glanced over his shoulder at the women. "Either discussing some scandalous novel or the latest Paris fashions. Perhaps both."

"Not Chance's death?"

Desmond shook his head. "Nothing so morose."

"A man dies in their midst and they're talking about clothes? They act as if nothing happened at all."

"People die every day," he informed her.

"Surely not every day."

"You sound so surprised. Don't tell me they've found a way around that in your time."

"With our medical knowledge and way of life, I suppose it's not as common as it is here."

"Your world must be a wonderful place."

My world doesn't have you in it.

"I wouldn't say my time is better, just different, each has its good and bad points." The soft light in the room cast the most flattering shadows, contouring his face, obscuring his eyes almost completely. Every now and then when he tilted his head Margaret could see the reflection of flickering candlelight.

He looked very handsome. Good thing she was sitting down. There's no way she could have remained standing.

"Are you afraid?" she asked him, breaking their silence.

His eyes shifted from staring across the room to gazing at her. "Are you?" came the immediate response.

"I am for you." Margaret looked from Desmond to the various groups of people. One of them could have been the killer. She wondered if he thought about that too.

Half of them could be eliminated from suspicion. On the other hand, there was no way to be certain the killer was here. Maybe he was an uninvited guest they didn't even know was among them or perhaps a member of the staff.

An old house like this one must have scores of hidden recesses, secret panels, and long lost passageways that could be utilized for sneaking around, killing off people. And perhaps, hiding bodies.

"If all goes as history has recorded," Margaret said, "the next week should be the end of this."

"If I return home tomorrow and lock myself in, will that ease your fears?"

She smiled. "It certainly couldn't hurt."

Desmond leaned forward and took her hand, rubbing the back of it with the pad of his thumb. The motion was almost hypnotic.

"The passage of time would be far more enjoyable if you were there with me."

She was tempted. And he wasn't helping. Margaret stared into his eyes, they were blacker than the surrounding darkness. He pressed a kiss onto her hand.

She wanted to feel those lips on hers. Margaret hadn't been

ready the first time, but she promised herself she'd be ready for the next.

Locked in a house, alone with him? A good idea for him, but it might not be in her best interest. Well, that'd be tomorrow, and she'd face that...tomorrow.

"I can see the indecision in your eyes."

"I never said I wasn't attracted to you," she confessed.

"So you are interested." His lips curved into a gentle smile. "I have no intention of taking advantage of the situation. But I can assure you I will do my utmost to persuade you."

Of that, she had no doubt.

A few hours later, Margaret studied the change in the room's occupants. Most of the guests had retired for the night. Only a few couples remained shrouded in the darkness. She didn't look too hard for their identities, thinking they'd want to keep their anonymity.

"The hour is getting late. You will allow me to see you safely to your room?" Desmond stood, offered his hand, helping Margaret to her feet.

"Who will see you safely to yours?" she asked him. "I'm not the one who's in danger."

MARGARET WOKE FROM HER SLEEP. It was the middle of the night. She laid still. Had she heard something? A rustle of fabric? The creak of a floorboard?

Was it Desmond? Dare she hope...no, she *feared* it might be him. Margaret wouldn't put it past him to sneak into her room. Maybe he had discovered something after she had gone to bed and couldn't wait to tell her. Or maybe he would press her for her favors, future lady or not.

Lifting up her head and shifting onto her elbow, Margaret

waited. "Desmond, is that you?" She waited for a response. Must have been her imagination.

She settled her head onto the pillow. Within a few minutes, she drifted back into a sleepy state. Margaret let herself imagine what it would be like if Desmond were to creep ever so quietly into her room.

She knew she would feel the intensity of the heat of his body grow as he neared. He would hold her close and kiss her with tenderness and passion. His adept hands would apply loving caresses down the length of her body. She could very well succumb to him without a struggle in her dreams where she was safe enough.

Last night, fear blurred her memory of his body against hers. Her mind kept piecing the fragments together and her fertile imagination filled in the gaps. Margaret pulled the covers around her shoulders to her chin. Her body tingled. What would it feel like to lie naked beside him? Kate had described him as a Greek God. Perhaps he was sculpted out of marble with a hard, muscular body, but made out of flesh and blood. He'd press up against her with desire.

Just when the warm and dream filled world began to win the battle over the domain of the waking one, a hand shot out of the dark and clamped hard over Margaret's mouth.

CHAPTER 13

This was not Desmond.

He straddled Margaret's waist, capturing her arms and pinning her to the bed. His hand covered her mouth, muffling her scream.

She hadn't a chance.

There was no one to hear her.

It was too dark in her room and she couldn't see who it was. But she could hear him, breathing in shallow, labored breaths and gasps. The sounds of her struggle filled the air. It felt as if it went on forever before a taunting voice called from the hallway.

"Mrs White?"

It was Gerald.

Oh God, please let him help me.

Margaret felt a hand wrap around her throat, soon joined by a second, squeezing, cutting off her air.

She had to do something. Everything was growing dimmer. Margaret knew she didn't have long before she would unconscious.

Margaret managed to pull her left arm free, but it didn't help her. There was no escape. She had to do something. She needed a weapon. She needed something to smash her attacker's skull.

She reached out next to the bed. Her grappling fingers brushed against something on her nightstand. The lamp. It was just out of reach. Stretching and stretching her arm, just to touch it, she kept trying until she finally managed to tip it over, sending it crashing to the floor.

A frantic call from her brother, "Margaret!" The door flew open and the assailant leaped off the bed only moments before Gerald stepped into the room along with the light from the hallway that came flooding in. "What are you doing in here, Sumner?"

Sumner? Margaret's vision was blurry. Her windpipe felt crushed, she couldn't speak.

Mr Carroll Sumner straightened the cuffs of his shirt. "If you must know, I was invited by your sister."

Gerald looked at Margaret. She was out of breath, gasping for air. That idiot Gerald probably interpreted her appearance as recovering from the throws of interrupted passion.

"I think not." Gerald's gaze moved from her back to Sumner. "My sister does not dally when she has a beau."

"Are you calling me a liar?" he spat, insulted.

"You have attacked my sister, sir! I shall be returning to London in the morning," Gerald said with deliberate calm. "I shall wait for your seconds to call on me at Ashworth House."

"Glad to take care of things once and for all, Sinclair!" There was a seething undercurrent in his voice. Pure loathing. Why did he hate Gerald so much? She could tell there was more than what went on here. Sumner stalked by Gerald and out of the room.

Striding down the hallway, Desmond nearly ran into the exiting Sumner storming out of Margaret's room.

Inside her bedchamber, Gerald sat on the bed next to Margaret, consoling her.

"What the devil's going on?" Desmond's anger melted into concern when he saw Margaret. He rushed to the bed, knelt by her side, and took up her hand. The usual comely blush on her cheek was absent. The life in her eyes nearly extinguished and her trembling hand stayed at her throat. "What's happened, Sinclair?" Desmond glanced at Gerald for answers but he said nothing.

Margaret motioned her brother away. Before leaving, he leaned close and kissed her cheek. "Remember, we shall be departing first thing in the morning. You'll look after her now?"

Desmond nodded, he would. Gerald left her in Desmond's capable care.

Margaret's grasp tightened around his fingers and waited until her brother left.

"Strangled," she whispered, her throat clearly pained her. "Gerald saved me." Her meaning was quite clear.

"Sumner? By God, I shall enjoy killing him!" When Desmond started to move away from the bed, she took hold of his sleeve, preventing his departure.

"Gerald's called him out."

"*I* want to be the one who—"

Margaret cut him off. "Gerald has every right. He is my brother."

With the lift of a sardonic brow, Desmond said, "Then I shall enjoy watching Sumner die."

"I think it's him!" The words, barely audible, must have hurt.

"What?"

"The killer." She struggled, forcing the important words out.

"Sumner?"

She nodded.

"Why on earth would he want to kill you?" Desmond did not doubt Margaret, but he clearly questioned her allegation. He thought back. "I think he was there when I said you had predicted Chance's death." His gaze bore into her. "He might have even overheard us and deduced you might know more than you've let on."

Margaret returned his gaze. She could see the fear in his eyes, not for himself but fear for her.

"Now, you're in as much danger as I am." He paced a few steps. "I cannot in good conscience leave you alone."

"But I can't prove a thing." Her voice still sounded raspy and cracked.

"Let me get you something to drink."

"Desmond" —she reached out to him— "Please—don't leave me alone."

"No more talking." He laid her hands onto the counterpane. "No need to worry." He sounded so cavalier. "I'm going to die anyway, remember?"

❧

Margaret shot upright in bed when Desmond returned to her room with a glass of water.

"Everything will be just fine," he reassured her. He held the glass to her lips. "Here, sip this."

She placed her still trembling hands over his, cradling the glass. In the room's dim light, Desmond saw the red marks around her neck. She looked so helpless, so vulnerable like this.

Margaret looked no different than any other woman. Coming from the future hadn't made her different. It was the way he felt about her that made her special.

Desmond set the glass on the small table next to her bed.

"I wish you didn't have to go."

169

"I have no intention of leaving you by yourself," he reassured her. "Do not worry. No one will think it strange, me being in your bedchamber."

No, they wouldn't, would they? She smiled. "Are you my protector now?"

"As you are mine."

Margaret squeezed her eyes closed, fighting back tears. "I'm afraid I might not be as brave as I thought." With the relief of Desmond standing over her, protecting her, comforting her, Margaret began to cry.

"Brave? Someone's just tried to kill you. Your composure is... exceptional." Desmond pulled her to his chest, cradling her, showing no other interest in her except to banish her fears.

She nestled closer into the crook of his neck. Her cheek rested on the velvet of his dressing gown. Peeling her off his body, Desmond laid her on the bed.

"I think you should try to get some sleep." He tucked the bedcovers around her.

Desmond watched her lying there. She was a stranger in his world. He wouldn't let anything happen to her. Ever. How could he allow his feelings for her go so far? Entrusted with her secret, he was the only one who knew the truth about her.

The whole truth.

❧

THE NEXT MORNING, Margaret dressed herself in a high collared dress, hiding the bruises around her neck and gone down to the breakfast room.

There wasn't a trace of Sumner or his wife in the house. Margaret knew the way gossip traveled and wondered if everyone knew what went on last night. She sipped her tea and kept fingering the collar of her dress. It felt snug and it still hurt to swallow.

Desmond had left her room without causing a scandal very early that morning. She nearly had to kick him out so she could change out of her nightrail. He left under protest.

"Your brother is mad!" Kate stalked into the breakfast room.

That wasn't news to Margaret.

"Another duel! Can you imagine? He knows dueling is against the law. I own one day he'll be arrested for it!" How could Kate take this dueling business so lightly?

"Aren't you appalled?"

"It's so exciting!" Kate didn't seem overly concerned about Gerald's well-being.

"Exciting? Gerald might be killed."

"He is bound and determined to go through with it. I don't know why you'd object. It is your honor that's at stake."

"Honor? What about *his* life?" Margaret dropped her napkin on the table and stood to leave. "Where is he?"

"I left him in the Gallery."

"I can't let him go through with this." Margaret left to see what she could do.

MARGARET STOPPED at the door of the Gallery when she heard the crisp sound of a thin blade slicing through the air. This is where she first had that *déjà vu* feeling and now she knew why. Gerald stood at the far end. He executed several advancing, offensive combinations, heading in her direction. Breathing heavily, he came to a standstill not far from her.

"What are you doing?" she asked.

"Practicing," he answered between labored breaths, "for the duel."

"Do you think you'll be dueling with swords?"

He pointed the *épée* upward and carefully flexed the blade. The edge gleamed, showing its deadly beauty. Something wasn't right about this image.

"Sumner is as skilled at swords as I. If I were him, that's what I would choose."

"Pistols," Margaret said in a low, monotone voice. The words just came out.

"What's that you say?"

"He'll choose pistols," she repeated, a little louder this time and with more certainty. Margaret looked into Gerald's face. This was the duel in which he died. She recalled seeing in the museum at Ashworth House:

Gerald Ashworth, Viscount Sinclair, was killed in a duel on the morning of July 13, 1813.

That was two days from now.

"He'd be more of a fool than I think he is if he chooses pistols." Gerald sliced the blade through the air as an irritated cat lashed its tail. "I'm a far better shot than he. I can shoot him clean through with my eyes closed. He knows that."

Margaret laid a hand on his sword arm, staying the blade. "Gerald, you must not go through with this. Don't act as if you're doing me any favors. You're fighting this duel for you, not me—to impress Kate."

"I have no need to impress the lovely Catherine. For once Margaret, you're wrong about this. I don't know what Sumner was doing in your bedchamber, but I am quite certain it was not by your invitation."

She fingered the high collar of her dress. "How can you be so certain?"

"I know you're in love. Despite the occasional harsh words you two exchange, I can see it when you look at him." He smiled at her and chucked her under the chin. "I know you, my dear

Mrs White" —he now used the former derogatory moniker as an endearment— "you are a faithful lover. You lavish your attention on only one man at a time and at present, that man is Pierce Desmond."

Margaret hadn't thought she was that transparent. And it surprised her Gerald was not oblivious to what went on around him. Quite the contrary, he proved himself to be insightful as well. She could hardly believe it, he had some scruples.

"What would mother and father say? What kind of son would I be? What kind of brother? Would you have me look foolish?" He addressed her with a seriousness she had never experienced since knowing him.

"No, of course not." She knew nothing of his and Lady Margaret's parents but imagined no parent would wish harm to come to their children.

"Besides, I'm more afraid of what Desmond will do to me if I don't go through with it. And I'll tell you, I'd rather face Sumner on the field than Desmond in the front parlor any day."

He gave a chuckle that broke the serious mood. Margaret smiled too.

"Now off with you" —he urged her away— "We'll be leaving for Ashworth House in a few hours."

Gerald watched her head to the door before he continued his session. After stepping outside, Margaret turned and watched him raise, saluting an imaginary opponent and point his blade toward the ground.

The downward thrust severed the tips of a palm frond, sending the green fragments spiraling to the floor.

Watching the image again set the certainty of impending disaster. It's not that she thought Carroll Sumner didn't deserve to die. He had tried to kill her and just might have succeeded.

Margaret just didn't think it was worth Gerald's life.

৶

THE TRIP back to London for Margaret was blurred with worry for both Gerald and Desmond. There had already been two deaths this last weekend, and she didn't want either of them to be next.

When she arrived at Ashworth House, she changed out of her traveling clothes. As she came downstairs, she watched two men leaving out the front door. Two other young men remained.

One was light-haired and the other dark-haired, neither known to her. When she entered the front parlor they both bowed, greeting her by name. Then she realized she was known to them.

"Gentlemen," she replied, not knowing how to respond to each individually. Were they seconds? Gerald's seconds? And the first pair of men who departed Sumner's seconds? Margaret glanced at Gerald. "Am I interrupting?"

"Thank you, Curry, Durham." Gerald nodded to them. "We have concluded our arrangements." He saw them to the front door and exchanged some last words before their exit.

They were talking about the duel and didn't want her to hear. If only she knew what they were saying. If only she had been downstairs earlier to hear about the details. Important things like what time they were to meet or where they were going.

Margaret knew the duel would take place in the early hours, tomorrow morning. Duels were not limited to dueling fields. It could take place on one of a dozen popular spots, far too many to try and guess.

Again, she was tempted to blame the portrait hanging on the far wall. If it was to blame for her present circumstance, it could be blamed for not helping her when she clearly needed it.

"Shouldn't you be resting?" Gerald came closer and touched her cheek. "You don't want Desmond to see you with dark circles under those lovely eyes tonight at Woodrich's ball."

Margaret could have cared less about the condition of her eyes. "I'm afraid I've forgotten about it." She had to go to another ball? "What about you? Are you still intent on meeting Sumner?"

"'Pistols for two, breakfast for one,' 'Grass before breakfast,' anything you wish to call it. Yes, I intend to." He stood there, staring at her. "Have you forgotten what he did to you?"

What was he thinking? There was something very intimate about the way he looked at her, touched her. Even though he wasn't really her brother, it felt very uncomfortable.

"This isn't like you at all, Margaret. Not that you've shown any interest in my well-being before, but you've never questioned my abilities." He balanced her chin on the tip of his index finger. A slow, easy smile spread across his lips. "I think I like this new show of concern for me."

Margaret quivered when he kissed her on the cheek, just brushing the corner of her lips.

"I think I'll be off to see Kate." He stepped away from her and retrieved his hat. "I shall tell her you'll see her tonight."

"You're not going to make it easy for me are you? You know I don't want you to fight." Venting her anger would do no good, but she would continue to make her point.

"I must say, sometimes you truly surprise me." Ignoring her, he set his hat in place, took up his walking stick, and left.

Gerald was going to fight. If he faced Sumner he was going to die. And she'll be damned if she was going to sit by and do nothing about it.

CHAPTER 14

NEARLY FIVE HOURS of the Woodrich ball had passed without incident. All talking stopped when she appeared. Margaret knew quite well those around her whispered about the scandal. It was unnerving. Shortly before two in the morning, a frantic Kate confronted Margaret who had been standing on the sidelines still trying to figure out how to stop the duel.

"This is madness! Margaret, you cannot allow Gerald to go through with it!"

Astounded by the change in opinion, Margaret replied, "You thought dueling was exciting. Now you want me to stop it?"

"Do you want me to admit I was wrong? Very well, I was wrong! I was wrong! Please, Margaret!" She rushed to the front window. "Look, they're leaving."

Margaret moved to stand by her friend's side to see Gerald approaching Curry and Durham who waited for their coach. Their somber features stuck out amidst the gaiety of the other guests.

"Now please, you must do something!" Why had it taken Kate so long to change her mind?

"Do? What do you think I've been trying to do? He's not about to listen to me."

"Please, Margaret, you are always so clever. I'm sure you can think of something." Kate grabbed Margaret's arm in desperation.

Margaret fingered the wide pearl choker that hid the marks on her neck. "I thank you for your confidence and I can assure you I have not given up." Yet, she had no idea what she would do.

"I knew I could depend on you."

Kate acted as if her agreeing to intervene made it so. It didn't. With one hand she dropped her fan open and waved it, cooling herself with the other, she discreetly motioned to someone across the room. An instant later Sir Cornelius appeared at her side.

"I am feeling a bit light-headed," Kate claimed. "I must sit down and rest."

"Come, my pet." He cooed in a tender, comforting tone. He slid his arm around her waist for support and led her away. "You are such a tender flower, this heat must be wilting your delicate petals."

It was hard to know if Kate was acting. Sir Cornelius was hard to take in any case.

But Kate's panic was contagious. Margaret felt her anxiety building. Gerald was about to leave and she had no idea where he was going. Margaret glanced around for...then she saw him, Desmond.

She found him in conversation with several other gentle-men. She waved her closed fan to attract his attention and within a few seconds, he stood by her side.

"Where have you been?"

"Whatever is the matter?" He acted as if they were here to have a good time.

"Look, Gerald is leaving." She pointed out the window where Gerald saw his friends into their transport. "Quick, let's follow them." Margaret grabbed Desmond's arm, thinking she would usher him out of the room and on the trail of the three men.

Desmond didn't budge.

He stood his ground. "I believe I wish to dance."

"Dance?" Margaret turned her head from Desmond to the main ballroom door. "There's no time to dance." Gerald was the last of the three to leave. Margaret sighed in exasperation. "If he leaves, how are we ever going to find out where they are going?"

"I already know where they are going," came the composed reply.

"What did you say?" His answer robbed her of breath.

"I said I would like to dance."

"No, you said you knew where Gerald is going. Do you know about the duel?"

"The time and place," he drawled and gave her an all-knowing smile.

Margaret stared at him, waiting, almost unable to remain calm. "Are you going to tell me?"

"Are you going to dance with me?" Desmond held out his hand.

She stood motionless, undecided whether she would or should indulge him. This might be a bad precedent to set.

"I promise you will not miss the event."

Margaret looked at his outstretched hand before taking it. His relaxed body language told her she had nothing to worry about. Desmond led her onto the dance floor.

"Are you going to tell me now?" she asked, after taking only five steps.

"Can I not enjoy my one dance?"

Margaret ceded the point and remained silent. "I don't

think I can stand any more of this," she confessed after keeping silent for several minutes. "I feel as if I'm going to scream."

"Well, don't do it here."

"Then take me home."

"I'm afraid I can't do that either. There your brother prepares himself." Desmond held Margaret tight, preventing her from flight. "You should not disturb them. Soon they will spend some time busy with numerous last drinks, toasting his bravery."

Male bonding ritual, she imagined.

"I cannot stay here and pretend to enjoy myself."

"You're not enjoying yourself?" He looked hurt.

"It's through no fault of yours," she whispered. "It's this dueling business."

"Quite understandable. Then we shall leave."

❦

MARGARET AND DESMOND traveled in the darkened coach through the streets of London in silence. It felt as if they'd been traveling forever. Glancing out the window, Margaret barely made out the street sign in the gaslight lamp, *Curzon Street*, as they passed. They finally stopped in front of a townhouse and disembarked. By the time they stepped onto the midpoint of the walk, the front door had opened.

After stepping inside the townhouse, Desmond took Margaret's cloak and handed it to the butler, Maypink, before shedding his outerwear.

"I believe Lady Margaret is in need of your homemade remedy, Maypink, would you be so kind?" Desmond asked.

"At once, sir." Maypink headed off.

Desmond led Margaret down the hall. They passed the

handsomely decorated parlor on the right, on the way to the library.

Clearly, the library was his favorite room. And why not, it felt warm and inviting just standing here. She recalled her first visit when she thought he had been injured.

"Will you be seated?" He patted the winged-back chair.

"No. I think I'd rather stand, thank you." Margaret found an area on the far side of the blazing hearth and began to pace.

"Perhaps you would care to have your mind taken off your troubles for a bit?" He sat upon his mahogany desk and ran his hand in a very slow and deliberate way along its smooth, hard surface.

Didn't he ever give up?

The butler entered carrying a thick, ceramic tankard on a tray.

"Thank you, Maypink." Desmond took the tankard and without a word, the butler left, closing the door behind him, leaving her alone with Desmond.

Stepping into Margaret's path Desmond halted her pacing. "You're going to wear a spot on the carpet. Here drink this, it should help calm you."

Her hands cupped the warm mug. "What is it?"

"A posset. Maypink's old family recipe. He won't divulge the ingredients to a soul."

Margaret slowly inhaled the contents to see if she could guess what it contained and exactly how much alcohol. She wouldn't completely put it past Desmond to ply her with booze and then take advantage of her. "Exactly, how much alcohol does this have?" She guessed it was a conglomeration of warmed milk, assorted spices, and an abundance of brandy.

"Not enough to leave you ailing in the morning, but it will ease your anxiety."

Margaret took a sip, sampling the supposed healing concoction. It tasted okay. Then she took a deeper drink, hoping it would help settle her nerves.

"I can understand Gerald's reason for going through with this, but I can't fathom why Sumner would agree to risk his life. For what?"

"Did you know Sumner caught Gerald dallying with his wife last year?"

"No, but I'm not surprised." Margaret rolled her eyes. "Men! You never change."

"Is my Gender to be blamed for the duel?"

"No, but male-aggression is not something that disappears over time."

"Has there been an improvement in *your* Gender over the next few hundred years? I find you are quite different from the females of my time."

"I *am* different from any other woman you know." There was no doubt in Margaret's mind, it didn't make her any better, just different.

"But you are still a woman, are you not? Regardless of what century you are from, you are female nevertheless. A pleasing one from what I can see."

She felt him take a long, lingering look at her. His gaze hugged her curves, charting territory he wanted to explore. It made her feel uncomfortable yet his interest intrigued her.

No doubt he was used to getting what he wanted when he wanted. He somehow sensed this Margaret was as inexperienced as he was experienced. He reached out and touched her cheek. Did he know what he did to her insides? Did every woman fall to his charms?

"It don't matter where or when you come from."

Was it just a line? Was he saying all this to have his way with her? She hoped not. No, he probably hadn't said that exact line to anyone before.

Margaret knew love and trust were not the same, and she desperately needed to trust someone. She was hoping that someone would be Desmond.

His lips replaced his fingers on her cheek. Then he moved down her neck, which sent a rush of heat flooding through her body.

Margaret probably knew more about the actual biological aspect of what happened between a man and a woman. But in the field of actual practice, hands-on, as it were, she was a novice.

"I'm sure you've kissed hundreds of women."

"But you shall be the last," he whispered. His hot breath seared down her neck.

She couldn't let it happen. What was she thinking? Desmond was eventually to marry Lady Margaret. Would she still be Lady Margaret when they married? They very well might make love in the future, but now was certainly not the time. Margaret had to put the brakes on before this went too far.

"I think it's very nice we have become friends," she said, trying to distance herself and hoping it would help cool Desmond ardor.

"*Friends*? Is that all you think we are?"

"Why of course. Do you not think of me that way? I've trusted you with my deepest secret." Margaret thought she meant as much to him as he had to her. "I haven't told any other person that I'm— I'm from...you know where."

Desmond gave an amused chuckle. "I'm afraid men and women cannot be friends."

"Of course they can."

He moved his head from side to side, denying her statement. "Men and women can be acquaintances, lovers" —his eyes softened to that of his voice— "or perhaps" —his voice hardened— "enemies. But never friends. It's an impossible notion."

"Desmond," Margaret said, exasperated. "Pierce," she said in a softer tone. "I might have been mistaken, but I thought we understood one another. I thought you and I were...that we had something special between us, something more."

"As did I." He smiled. It was a welcoming, seductive one, and he tried to pull her close.

She resisted his embrace. "But you deny me your friendship."

"You ask for something I cannot give."

"You're not hung up on that nineteenth century belief that women are only good for one thing, are you? I thought you better than that."

"Are you referring to my unrepentant feeling of lust?"

She did, but she didn't admit it to him.

What woman would not want to be loved by the man she adored? The problem was he didn't love her. He only desired her. Margaret couldn't allow herself to become distracted by his unending passion.

She had to keep focused. And her focus was to keep Desmond alive. Lady Margaret and Desmond were destined to be together. Maybe there would be time for love later.

That should keep Desmond happy. But she did not tell him. Nor would she.

"I find nothing unorthodox about them. My urges, that is." He released his hold and stepped away from her. "I am a nineteenth century man. I beg your pardon if I cannot conform to your ideal. I am the only man I know how to be."

He was right. She was expecting him to behave like a modern man—from the twenty-first century.

The line of trust Margaret trod was a narrow one. An occasional misstep landed her in his arms. If she fell, she would most likely land in Desmond's bed. Or—she eyed the large desk—an equivalent substitute.

Did he really feel nothing more than lust for her? That would be very disappointing.

She stepped toward him. "One would think you might not have a heart." Margaret rapped on his chest. Where, if he had a heart, it might exist. A hollow, metallic sound emitted, proving to her, she was right. He hadn't a heart. At least not a flesh and blood one.

Desmond's hand swept between her fingers and his coat, but Margaret had moved quicker than he. Her other hand plunged into his coat and plucked the item which made the suspect sound.

"Now see here," Desmond protested. His coat prevented him from raising his arms high enough to reclaim the object from her.

Margaret spun away. It was a slender, silver box. Probably for cheroots.

"No, do not open that!" he pleaded.

"Why ever not?" she sniffed. "Don't be ridiculous."

"*Please.*" He pleaded.

She ignored him and used both thumbs to pry it open, exposing a collection of small items: a gold-covered button, a length of gold-edged blue ribbon, a small lace handkerchief with a monogrammed M on the corner, and a small piece of folded paper.

They were all mementos of her. He had saved them—saved them all.

"What kind of man are you? Margaret lifted the length of ribbon. "What kind of man refers to friendship between a man and a woman as nonsense then saves the most insignificant objects as keepsakes?"

"The kind of man who is in love," he answered with great reluctance and sounded vulnerable when speaking his truth.

He removed the items from her hand and pulled her into his

arms. The closer he held her the more she could feel her defenses weaken. Margaret was beginning to understand just how much he had wanted her. She couldn't help but admit she wanted him too.

It was happening. Margaret felt the cracks in her resolve beginning.

Desmond pulled Margaret into his arms, enveloping her in warmth, nothing could have felt more right. His lips pressed onto hers, soft and welcoming. He wanted her to confess she wanted him as much as he wanted her.

She wasn't going to do that. She could not do that.

His hands ran down the length of her back and pressed her to him, letting her feel him, his strength, his desire, his confidence, his support.

She wasn't alone. He was there and would continue to be there.

Desmond released her. "Since I've been found out, you might as well know my one, remaining secret." He stepped to the hearth and pushed the center of the utmost left medallion on the chimneypiece. A small door opened, exposing a removable drawer. "This by itself is a place to store a few small trinkets. It in itself is not of significance."

He walked to the adjacent wall and pushed one of the panels. It sprung open, revealing a second, much larger, concealed compartment with several narrow shelves.

"This is where I keep everything of importance." Desmond retrieved the silver box and its items, placing them on the middle shelf and closed the panel. Glancing at the mantle clock he announced, "Come now, my dearest, I think it's time we leave."

DESMOND HAD his coach brought around and they were soon on their way. The gravel crushing under the wheels sounded especially noisy during the quiet early morning ride. Margaret didn't know where they were headed. It didn't matter really, as long as she got there in time. Now that she was on her way to the duel, how was she to stop it? Gerald had proven impossible to convince. Sumner would probably be equally as reluctant to give up his next victim.

Chauncy Waite and Sir Julian Montgomery were both killed by Sumner. Alison's accident must have been his doing as well. Margaret could never forget he had tried to kill her but that had been a failed attempt. He was an experienced killer and it would take more than just *coming from the future* to outsmart him.

"We're going to need a diversion," Margaret said, thinking out loud.

"Why don't you try swooning in the middle of the field? Once they get an eyeful of your heaving bosom, it's bound to delay them some."

"I would appreciate if you would leave my bosom out of this."

The coach stopped next to two standing transports. Desmond helped Margaret out of the carriage. Gerald, Sumner, their respective second, and a surgeon stood around a table set near a long, wide expanse of the cropped field of grass only thirty or so feet away.

The morning air felt cool, quiet, and eerie. The premonition of death hung heavy in the atmosphere. Someone would die this morning. The light crept over and through the trees on the south-eastern side of the desolate field announcing the start of the ritual. Only the morning mist that was once fog remained, collecting in the low spots. Soon the duel itself would begin.

The circle of men parted, revealing an open black box on

the table. The pistols. The men spoke among themselves, much too quiet and too far away for Margaret to hear. She could see Gerald holding one of the pistols, examining it. Seeing the weapon in his hand magnified the premonition, making it all the more immediate that something had to be done.

"I want you to get them away from the table and try and talk them out of this," she told Desmond.

"What are you going to do?" By the look on Desmond's face, he didn't know what she was up to. Hell, she didn't know what she was up to.

Margaret glanced at the black box then back to Desmond. "I'm not sure yet."

Desmond walked toward the center of the open field. The men around the table headed in the same direction—away from Margaret to speak privately. Gerald replaced the pistol in the box and followed.

Margaret watched the men gather into a tight group. She inched toward the table. The morning dew soaked the hem of her cloak and dress, making her feel weighed down when she was trying to move with stealth and speed.

The momentarily abandoned pistol case sat unguarded on the table. The handsome set of dueling pistols lay in a bed of red velvet. Margaret lifted each pistol and looked at it in turn, keeping her attention on the men all the while.

"Take her home, Desmond," Gerald ordered. "A lady should not have to see a coward die."

Margaret moved away from the table, returning to her original position near Desmond's coach.

"You shall regret those words," Sumner returned, stomping toward the table where the weapons lay. He looked more than eager to get the business over with. With a cold, steely stare he took his last look at Margaret.

Desmond tried to continue his stall tactics. She waved and called out to him. "Please, Desmond, take me away from here."

They boarded the carriage and departed without delay. Margaret turned in her seat to look out the back window at Gerald and hoped all would turn out all right. She faced forward once again and closed her eyes.

"Knowing what that scoundrel did to you, it was all I could do not to kill him on the spot," Desmond said through gritted teeth.

"I am glad you restrained yourself. I assure you, justice will be served." She placed her hand on his. "Only one so sure of victory would rush into such action. History, as I know, shows Gerald Ashworth died in a duel. I believe it's this one."

"Impossible. He's a crack shot."

"That may be, but as I recall it seems his gun misfires."

"Has it been tampered with?"

"I should think it fitting that Sumner dies by his own devices, don't you? There's a saying where I come from, what goes around, comes around." She smiled. "I have a confession to make. I switched the pistols in the case."

"Justice will be served then." Desmond looked to be relieved too. "Can I also assume the danger to me has passed?"

"I would think so."

Desmond's coach stopped in front of Ashworth House.

"What about us? I love you, Margaret."

"Lady Margaret is a married woman." And in this time that was who Margaret was. "I have yet to meet my husband, Mr White, that is."

"And you never have kept his company," Desmond told her. "I don't see why that should change."

"Never?" It felt strange having someone know you better than you knew yourself. But she wasn't the real Margaret.

"Never," he confirmed with complete certainty. "We belong together."

She'd always known it. "But what am I to do?"

"Say you'll stay with me."

"I cannot." As much as she loved him she could not promise fidelity when bound in matrimony to another.

He took her hands in his and stared into her eyes. "We will be together, I promise."

From the determination glinting deep in his eyes, she believed it.

"I know in my heart I should never love another but you," he vowed.

He was the man for her. But it wasn't right. The time wasn't right.

"I must ask something of you."

He did not immediately agree but waited for her to continue.

"If I return to my century...go back to my own time," she began.

"I shan't allow it to happen." He took up her hand as if he could physically keep her next to him.

"I doubt you or I have any say in the matter. Pierce, you must promise me. If I return to my own time, promise me you will marry."

"Marry another? How could I?" His eyes narrowed and she saw his eyes moist with tears. "How could you ask such a thing of me?"

"Don't you see? You must continue your family line. If you don't, your great-great-great-great grandson will not be born. He will never deliver that book to me in my time so I can return to 1813 to fall in love with you here. You must do it so in two hundred years from now I will come back to you."

"What will it matter if we cannot be together now?"

Desmond stilled and stated with quiet conviction. "I want to be with you."

"I'm not sure how but it does matter. And more than anything I want to be with you." And she did. She loved him—but inside she could feel this was not the way it was to be for them.

He pulled her into his arms and hugged her tightly. "Then I'll find you again. Wherever, *whenever* you are, I'll find you."

When Margaret opened her eyes, she sat upright and leaned toward the window, pulling away from him, entranced by the beginning haze swirling on the ground.

"What is it?" Desmond grasped her arms, again drawing her near. "There is nothing to fear, it is only the morning fog. Let me see you safe inside."

Once inside the house, Desmond followed Margaret into the parlor where she could see his coach waiting outside.

"You must go upstairs to bed. There's no use waiting up to hear the details. I imagine Gerald won't be home for hours, he's probably enjoying a victor's revelry." Desmond pulled her close and kissed her cheek. "I shall come to call in a few hours when word of the outcome is announced. I promise."

"All right." She'd like that. To know that Desmond and Gerald were both safe, and that villain, Sumner, got what he deserved would be a wonderful start to her day. Keeping Desmond pressed at her back, Margaret turned to the window. The mist had crept forward, now extending in front of the house.

The sight of it chilled her, causing a shiver to run down her arms.

It was a rude awakening. At ten-twelve in the morning to be exact. It couldn't already be time to rise?

It was Maypink who woke and informed his employer that a Mr Samuel Bevans was waiting to see him belowstairs, insisting the matter was quite urgent.

"What the devil are you doing here so early?" After only four hours of sleep, Desmond was tired and grouchy.

"Very important business," the solicitor stated.

"So I hear." Desmond tried to keep a civil tongue. "All right, come into the breakfast room. I'm sure there is at least coffee, isn't there, Maypink?"

"At the very least, sir."

Desmond turned almost completely around to look at his butler. Either he was muzzy headed from last night or he was hearing things. He walked into the breakfast room and found his seat.

"I thought you should know right away, my lord." A knowing smile flicked over Bevans' face.

"What? Why are you *my lording* me?"

"First, I believe an apology is in order." The solicitor remained standing.

Desmond had no idea what was going on in his house this morning. He swallowed the entire cup of coffee and held it out for seconds. Maypink obliged by refilling the cup.

"I could not say before, the matter to which I am referring prohibited me from speaking about it to another."

"Will you come out with it, man! What the devil are you talking about?" Desmond had no patience for this today. There was much to do and he wanted to get back to Margaret.

Bevans took a deep breath. "Twenty-some years ago, your father, along with a dozen or so others came to the offices of Bevans, Blake, and Whitford to set up a certain type of an annuity."

"An annuity?" Desmond lowered his cup with the realization dawning upon him. He saw the whole of it then—the tontine.

"The principal members, who were sworn to secrecy, have been deceased for many years. As of this morning, all but one of the participants of the tontine remain."

Desmond felt his blood leave his face. "Are you saying I am the only one left?"

"It appears Mr Waite was not the only unfortunate guest to expire at my home this weekend. I was informed that the body of Sir Julian Montgomery had been discovered shortly after the guests had departed. I will spare you the details. However, I have removed his name from the list of survivors." Bevans cleared his throat.

"News of Mr Carroll Sumner's death came to me only an hour ago. I have confirmed he was killed in a duel earlier this morning. It appears his opponent did not have a chance to fire a shot. Mr Sumner raised his weapon and discharged into the air, his pistol misfired, killing him instantly." Bevans pulled out his *pince-nez*, set them on the bridge of his nose, and flipping open a small tablet, consulting his notes.

"As the surviving member, you have inherited several hundred thousand pounds, still invested by the firm, and according to one of the member's alternate agreed-on contributions, certain, and perhaps questionable, inheritance papers were drawn up and signed by the fourth Viscount Alison to pass on his lands, all subsequent holdings" —he glanced over the top of his glasses— "such as they are, to the winner." He flipped the notebook closed and pulled the glasses off his nose. "Not only have you inherited substantial funds, making you a very, very wealthy man, you are now the sixth Viscount Alison."

Desmond sat back stunned.

My God, Margaret was right.

BY THE TIME Desmond had dressed and raced to Ashworth House with his news, it was well after noon. He sat nervously in the front parlor, waiting for her. He'd been waiting for a good half-hour.

What the devil was taking her so long?

He would have thought she would have run down in her nightrail on hearing of his arrival.

Desmond glanced up at the portrait of Lady Margaret. It was supposed to be Lady Margaret, but... he stepped closer, peering into the picture. Then he moved back to study the painting more fully.

It didn't truly resemble her, he thought.

The face of the Margaret he knew was rounder, softer around the jaw. Her eyes were different, they held more intelligence. Her nose was more refined, and her lips more shapely.

This wasn't the first time he had seen this painting. How was it he had never noticed the difference before?

The rustle of skirts told him someone had arrived. He heard Margaret's voice call to him. "Mr Desmond?"

Desmond turned around and stared at the stranger standing in the doorway, and he knew *his* Margaret was gone.

CHAPTER 15

Margaret woke and stretched. She would have thought the uncertain outcome of Gerald's duel would have surely kept her from finding nocturnal bliss. For once she was pleasantly disappointed, she had had a very restful sleep.

Sunlight peeked out from under the heavy drapes at her window. It was past time to rise. Where was Betsy with her morning chocolate? Where was Nora to help her dress?

Margaret slipped out of bed and drew back the drapes, sunlight filled the room. Not the soft, diffused light of morning but the indirect rays of afternoon. She could see the sun behind the trees across the street where it would sit at the end of the day.

How could it be late afternoon? Exactly how long had she slept?

Perhaps someone had tried to wake her earlier and she was too deep in sleep to be roused. But she didn't think so.

Something was wrong.

Desmond said he would call that morning. She was certain he would do so and he would not have left Ashworth House until he had seen her. He would have waited until she woke. Or waken her himself, she'd not put that past him.

Something was very wrong.

"I don't like this," she whispered.

Noticing the wardrobe before her—it was as if it beckoned to her to near. As if it wished to reveal its secret to her. Margaret slipped off the bed and approached it with purpose. She closed her eyes and gripped its smooth, worn brass knob. In a single motion, Margaret pulled on the door handle and opened her eyes. There were her clothes. All neatly hung and folded, just as she had left them. Blouses, slacks, and her underwear sitting on a shelf. And all the way on the left on a hanger was her Regency costume ready to wear.

She understood what had happened and didn't want to believe it was true.

Stepping away from the wardrobe, she moved to the bedroom door, opened it and looked down the hall, checking to the right and to the left, looking for someone... anyone. There must be people downstairs. She made her way to the staircase and descended to the ground floor. The hall table and the long clock that stood in the foyer were still there. They looked the same. Everything looked just as she remembered.

When she stepped into the front parlor, Margaret froze—glued to the spot where she stood and stared at the painting, Lady Margaret and her husband. Her husband—Sir William Carlisle. She approached, getting closer to read the small brass plaque on the frame to make certain her eyes weren't playing tricks on her.

There was no mistake, it said: Lady Margaret and Sir William Carlisle.

She was back in the twenty-first century.

How could this have happened?

She didn't know exactly how it happened the first time

either. And as for when—she knew exactly when it had happened.

While she slept—two centuries had slipped away.

"Margaret? What are you doing down here? And dressed like that, no less."

Margaret turned to face the landlady.

"You all right, dear?"

"I'm fine." Margaret crossed her arms, feeling a sudden chill.

"Why, you've been crying." Mrs Taggart stepped toward her.

It was true. Margaret swiped at her cheeks, wiping away the tears she'd unexpectedly shed. "I had a bad dream, that's all." It wasn't really a lie since she wasn't sure of exactly what had happened to her. "I don't sleep well during the day."

"I know what you mean," Mrs Taggart said. "I canna remember what day it is sometimes, much less if it's morning or night."

"Exactly," Margaret replied. She didn't bother to mention she was having trouble identifying the century.

"You should change for your dance, you're going to be late." Mrs Taggart pointed upstairs. "You'd best get ready, you and Mr Montgomery are the last to go."

"Mont... Mont—gomery?"

"Aye, you know, the funny young man from the States?"

"Oh yes, of course." Somewhat differently, but she remembered him.

"He's still gawking at himself in front of the mirror. Catherine's just left, she says she'll keep an eye out for you. Is there anything I can do for ya?"

Margaret stiffened at Mrs Taggart's use of *Catherine*... of course she meant *Katie*. "No, I can manage. Thank you."

"You'd best move on, then." Mrs Taggart retreated, motioning Margaret to do the same.

Back in her room, Margaret approached her bedside table and trailed her finger over the cover at the slim book sitting next to her cell phone.

Her cell phone.

Could it all have really happened? Or had it been a very real, very vivid dream? It had all seemed so real. But the portrait...Lady Margaret and her husband *Sir William Carlisle*? That had changed, hadn't it? She was sure that painting hadn't hung there before. And what about Desmond?

Margaret picked up her phone, opened a browser. It was surprising how easily the reflex of using her cell phone returned after not using it for what seemed like weeks. She typed in: *Pierce Desmond*.

Nothing. It was as if he had never existed.

It was not true. It couldn't be true. She remembered him... vividly.

It couldn't have been a dream. But the painting downstairs... It should have been Desmond, no... Viscount Alison as Lady Margaret's husband, not Carlisle. Margaret could not allow this to distract her. She pushed the confusion of the portraits aside and set to her task of preparing for the ball.

It took a good half hour for Margaret to pull her hair into a chignon and slip into her dress. She looked far different from the fancy-dressed, head-full-of-ringlets earl's daughter who had dressed with the help of a lady's maid.

After having an elaborate wardrobe of a Regency lady at her disposal, Margaret found her own Regency costume drab. She remembered her frothy pink frock with the line of gold buttons down the back.

If she had really gone back in time, what could have possibly been the reason? What purpose had it all served? Was it to have Lady Margaret marry Sir William Carlisle instead of Desmond?

Then what had become of Desmond? And what had become of Gerald? Had he truly survived the duel in which he had originally died? Checking up on him should be simple enough.

She left her room and went to the back parlor on the ground floor to find the Westchester family history. Entering, she immediately recognized Lady Margaret's painting, the one that had once hung in the front parlor. And Margaret had no difficulty identifying the portrait of a fifty-year-old Gerald, now the sixth Earl of Westchester on the adjacent wall.

The information in the display said that Gerald became earl in 1817 and subsequently married the recently widowed Lady Catherine Holloway. Some said, much too soon after her husband's death.

So everything had turned out all right for Kate and Gerald. But what about Desmond?

In a smaller notation, almost completely obscured, said that the London townhouse, Ashworth House, was sold to Viscount Alison in 1823.

Margaret knew this reference to Alison must have meant Desmond. Desmond. Pierce.

"Excuse me, Margaret?"

Margaret turned around. From the simply tied cravat around the young man's neck to the black silk pumps on his feet was whom she recalled as Sir Julian Montgomery.

"J— J— J—" Margaret stammered. It was like seeing a ghost.

"Are you going to start calling me Jonathan or Mr Montgomery too?" He sounded a bit exasperated. "Mrs Taggart's has us all change our names. She's told me to find you and tell you our transport to the ball will be here any minute."

"The transport..." she repeated.

He gestured for her to go before him and Margaret led the way.

"I think we're the last ones here," he said. He fingered the lapels of his coat and ruffles of his shirt. Margaret half expected him to pull a small red enameled snuff box out of his coat pocket.

"But you know," he continued with a smile. "We'll be fashionably late and make at least a semi-grand entrance."

Margaret understood better than he could ever imagine.

ও.

"A courier has brought your invitation to the party, sir." The butler laid the envelope on the small table next to the door of the bedchamber.

"Thank you, Maypink." Pierce Chapman, Viscount Alison, turned from the full-length mirror hoping his servant knew more than Perry about his get-up for the evening. He had slid on the stockings and managed to step into his breeches. The shirt, with its copious amount of fabric, was another matter.

"I didn't realize it was a fancy dress party." Was there a choice of costume? Perry didn't think he would have chosen this one. He stared into the mirror, examining his reflection, and didn't know what to do next. "Do you have any idea how to... Or perhaps someone who might be able to..." He made a general gesture indicating his clothing. Perry didn't even know what to call it. The *shirttails* were proving to be quite troublesome.

He recognized the rigid confidence of his butler when he entered the bedchamber. "You will be attending a gathering in the manner of an early nineteenth century ball comprised of English Regency era enthusiasts." Maypink informed him and proceeded to take matters in hand straightaway. "It is fortunate, sir, that I am familiar with the assembly of these garments."

"How could that possibly come about?" Perry knew well the Maypinks had been in the service of his family for many, many generations. They were all very clever and had some unusual skills. Thus, Perry wasn't completely surprised to learn this latest bit of information.

"My grandfather was the one who instructed me and he learned from his grandfather." Maypink informed him.

"I wonder why they thought it would be worthwhile. Seems an out-of-date bother to me."

The pale, embroidered waistcoat went on next, Maypink worked the buttons, closing the front. "I cannot say, however, I was told it was imperative I should master the skills to dress a *Mister Darcy*."

"Your grandfather told you that?" Even Perry, who had never read a Jane Austen novel knew of Mr Darcy. "That seems odd."

"Agreed, sir, but my grandfather was most adamant and as a lad and I did as I was told."

"It's a good thing for me he insisted, else I'd be out of luck."

When the servant stepped away, Perry checked the long mirror and his reflection showed a marked improvement. Dressed all in white, or as he had been previously corrected... ivory, although he did not see the difference, he looked very smart, indeed.

"I have taken the liberty of generously starching the linen." Maypink lifted the long, thin length of cloth Perry had seen laid out and had no idea as to its purpose.

"Whatever you think is best, I suppose." Perry stood still, allowing Maypink to stand the shirt points on end and circle about him with the neckcloth. It felt a bit tighter around his throat than he would have liked.

Noisy footsteps of someone climbing the stairs and quickly approaching his bedchamber sounded. "Is that Sean?"

Maypink glanced over Perry's shoulder, watching for the visitor's identity. "Unknown, sir. I informed Mr Howard, when

I spoke to him earlier, that you needed to leave at half-seven."
Answering did not distract his concentration on his current
valet task.

"Let myself in if you don't mind. Tried calling your mobile,
Pere, it's going straight to voicemail." Sean's words preceded his
arrival.

"I've turned it off, don't want to be disturbed." Perry found
that standing still took quite the effort. He could barely hold a
conversation.

"Just stopped by to tell you know the technical issues have
been fixed, everything is all up and running again. We're all set
to schedule another meeting with—" Sean strode into the room
and took in Perry's garments with a gasp. "What the—you can't
wear that tomorrow night, you'll be a laughing stock."

"This isn't for the Gala." Perry remained still, not looking at
his co-worker/friend.

"That's a relief. Are ye off to some dress-up do?" Sean had
difficulty standing somewhere where he could speak to Perry
directly and swung around him, avoiding Maypink's minis-
trations.

"I am." Perry did his best to answer coherently while
glancing at his friend to make eye contact.

"Sir." Of course, Maypink did not sound impatient but
Perry could tell he'd best pay attention. "If you could remain
stationary for just a moment longer...there." Then he stepped
out of the way.

"I say, Maypink, that's quite smart." Perry smiled at his
reflection, admiring the frothy effect the butler had sculpted
beneath his chin. He looked like he'd just stepped out of a BBC
period drama.

"I believe it's a well-crafted cravat, sir. I am quite pleased."

"I'll say it is." Perry could not help from smiling. Part of him
thought he appeared ridiculous, another part thought of him

quite dashing. "Your grandfather, not to mention your father would be very proud. Well done."

"If you will excuse me for a moment." The butler removed himself, allowing Perry and Sean a moment's privacy.

"You're going out in public...dressed like that?" Sean raised his arms in a helpless motion. "I hope the *Evening Standard* doesn't get wind of this."

"I'm certain there are far more noteworthy topics than my appearance."

"You're true and well playing His Lordship now, aren't ye?" Sean remarked rather pointedly. "Don't blame me if we're in total disgrace and our reputation is in the loo by morning."

"It's only a party, Sean."

"If you say so, then I'd better get a wriggle on." With a cursory wave of dismissal, he left.

Maypink returned with another garment. "Your jacket, sir." He held it still so that Perry could slide his arms in, one at a time. The butler adjusted the shoulders and ran a lint brush down each sleeve. Stepping to one side, he set aside the brush and presented, "Your dancing pumps, sir."

"*Dancing...*" Perry couldn't say it. "I don't think I'll be needing those."

"They are *de rigueur*." The butler informed him with raised eyebrows.

"Well, then. Proceed." Perry wouldn't think of breaking fancy dress rules.

Maypink set them on the floor and Perry slipped his foot into each one without any trouble.

"I still don't think I'll set foot on the dance floor. No matter." Perry turned to the full-length mirror once more. "Well done, I say. I cut quite the figure of a Victorian gent, don't you think?"

Maypink cleared his throat and eyed his employer. "Actually, you are dressed as a *Regency* Gentleman, sir."

❧

THE NOISE of the traffic and modern day London followed Margaret up the stairs to the assembly rooms. She trailed behind the guests who traveled down the wide, unfurnished corridor and into the dancing room, where everyone was gathered.

A modest quintet played dance music and the harsh glare of electrically powered lights from a large ceiling chandelier and wall sconces provided the room's illumination.

This was a one-eighty degree difference from Lady Heathcote's lavishly decorated ballroom with its damask drapes, guild-encrusted furniture, and twenty-piece orchestra.

"Over here!" Katie called out, waving to Margaret when she entered the assembly room. "I thought you'd never get here. What took you so long?"

"I overslept." It startled Margaret how much Katie resembled Kate— Lady Catherine.

"Overslept? I thought you'd be too excited to sleep."

Not that she could remember what had gone on, Margaret said, "I was, but when I went out—I really went out."

"I guess so." Katie motioned Margaret near and lowered her voice. "Now tell me, what was in that package?"

"What package?" Margaret couldn't quite remember all of the details before she left. It all seemed so long ago.

"You know, the package." Katie's hands indicated rough dimensions. "That small parcel that came this afternoon."

Had it been delivered just that afternoon?

"You know, the package? The one Viscount Alison brought? Come on—"

Margaret did remember. She remembered receiving that package weeks ago. This felt so weird. Way beyond *déjà vu*. And she had already had this conversation. "It was a book, I already told you."

"Just a book? And you did not already tell me."

A man with dark, curly hair entered the room, catching Margaret's eye. He looked a little like Lord Byron and the thought shook her for a second until she realized it couldn't be the real Byron. Not this time.

"Margaret?"

"What?"

"I asked you—what book was it?" Katie repeated. "Are you listening to me? What was the book?"

"Oh, *Childe Harold's Pilgrimage* by Byron."

"Why would Viscount Alison give you a book?"

"I don't know." Margaret had already solved the puzzle of the book and had moved on to more difficult matters. The most recent was assuring Desmond's tontine victory, saving Gerald's miserable hide, and perhaps, almost single-handedly changing the past.

Within the next ten minutes, Margaret partnered with the *Sir Julian* look-alike Jonathan Montgomery, joined Katie and a *Sir Cornelius Poole* looking Paul in a country dance.

She wondered why people here resembled people she knew from 1813. Or was it the other way around? Maybe that was part of the reason why she had gone back in time.

Were the same people drawn together in specific places during time itself? But there was no way she would ever really know.

This Regency gathering was only a painful reminder of what had been, more specifically, who Margaret had been with. Whom she had to live without.

Pierce Desmond. She'd never see him again. Never. And she would have to get on with the rest of her life.

After the dance, Margaret excused herself and found isolation on the terrace. The soft glow of the ambient city lights silhouetted the chimneys and rooftops of the surrounding buildings. It was beautiful, but it wasn't the nineteenth century London she had grown to love.

What was she going to do? How was she going to cope?

Stepping back into her old life was going to take some time. Her old, comfortable life wasn't that comfortable anymore. She wanted to go back. More than anything—she wanted to go back to 1813.

Could one travel back and forth through the fourth dimension a limited amount of times? More than likely she had reached that limit.

If she couldn't go back, maybe Pierce Desmond could come forward. She was sure he missed her as much as she missed him. Maybe if she wished really, really hard. Perhaps if they wished at the same time, their wish would be granted. Why not? It was certainly worth a try.

Margaret closed her eyes and wished to see him again—to bring him forward in time... to her. As hard as she could, Margaret wished Desmond here—now.

"I beg your pardon?" came a man's voice.

Margaret turned toward the doorway and saw a man wearing an evening coat, knee breeches, clocks, and pumps. The light from the ballroom obscured the details of his features.

Margaret's heart skipped a beat. Maybe two.

He couldn't possibly be who she thought he was.

He stepped out onto the terrace, and into the light. Margaret saw the familiar features of his face and his combed-back hair.

"Oh, my—*Desmond!*" Margaret called out just before everything went black.

CHAPTER 16

"Is she going to be all right?" Katie asked.

"I believe she'll come round in a bit. Let's just give her some air and a chance to breathe. She'll need something to drink. You could fetch her some water," the stranger suggested.

"I'll be right back." Katie disappeared into the assembly room.

When Margaret opened her eyes, the man, it looked to be Pierce Desmond, knelt next to her. Had her wish come true? Had she summoned him here from the past? Was he really with her now?

"Is it you, *Pierce?*" her voice came out in a whisper. She tried to sit up.

"Let me help you to the chair." His smile was calm, reassuring, and familiar.

She accepted his aid by allowing him to take hold of her arm. Margaret tucked her legs under her and stood, she rested her other hand on the stone bench to steady herself.

Katie returned to the terrace, carrying a glass of water. "How is she, Lord Alison?"

Lord Alison? Katie called him *Lord Alison.* Margaret took a closer look and realized he was not exactly Desmond but maybe a modern version but not Lord Alison.

"Our patient is finally awake, but she seems to be a bit disoriented."

He took the glass and slipped his other hand behind Margaret's back for support while holding the glass up to her lips. She took a few sips but still couldn't pull her gaze from him.

"How are you feeling?" he asked.

"Fine. Really, I'm fine." But she wasn't. Not even close. Margaret had a hard time catching her breath and couldn't keep from staring at him. At his face, his smile, his eyes.

"Thank you," she said to Lord Alison and Katie.

"You scared me half to death," Katie told her. "You've never fainted before in your life."

Not in this lifetime.

"I know, I'm really embarrassed," Margaret admitted. She still felt a little woozy but didn't want to cause a commotion. "I think I'll just sit here for a few minutes."

"I'll keep her company." Lord Alison volunteered and sat next to her.

"I know a hint when I hear it." Katie bent and whispered to Margaret. "I'll just be in the next room if you need me."

"I'll be fine, Katie," Margaret reassured her. Then she remembered. She had come back to her own time from...from... the past.

Lord Alison waited until Katie left the terrace before he spoke. "Do you know who I am?"

"Not precisely," Margaret confessed. He could not be who she thought he might be. The butterflies causing her lightheadedness had now migrated to her stomach.

"Just a few moments ago you called me Pierce."

"I did? Is that your name?" She wasn't exactly sure what was going on or how she should answer.

"Well, yes it is. I supposed you've heard of me from Mrs Taggart, I am Pierce Chapman." He motioned around to the terrace floor. "And from your friend Katie, I am Viscount Alison. My friends call me Perry. You may call me what you wish."

"Perry, if that's all right... *Have we met before?*" She was unsure how to phrase her question and simply asked him.

"I hardly call our first meeting proper. If you'll remember I was the inconsiderate chap who almost ran you over on the walk of Ashworth House this afternoon." He ran his hand through his hair, pushing a lock that had fallen forward.

No. That can't be right. That man had very short, very dark hair and bright blue eyes. Perry Chapman was someone entirely different—he looked like a true descendant of Pierce Desmond.

"I think I'd like to stand now."

"Do move slowly—or else you're bound to feel woozy all over again." He had a hold of her hand and his arm around her for support until she felt steady on her feet.

With the achingly familiar feeling of his touch, tears came to her eyes. He wasn't quite the same. He looked somewhat like Pierce and in some ways felt like Pierce, why couldn't he be *her* Pierce?

Perry helped her take a few steps. "How are you managing?"

"I think I've recovered. Thank you." Still feeling somewhat confused, she stepped away from him and tried to regain her composure. "I'm sorry about that little scene I caused when you came out here. I don't know what happened to me."

"Well, I don't usually have that kind of effect on women." He glanced at her in a moment of nervous silence. "I must confess, I haven't been entirely truthful about my presence here."

Margaret's breath caught. Although it might be what she wanted to hear, she was sure he wasn't going to confess that he was really Pierce Desmond from the nineteenth century.

"I came here tonight to apologize for my behavior this afternoon on the front walk. I was quite rude."

Oh, that. From what Margaret could remember, she was the one who almost tripped him. "You weren't rude."

"Inconsiderate, then. I hate to sound like a whining, incompetent imbecile, but I've been somewhat inconvenienced today. I'm afraid I've taken some of my frustration out on you."

"Had a bad day?" She could sympathize with him, she was having one heck of a day herself.

"The absolute worst."

Margaret paused, politely waiting to hear the details if he cared to continue.

"I really don't want to burden you with my problems. No matter, everything has been set to rights now."

"It's not a burden. Please," she encouraged him. "I'm really a little curious."

"Very well...I had this meeting with some House members and other advisors when the broadband went out. Only our broadband, you understand. The rest of the businesses in the building were fine, and the meeting in which I was participating went on fine.

Without broadband one really can't do much of anything. I have my mobile but really...it's rather worthless except to call the broadband company for emergency service."

She might have thought Perry Chapman could have been Desmond's clone, but he wasn't Pierce Desmond. This Pierce was a twenty-first century person, coping with twenty-first century problems.

"Then I was tasked with an errand, a family commitment I could not ignore which brought me to my visit this afternoon. If I had been the gentleman I profess to be, I should have seen you and your friend into the house. On reflection, I distinctly remember your friend *Katie* standing on the pavement, a shopping bag in each hand and burdened with several more in her arms."

As Margaret recalled, Katie saw well enough from behind the packages to see the viscount, the other one, that is—the one Margaret remembered, step into his green Aston-Martin and drive away.

"Instead of leaving the parcel with Mrs Taggart at the front desk, I could have—no, I *should* have waited for you." He paused for a moment. "For some reason, it was supposed to be hand-delivered. I just hadn't the time this afternoon."

"It's all right," she said, hoping to ease the guilt he obviously felt. "Really, it's no big deal."

"Oh, yes—well, anyway," he continued, getting back to the story of his day. "I made some inquiries and discovered you were attending this fancy dress party and I...well, it seemed I owned the appropriate costume so I thought I might come and join in on the festivities."

"You crashed the party?" He could make it sound as nice as he wanted, it all boiled down to the same thing.

"Me? *Crash* the party? Nonsense. I merely acquired a last minute invitation."

"It would be easy for you, wouldn't it?" She knew his viscount status would be more than welcome at the re-creation ball. He would lend an authentic air with his presence.

"I must admit, I did not find it at all a problem. Actually, I find this all really very pleasant. Not all my duties are this interesting."

"Like taking the time out of a chaotic day to deliver a silly little package?" She tried to lighten their conversation. It must have worked because his smile widened.

"Do you know that package has been in the safe at Alison House ever since I can remember? I never expected to be the one to see it to its final destination." He paused as if just realizing what an honor it had been. "You see, there was a note attached, with explicit instructions that the package be delivered to a Margaret Swanson at Ashworth House on July 5th of this year.

"I can't say for sure how long it's been there. But before he passed away, my father told me he remembered seeing that wrapped parcel as a child. I can't even guess how long it might have been there before that."

Margaret didn't want to offer an answer.

"With the difficulties this morning I had completely forgotten about the task. My butler did not fail to remind me, thank goodness. The instructions were very specific and said I had to personally deliver the parcel. I'm afraid this will sound quite odd." Perry brushed the back of his fingers up his neck and to scratch his jaw. "But the thing of it is, I have no idea what it is."

Margaret froze, staring at the gesture. She'd seen Desmond do the very same when he was irritated or in an uncomfortable situation.

"I would have stayed to see, mind, but I had some pressing matters and had to dash back." He stared into her eyes. "But I must confess I am curious." He remained silent, encouraging her to speak.

"Didn't you know?" Here we go again, she thought. "It was a book. Lord Byron's *Childe Harold's Pilgrimage*."

"Why on earth would you get that?" He stared at her.

"Why on earth would you give it to me?" She returned his gaze.

211

"Good point." His brow furrowed. "I haven't a clue."

It had just occurred to Margaret that it probably came from Desmond, who had followed her instructions, to ensure her travel to 1813. Now that she was back in her own time, was something more supposed to happen?

Katie stepped onto the terrace interrupting them. "Just checking up on you. I see you're up and around."

"Yes," Perry took the liberty to answer. "Miss Swanson...eh, Margaret, has made a very nice recovery. Shall we all join the others?"

Katie, Margaret, and Perry finally returned to the party. The gathering was not quite a crush, but there were a lot of people in the small assembly room. Some congregated around the refreshment tables, others stood along the edge of the dance floor watching the musicians play or the couples dancing.

"I can hardly believe you Americans came here to do...this." What Perry must have meant was playing dress-up and having a tea party.

"Not all these people are Americans, some are British," she told him.

"Really?" He glanced about the room and she could just imagine him trying to distinguish the two. It was difficult if not impossible, even for Margaret.

"The American Chapters of the Regency Society were invited by the London Chapter and we all get along just fine."

"I had no idea such a thing existed before now. It's all quite fascinating."

"Do you think we from the Colonies started it all?"

Perry shrugged. "You've got a point there."

"It's not called *Regency* for nothing, you know. It's you English who had Prinny, the Prince of Wales, future George the fourth rule as Regent of England for his father George III."

"I never thought about it that way. I suppose it was a British invention." Perry pointed to the dancers, just completing their set. "Do you..." He waved his fingers in a circular motion indicating the activity on the dance floor.

"If you're referring to the Regency dancing...yes, I do." It had taken Margaret years of practice. She wouldn't exactly call herself an expert but she had become quite accomplished and her visit to the nineteenth century had helped.

"I find I'm embarrassed to admit that I can't even attempt a simple minuet. I suppose I should feel awfully ashamed of myself. As you said, it is a part of *my* country's history."

The musicians tuning their instruments before the start of the next dance, setting the dancers into place. Thomas from her tour group rushed up to her.

"Peg— er, Margaret—" His apology for interruption was brief before he continued. "I need a partner for the Duke of York, could you?" He glanced at the man standing next to her. "I'm sorry for interrupting... Would you?"

She looked at Perry. It would be impolite for her to leave him standing here alone.

"Please go ahead," he encouraged her.

"Are you sure? I hate to leave you alone."

"I'd love to watch," he said, sounding sincere. "I'll be right here when you've finished."

"You really shouldn't feel as though you ought to stay," Margaret said. "I'm sure you must have other, more pressing matters to attend to."

"I'm fully entertained and receiving a much-needed education all at the same time. At the moment, there's nothing I'd rather be doing."

He did seem rather taken with everything going on around him. Although she didn't quite know why.

"You're a prince," Thomas declared and walked off with Margaret by the hand.

"Not quite," Perry replied, smiling. "Merely a viscount."

Margaret left with Thomas to join his wife, Karen, and Paul and two other couples to form a square. When the music began, the dancers sprang into action. The gentlemen bowed and the ladies curtsied before the couples began the steps of the dance.

Perry watched her step onto the dance floor. He found the people in their fancy dress and synchronized steps mesmerizing, almost hypnotic. Merely watching the swirls of color gave him the oddest feeling, other-worldly as if he were observing something, not of this time, which it wasn't.

Margaret looked lovely. She moved around and around, to and fro, her steps dainty and— when on Earth did he think of a dance move as "dainty steps"? And why did it now appeal to him? Pink flushed her cheeks and he had the strangest urge to stand next to her, *dance* with her but he had no idea— well, he couldn't.

It wasn't just the gathering Perry found entertaining. It was this American, Margaret, whom he found utterly and completely enchanting. Perhaps he found her somewhat exotic.

Everything he told Margaret tonight had been true. He had felt guilty about that afternoon and he did wish to apologize for not being more of a gentleman, he should have waited for her return. As it turned out, it would have been only a few moments.

While speaking to Mrs Taggart, Perry learned of the ball. It was the last event on their tour, and the whole house was filled with anticipation. Never did it occur to him to join in the festivities.

A few hours later, something odd had happened to him. Perry had been sitting in his office with Lisa Chang, Chapman Enterprises' VP, and Sean the CTO, all were participating in a video chat with a half-dozen other people. During one MP's discourses, Perry began to lose focus and he began to daydream.

He was reliving the meeting with Margaret on the walkway of Ashworth House. After delivering the parcel, he had left the house and while moving down the front walk, he nearly tripped over her. Only this time, he imagined their eyes had met and held for an instant but in that instant, something had happened. Right then something changed. Something changed inside him.

Not just *in* him, but changed *him*, every piece of DNA down to his last chromosome.

Thank goodness the internet had crashed then.

"What? Are you kidding me?" Sean launched to his feet and ran to the control panel to check the router.

"Did you touch something, Perry?" Lisa accused him but hardly unjustly. Perry was known to have an adverse, anti-technology effect on all sorts of electronics.

"That's it! You get out of here so we can get this fixed, *Pere*. Go on." Sean peppered his outrage with some choice expletives.

With pleasure. Perry stood from his desk and headed to the lift.

"Don't forget we have that Gala tonight!" Lisa called out. "And don't be late! It makes us all look bad."

"I'll let you know when we've got everything up and running," Sean swore again. "And I'll see if I can get a summary of what we missed."

None of this was important anymore. All Perry knew was that he had to see Margaret again.

"You AREN'T BORED STIFF, are you?" Margaret returned to Perry's side to find him wearing the strangest expression. "I'm so sorry."

"No, I was just..." Perry drew in a deep breath as if he were waking. "I found the dancing entertaining and the costumes look very...I'm sorry I cannot dance with you myself."

"Well..." Margaret thought about the alternate activity one would partake in during the Regency period. "Would you care to take a *turn about the room*?"

"What does that mean?" He didn't look shocked but the phrase baffled him.

"You offer me your arm and we take a subdued stroll around the exterior of the room, admiring the paintings, tapestries, and other embellishments we come across." The range of expressions crossing his face was priceless. Margaret managed to keep from laughing at him.

"Well, then." Perry literally stuck his arm out. "Let's do it."

"Just a moment." She lowered his arm and bent his elbow, to a more comfortable position, then gently laid her gloved hand upon his sleeve. "I think we're ready."

"Now we walk around the outside of the room." He was taking all this very seriously.

"That's right." Margaret allowed him to lead the way. "*Take a turn about the room.*"

"Must we admire the art and such?" He did have a point, there weren't any original paintings on display. This was, after all, a rented hall. Perry led Margaret past the other guests, navigating his way to the wall.

"This is just an excuse to share a *tête-à-tête* during a public event when one cannot, for whatever reason, manage the dance floor."

"Perfect, then." They spent some time walking past vast, empty areas and not any art to comment on. "So tell me, how long have you been in the UK? And how much longer will you be staying?"

"Our group is on a two week tour. It's nearly over now and we'll leave this Friday."

There was a pause in his step. "You have two days left?"

"Sad, isn't it?" Margaret could easily see herself spending the rest of her life in this country. In reality, she wasn't sure she'd even make a return trip in this lifetime.

"Do you have any plans for your last few days?"

"Not really. I suppose we'll figure it out. This was the highlight of the tour and no one has thought beyond today." Margaret hoped by then her mind would have calmed and she would have figured all this out before she got home.

"I'm sure you'll have a delightful time, no matter what you decide."

"You're right." She beamed a smile at him. "We'll have two wonderful days and then Friday will be a sad day."

"It's a traveler's regret. Enjoy every moment you have left." He patted her gloved hand and slowed to a stop. "I see we've reached the other side of the room and, I suppose, I should leave you to the rest of your evening." His attention moved from Margaret to the other occupants in the room.

"It's probably a good idea." She felt a lump grow in her throat and she blinked back her tears. "Thank you for coming by. It was very nice to meet you." Margaret pulled her hand from his arm but he captured it as if reluctant to part from her.

His hold caused her to focus on him. Perry was so handsome, extra handsome dressed in his pristine cravat, Regency period dress, and untried dancing pumps.

"Lord Alison?" What had just happened? Why was he—

"Perry..."

"Perry...what is it?"

"Would you mind if I asked to see the book?" His request came out in a rush.

"The book...*Childe Harold's Pilgrimage*?" She didn't mind but....

"Could I? That would be brilliant." His eyes widened and

he smiled. "It wouldn't be an imposition, would it? After all, you only have a few days left of your holiday and I don't wish to waste your time by—"

"I think it would be fine. It doesn't take *that* long to look at a book." Margaret shrugged. It seemed to her he was awful excited to see a *book*.

"Drop by tomorrow morning, shall I? Nine? Ten?"

"Let's say ten. I think I'll be sleeping in a bit tomorrow morning."

"Oh, right. Excellent." He seemed to brighten up, almost happy at the prospect of seeing her again. "I'm glad I took the time to attend tonight. I suppose I'll see you at ten, then?"

"Until tomorrow." Margaret nodded.

"I suppose I'll be off now." He released her hand and took a few steps away from her. "I'll just see myself out."

It was difficult to say who had a sillier smile. The American tourist or the British viscount.

❧

"DID you find your evening a success, my lord?" The butler closed the heavy front door of the townhouse.

"Yes, Maypink, I believe it was." Perry had had a grand time tonight. He couldn't help but smile.

Maypink stopped at the foot of the staircase, taking Perry's outercoat. "Would his lordship be changing out of his evening's" —the butler eyed his employer from the top of his head to the tips of his silk dancing slippers— "costume?"

Perry glanced at his attire and pulled off his gloves, smiling. "No, I don't think so. I'm comfortable enough for the time being." He started down the hallway and then stopped. "Would you please join me in the library?"

"At once, my lord."

Without another word, Maypink followed his employer into the library. Perry sat in one of the leather wing-backed chairs next to the glowing hearth.

"Would you care to sit?" He gestured to one of the chairs.

"That will not be necessary."

"All right, then." Perry crossed his legs and rubbed his chin a bit. "I'm not quite sure where to start."

"I shall endeavor to remain patient, sir." Maypink busied himself by pouring brandy in a snifter and setting it on a silver serving tray.

"Your family has been in the employ of my family for at least two hundred years, haven't they?"

"As I understand it, yes, my lord." Maypink lowered the silver tray next to Perry's elbow.

Perry cupped the snifter in the palm of his hand and swirled its contents along the inner walls of the glass. "What do you know about the package that was in the safe at the main house?"

"I doubt that any of the former employees of my family would have participated in anything as common as gossip."

"Come now, Maypink, there must have been something said about the package. After all, it's been there a good fifty—maybe sixty years at least."

As proud a family as the Maypinks must have been, Perry doubted that in all the years of their employment they had never heard a whisper or two, some stories associated with the parcel that has been passed down the generations.

Maypink gave a deep, rueful sigh. It appeared he was most reluctant to continue. If he didn't know any better, Perry could have sworn the butler rolled his eyes.

"I do not know all the exact details of the story itself, only the summarized version. I shall repeat what I know of it if his lordship wishes. However, it is one that takes on the elements of a fairy tale."

"Yes, yes, I understand." Perry sat forward, anxious for Maypink to begin. "Do go on—go on."

"I had this from my father, who was told by his father and so on, back approximately four generations." With the straightening of his posture and the slightest lift of his chin, Maypink continued. "It was said that the item had to do with reuniting a couple destined for true love."

"True love? Destiny?" Perry sat back. "Gad, that does sound like a fairy tale."

"As I have said, my lord. I believe all in all a story to be included in the company of Rumpelstiltskin and Sleeping Beauty. Will that be all?"

"Yes, Maypink. More than enough." Perry wondered why he had bothered to ask.

Maypink left without a sound.

Perry didn't believe, nor would he ever believe in such nonsense. Was his life really predestined? Had he no choice?

His delivering the book to Margaret—his meeting Margaret—his sudden interest in Margaret. Were they not all coincidences?

Maybe tomorrow will tell.

MARGARET HUNG her Regency gown in the wardrobe and sat on her bed. The high point of the tour was over, finally over. She felt so many things—too confused to think about tomorrow—exhausted from traveling and somewhat relieved that it was all about to come to an end—and excited but perplexed at Perry Chapman's presence at tonight's party.

Margaret thought she had left the man she loved in the past. Yet, a few hours ago she might have sworn he had followed her to the present. Although Perry may have looked like Desmond, it was all too clear Perry was not Desmond.

Margaret sat on the bed and took up the Byron novel. What answers did it hold for her now? Opening the cover, she read the inscription on the inside and turned the pages one at a time. Then two and three at a time, until she got halfway through the book. Then she found a folded piece of paper, tucked in tightly between two pages.

She hadn't remembered there being anything in the book before. She pulled it free and unfolded the paper. Margaret recognized Desmond's handwriting.

My Dearest Margaret,

Words alone cannot express the gamut of my feelings--the joy in knowing you, the devastating loss after you had gone, and the hope I have that one day we will be together.

I would not wish you to experience the profound sadness I have been forced to endure for the six months since your departure. Not a day passed that I did not wish for your return. You cannot imagine how difficult it was to go on day after day, knowing I would never hold you in my arms, never see your gentle face, and never again hear your sweet voice.

It took a great deal of time to emerge from that darkness and accept what I must do. I kept a very close watch on Lady Margaret after you left. I confess that there was never a confusion between the two of you. I retained close ties with her and her family for your sake.

I must tell you that not even a fortnight had passed before she was determined to dispose of the book that Byron had gifted her. Luckily, I was there to unburden her of its presence, promising that she would never see it again.

Although I do not fully comprehend the reasons why be

assured I have done what I must to ensure your return to the past. I have compiled the facts from personal recollections and the scant details you have relayed to me during the short time we shared.

I have done as you asked and married. She is an agreeable lady who has provided me with three sons. I have tried to be a good husband and kind father for all those many years since you left.

Fortunately, time for me will soon come to an end. I am not an old man but the doctors are at a loss to explain my present condition. I am thoroughly convinced I lay here dying of a broken heart.

Margaret gasped and pressed the letter against her chest, choking back a sob. It hurt her so very much to read about him, the end of his life. How many years had it been since she'd seen him? And he had to live the rest of his life without her.

"In my last remaining days, I complete my final task and prepare the book for its journey to you. I enclose my last words in this letter and seal it within the tome that I have every confidence will have the good fortune of encountering your hands.

I have no knowledge of how Fate will play her part in our reunion, and I truly believe, deep within my heart, there is to be one.

It is my fervent wish that you will not know a day without my presence...without my love. If it were within my power, I should be the first person you see when you open your eyes upon your return home.

I promise we will not be robbed of our time together again. This I swear.

With eternal love, yr humble servant,
Pierce, Viscount Alison"

Margaret pressed the paper to her heart and let the tears trickle down her cheeks. He wanted them to be together.

Could Perry Chapman be a modern day Pierce Desmond? She sniffed and swiped the tears away. Had Desmond's soul traveling through time and adapted to the modern era along the way?

Desmond grew up in the 1800s—he couldn't help it if men were arrogant and chauvinistic. He couldn't even see being friends with her.

Perry displayed the manners and conduct of a modern gentleman—kind, considerate, and sensitive. Could he really be Pierce Desmond reborn?

Was it even possible?

How could she know for sure?

And more importantly, did Perry know?

CHAPTER 17

THE NEXT MORNING, Perry Chapman, ninth Viscount Alison entered Ashworth House filled with a great sense of disquiet. On one hand, he felt enough adrenaline to run the London Marathon, on the other he knew this was a casual, social visit. Then why was he experiencing such turmoil? He'd spent an inordinate amount of time choosing what he should wear, careful not to overdress for the simple task of *viewing the book*. And why had he gone to such lengths?

He couldn't deny he had been curious about the parcel he'd delivered but when he met Margaret... Last night had changed his life. That sounded overly-dramatic but it didn't make it any less true. And here he was fussing with his open shirt collar wondering if he should have worn a lightweight jumper instead of a suit coat. Should he button the front of the jacket? Leave it open? Maybe do-up a single button?

"Why, Lord Alison." Mrs Taggart set her pencil down and pushed her papers aside when he approached. "What possibly could have brought you to us two days in a row?"

"Hallo there, Mrs Taggart, I'm here to see Miss Swanson." He tried not to sound too chipper. Although it was true, Perry didn't want Mrs Taggart to think him overly anxious, which he was.

By the look of her quaint smile and rosy glow on her cheeks, she must have suspected something was going on with him. "Ah, Margaret again, is it?"

"She's expecting me." Perry could feel his face warm and it was a good bet he wasn't fooling her one bit. "If you could just tell me her whereabouts."

"You can find her in the breakfast room."

Perry hurried off, throwing a polite but quick, "thank you" over his shoulder and headed down the corridor.

It didn't stop Mrs Taggart from calling after him, "You'd better make haste, Lord Alison. She leaves the day after tomorrow."

IN THE BREAKFAST ROOM, Margaret couldn't shake the feeling that her life was still a bit *off*. She thought she could find out what Katie remembered of the man they came across on the front walk from the day before.

"You do remember seeing him yesterday, don't you?" Margaret sat across from Katie, the Byron book on the table in front of her, with her back to the door.

"Remember him? You've got to be kidding. You'd have to have amnesia ten times over to forget him."

"Lord Alison, I mean. He *looks* the same, doesn't he? You don't think he's changed—the color of his hair, maybe?"

"Change? Why in the world would you want to change him?" Katie looked from Margaret to the ceiling, her eyes glazed over. "His hair...don't you just want to run your fingers through it?"

Perry's hair grew in dark but had lightened at the ends.

Margaret had wondered about it when she saw Desmond's portrait, but with Perry, she knew it was due to heredity.

"And those dreamy brown eyes...you could lose yourself in them."

His dark lashes accentuated his eyes and the resemblance to Desmond was...incredible. A little voice inside told her, much too incredible to be a coincidence. Or is that what she wanted to believe?

"And I don't even have to tell you about his body. It's has got to be that of—"

Margaret already knew—*a God's.*

No matter what Katie or Perry had said, Margaret knew this was not the same man she had met yesterday afternoon.

"I still can't believe you're dating a viscount." Katie was at it again.

"We're not dating," Margaret repeated, for what must have been the fiftieth time. "He just wants to see the book."

"The book? *Sure.*" Katie pretended not to sound convinced. "Do you think you'll be able to tear yourself away from him to meet us for lunch?"

"I can't imagine looking at a book will take that long." Margaret didn't want to make a big deal about it, obviously, Katie did.

"He is not coming here *just* to look at a book. I don't care if it's a First Edition or not. You could bring him along."

"We have no other plans together." Margaret maintained. There was no use making a mountain out of a molehill.

"It could be a date. A lot can happen between now and then." Katie's eyebrows lifted, and she gave that smile Margaret found so disturbing.

Had Katie expected him to fall in love with Margaret over browsing through *Childe Harold's Pilgrimage?* It would be equally wishful thinking on her part if she believed Perry were

Desmond. He couldn't help it if he looked like Desmond—and if she fell for him, it would be for all the wrong reasons.

Katie's relaxed posture stiffened when she waved her hand over her head and called out, "Lord Alison! In here!"

Margaret's breath caught with the anticipation of seeing him again. She thought their meeting for inspecting the book perfectly casual but apparently, her insides were telling the rest of her that seeing him again was a big deal.

"Good Morning, ladies."

Margaret did not turn to look behind her and did her best to resume breathing. Yes, she tried to act calm because it would have been an act, nothing could have been further from reality.

"I know I've come a bit early. I hope I'm not interrupting." Perry strolled into the room. He'd left his suit at home and today wore a simple light-blue shirt, gray slacks, and a jacket. It was very different from the nineteenth century garb of last night. His curious gaze went from Katie to Margaret.

"No, not at all. Please, sit down," Katie suggested. Thank goodness she said something because Margaret had been rendered speechless. "We were just talking about—"

"The dance last night," Margaret interjected, her voice finally returning and there was no need to include him in the topic of their previously discussed, dating or non-dating status.

"I can't tell you what an enlightening evening I had last night." His wide smile told her he'd meant it.

"It was fun, wasn't it?" Katie rested her chin in her open palm, looking wide-eyed at Perry.

"Where are you off to this morning, Miss—Katie?"

"We're going to get some of those lawn chairs in Green Park, sit in front of Buckingham Palace and enjoy our lunch. We have to leave now so we can get a good spot. Do you think you'll be able to join us? You're more than welcome to come along." She tried luring him with, "It's a picnic."

"Picnic, eh?" Perry smiled at the not-so-subtle attempt to tempt him.

"We'll get an extra chair just in case, see if you can convince him to come along, okay?" Katie said to Margaret, not in a quiet way. "Gotta go. I better see if I can light a fire under Paul. Well, good to see you again, *your lordship*. I just *love* calling him that," Katie whispered to Margaret with a giggle before moving to the door.

"And you as well, *Miss Holloway*."

Margaret thought she would melt at the sound of his voice. It wasn't Desmond's but the two shared some familiar qualities.

"Don't forget, Margaret, we're meeting at the fountain just outside Green Park tube station on the Palace side at 1:30. Don't forget your lunch."

"1:30. Bring my own food. Got it." Margaret waved. It was strange to think that she wasn't looking forward to lunch by Buckingham Palace in a couple hours. Not when Perry was here in her present.

Perry walked around to the other side of the table from Margaret and sank onto one of the hardwood chairs, chuckling. "Your friend Katie is very funny."

"I'll make sure to tell her. She'll be glad to know someone thinks so." Either Perry was extremely polite or he had the weirdest sense of humor. Margaret felt comfortable around him. He wasn't a complete stranger to her, not really.

A few minutes passed before his gaze settled on the book under her hands. "Is that it? *Childe Harold*?"

"Yes." Margaret had nearly forgotten this was the reason Perry had stopped by. She lifted the book off the table and held it out to him.

He took it from her with great reverence and eyed the object not quite skeptical but certainly wondering if it was what he thought it might be. He tilted it to see the back cover before spending several undisturbed minutes in silence inspecting the book. Finally, he flipped open the front cover and then the first few pages taking his time to read the inscription.

"It doesn't look as if it has been read much, does it?" Margaret finally commented. As far as she could tell the book had been opened and only a few pages were ever turned, mostly by her.

"It's in very fine condition. Basically new, really. Mint." He appeared completely taken with the volume.

Well, its circulation had been limited. It had gone from Byron's hand to hers to Desmond's.

"And it just-so-happens to be inscribed to you?" Perry glanced from the book cover to Margaret.

"Someone with my name. Some coincidence, isn't it?" She was not the real *Lady Margaret*.

"It's been sitting, wrapped in a safe for ages. I do mean ages. I am at a loss to explain why it should be delivered to you."

"I don't think I can tell you." Margaret wouldn't confess her crazy story to anyone.

"I suppose there is no use in torturing ourselves by discussing the matter further." He closed the book and made no motion to return it. "Now what about those lunch plans? At half-one, if I am correct. Would you mind if I tagged along?"

He hadn't meant it, had he? "It's up to you, really. Katie said they'd have an extra lawn chair for you." Margaret wasn't about to tell him what he should or shouldn't be doing. "I was going to take the tube to Green Park. There's a *Marks & Spencer* at the station right there and I thought I'd pick up lunch."

"Tube?" Perry drew in a breath and gazed into the room. "I haven't used the Underground in years, not since I was a lad."

"You probably don't even have an Oyster card." How many peers used public transport? "Did they have Oyster cards back then?"

"Course they did. I had one. I used to have one, no idea where it is now, probably long gone." He stood and held out the book to Margaret. "No worries, I'll buy a ticket. I expect they'll still have those."

"I'm pretty sure they do." Margaret followed suit and retrieved the book. "Let me drop this off in my room and grab my bag."

&

MARGARET LOOKED different than Perry remembered, must be the modern clothing. The last time he had seen her she had been wearing a period costume. Her hair was styled different but it was the same soft brown color. Her eyes held the same clever twinkle that captured his attention the night before.

He was fortunate indeed that he was able to meet with her again. A bonus was spending lunch with her and it seemed there would be an added traveling adventure as well. One didn't have that in one's very own city. Although he mostly grew up and currently lived in London, he hadn't really seen much of the city. It was just where he resided. He'd never spent much time in any of the museums or taking in the historic sites.

"You ready?" She had descended the stairs and stepped onto the landing.

"I can't say I'm used to a pedestrian's life. I'm afraid the Tube and bus travel went the way of my boyhood. Lead on!" He turned to bid farewell to Mrs Taggart only to find the office panel closed and he thought that odd. It looked to him as if the opening were never there. Perry dashed ahead of Margaret to open the front door for her. "Sorry, I was distracted."

"No need to, but thank you anyway." She looked at him with a beaming smile.

It warmed his insides. Why would her kind reply make his heart flutter in such a peculiar manner?

꙳

"IT'S NOT FAR to the station." Margaret pointed down the street and they walked side-by-side. "I guess this is not the normal way you travel around town."

"No, it isn't." He glanced around at the many people lining the pavement on both sides of the street. "Sometimes I drive myself, usually have a car and driver, occasionally I take a taxi."

Perry stepped to his left, avoiding several oncoming people. They headed toward the red circle and blue Underground sign. He followed Margaret into the station. There wasn't time to talk, there were too many people milling about and far too noisy. She led him to one of the machines to buy a ticket. Once that was done they made their way through the turnstiles then down the stairs to the platform.

There certainly more people using the Underground than he recalled but then again, he was only a lad and he most probably did not pay much attention as to what was going on around him.

Margaret stopped abruptly and glanced down briefly before meeting his eyes. "We're getting off at the third stop, Green Park, okay?"

"Right." Perry glanced at his feet, comparing their position to Margaret's, had more or less stopped where she had pulled his foot back off the wide, yellow line. He kept alert, watching the crowd of people around him. Some moving past him, some milling about, waiting for the next train to arrive.

An automated announcer over the station loudspeaker cautioned the passengers to keep on the watch for any unusual items or activity, encouraging them to: *See it. Say it. Sorted.* And report such to the proper authorities.

The approaching rumble and rhythmic clanking of the wheels, emanating from the darkened tube, grew louder. There were metallic screeches and hisses as the train came to a full stop before them. The doors opened and many passengers filed off.

After the shuffle of people settled, some seated themselves and some stood in the aisle and held on to the dark blue overhead handrail. Perry followed Margaret inside, they ended up standing in the corner at the end of the carriage. The doors closed and the humming of the engine began as they moved forward. No one in the carriage spoke nor even seemed to make eye contact, except Margaret and Perry.

He glanced at her and she had already been staring at him. He smiled and she returned his smile. They braced themselves for the first of three stops. There was a high pitched screeching of the brakes as the train rounded the corners.

An automated female voice announced, "Approaching Hyde Park Corner. This is a Piccadilly line service to Cockfosters."

Passengers ready to disembark moved closer to the door. The train whined, slowing to a stop. The doors whooshed open and the group stepped off the train shortly replaced by new travelers filling the void.

"Sorry, budging up a bit." Perry murmured to Margaret, stepping closer to her to allow people to pass. He did not find her closeness at all unpleasant. It was rather nice, really.

A few minutes passed while the passengers settled. The doors closed and the humming of the engine began as they moved forward. Margaret and Perry did not have to look far to make eye contact during this leg of the ride.

"Next station is Green Park. Change for the Jubilee and Victoria lines."

Perry felt almost sad at the thought of their journey coming to an end. The train slowed to the third stop, Green Park, and the doors opened, passengers filed out of the carriage, Margaret and Perry among them.

He followed her off the train and through the confusion of the lobby where people converged with the Jubilee and Victoria Lines, pushing all sorts of ways to get to their proper escalators and some through the turnstiles to exit. She grabbed hold of his hand to lead him as she navigated through the people and up the stairs. Moving to her left, she pushed open a glass door and stepped through bringing Perry along with her.

"We can grab something to eat in here." Margaret released hold of his hand and stepped into the shop. She seemed to know what she was doing and made her selection quickly but waited for him. He studied the rows of premade sandwiches and finally chose a package. "They have all sorts, don't they?"

Ploughman's Cheese, beef and onion, Chutney Bloomer, brie & grape, BLT, chicken & bacon, chicken salad, egg & water-cress, prawn & mayo, ham & mustard.

Perry chose the ham & mustard. As for the crisps: sour cream & jalapeno, sea salt & balsamic vinegar, sour cream & onion, four cheese & red onion, prawn crackers... He selected a safe bag of sea salt and cracked black pepper.

Then there was the choice of biscuits: custard creams, ginger rounds, shortbread, digestives...all sorts. One could never go wrong with Jaffa Cakes. Perry wrapped his hand around a small pack of those.

Pre-cut fresh fruit: Melons, Grapes, mangos, apples, and various selections of mixed berries. A cup of strawberries, rasp-berries, and blueberries seemed the right choice for him.

"Don't forget to get something to drink." She held up her

bottle of still water as an example. "I grabbed a bag of Percy Pigs!" Margaret said with some enthusiasm but he had no idea what that might be.

Percy Pigs?

Perry grabbed a bottle of sparkling water and joined Margaret in the queue. A few minutes later they had been rung up, paid, and were headed out the door.

He stared into the bag holding their picnic lunches. "I don't know what you think we're going to do with all this."

"Eat it, of course." Margaret resettled the shoulder strap of her purse and headed for the way out. "Come on."

They crossed Piccadilly Street in front of The Ritz Hotel and headed into Green Park. Just beyond the fountain where visitors stood, filling their water bottles stood Katie with a young man holding folded park chairs. Margaret glanced around at the multitude of people in the Park, Perry only knew Katie by sight.

"We're over here!" Katie's young man called out, waving his arm to catch their attention.

Margaret, with Perry in her wake, headed for her friends. "I'm glad we found you."

"You came!" Katie seemed particularly thrilled to see Perry.

"I was invited or have I misunderstood?" Perry glanced about checking their facial expressions to see if he had made a mistake.

"Yes, of course, you were." Katie rolled her eyes. "You didn't forget your lunch, did you?"

"We're all set." Perry held up the M&S logoed bag for her to see. "Allow me to carry those." He took the two green and white deckchairs from Katie.

"Let me carry our lunch, then." Margaret took their lunch bag from Perry. "Perry? Have you met Paul?"

"I do not believe so." Perry had thought to offer his hand but with the juggling of the deck chairs and bags, he thought better of it.

"I've heard so much about you." Paul inclined his head. "All good, of course. Nice to finally meet you. So you're a real viscount, huh?"

"I'm afraid so." Perry shrugged and nodded, feeling a bit out of sorts. He usually didn't feel this awkward about his title but for some reason, he felt uncomfortable around this group. "Basically grew up with it."

"*Niiiiii*-ce." Paul smiled. "Shall we choose a place to plant our chairs?" He motioned the group that they should move down the paved path. "Let's head this way. We'll want to get a good place for our picnic."

"Someplace where we can see the Palace." Katie motioned off to their right.

They finally found a spot where the people, the cyclists, and traffic did not hinder their view of the white stone of the building with the famous Royal balcony. Paul and Perry set up the chairs in a nice, semi-shady spot.

"Oh, it's beautiful, isn't it?" Katie stared at the full front of the Palace that lay before them.

"Katie, here you go." Paul offered her the first chair after he had taken some time to set it up properly.

"Margaret?" Perry called to her, distracting her from gazing at the Palace.

"Thanks." Margaret sat next to Katie and handed the lunch bag to Perry.

"You are so lucky to live in the same city with a Palace, Perry. I mean *the* Palace." Katie appeared to be vastly impressed by the Royal residence.

"I suppose." Perry hadn't known any different. He'd grown up with the Monarchy. "I've seen the front of Palace but I've never really *looked* at the front before." Of course, its appearance was exactly the same as on the telly but Grand wasn't a grand enough word for it.

They all opened their sandwich boxes, discussed the various types of sandwiches, nibbled on fruit, and shared their crisps while chatting. Katie and Paul were agreeable enough. Margaret remained quiet but not uninvolved in the conversation.

"I wonder what it would be like to drive through the front gate." Katie motioned with her right arm. "Past the guards at the post and under the arch to the courtyard."

"Normally I enter through the south gate." He motioned with his left hand and stilled when his comment drew wide-eyed stares.

"You've been inside Buckingham Palace?" Both Katie and Paul replied absolutely gobsmacked.

"Only a handful of state dinners and—" Perry's mobile rang. "I beg your pardon." He pulled it from his jacket and glanced at the screen. "It's the office. I need to take this." He stood from his chair and took a few steps away from the group.

"Did you hear that?" Katie whispered to Margaret. "He's been *inside* the Palace for dinner. I wonder if he's met the King?"

Margaret had ignored Katie and paid attention to Perry and his side of his conversation.

"Yes?" He glanced back at his fellow picnickers. "I'm at lunch at the moment." He paused. "Very well. Eh...at the Statue in front of the Palace. Cheers, thanks."

Although he ended his conversation with a 'Cheers' in no way did he seem cheerful. It was more than his facial expression that told Margaret he wasn't happy with the news. Something about his body language, the slight slump of his shoulders before he turned around to face her alerted her to the imminent bad news he had to tell her.

"I'm sorry, I'm afraid I have to leave." Perry didn't look happy about it. "The company is sending a car for me."

It was bad news and Margaret just realized this would mean goodbye, probably forever."

"Walk with me, will you, Margaret?"

"Of course." She capped her water bottle, set it aside, and stood.

"Katie, Paul, thank you for sharing your afternoon." Perry nodded his head and they got to their feet to say their goodbyes. Even they seemed sad to see their guest leave.

Perry led the way out of the Park and Margaret walked by his side.

"I didn't expect you would leave so soon." His sudden need to depart caught her off guard. Margaret had thought she could spend a bit more time with him.

"I had no idea our time would be this short either." Perry grew quiet. And for someone who asked for company, he did not seem as if he cared for her presence.

They headed toward the Palace. Both walked very slowly.

"You have one day left, is that right?" It was just something to say because she knew that he knew what day she left.

"Sad, isn't it?" Margaret could easily see herself spending the rest of her life in this country. In reality, she wasn't sure she'd even make a return trip in this lifetime.

"Is there a plan for tomorrow yet?"

"No. I suppose someone will have an idea, then someone else will make another suggestion, then some people will go to the first place and some people will go to the second just like today." Margaret hoped by then her mind would have calmed and she would have figured all this out.

"I'm sure you'll have a delightful day, no matter what you decide." He smiled. "I only wish—"

"You're right." She beamed back. "It'll be both a wonderful and then a sad day."

"Enjoy every moment you have left." He slowed to a stop when they reached the curb. "There's my car now. I should leave you to the rest of your lunch with your friends and—they're waiting."

"And you have to leave." She felt a lump grow in her throat and she blinked back her tears. "Thank you for coming by this morning. It was very nice to see you again."

He took up her hand. It caused her to focus on him. "I'm glad I took the time to do so. It was lovely to meet. I wish you a good rest of your trip and good-bye." With that Perry released her hand and left.

CHAPTER 18

THE ROYAL CRESCENT HOTEL, Bath

This was an early meeting. Very early because Perry had to drive over two hours to Bath that morning to accommodate one of the Parliamentary finance committees for the Conservatives and this had been thrown together at the last minute. As of now, he checked his wristwatch, he had been there for three hours.

This discussion was important. Sean appeared to be paying attention to the details. It was a good thing because Perry could not seem to keep on-task. His attention wandered to the ornate ceiling molding. He had no idea what design or pattern it was but it was old...Victorian? Margaret would like it. She would have loved it, the red-stripes on a yellow wallpaper with little ornate motifs. They even sat in period chairs with scrolls and carvings in the arms and legs, she would have known about them...and she would be gone tomorrow.

Why was he here and not spending time with her?

"Gentlemen." Perry stood. "I need to leave."

"What's that?" Sean straightened in his chair.

"We don't have time to reschedule again. The first time—"

"Mr Howard is more than qualified to speak for our organization." Perry pushed the notepad in front of him away and returned his ballpoint pen to the inside of his jacket. He stood and headed to the door to leave.

"If you'll excuse me for a moment—" Sean stood and left the four other men. "I'll be right back."

Perry bypassed the lift, not willing to wait, and took the stairs.

"You can't leave," Sean called after his friend. "Do you know what it took to set this up?"

"I know." Perry knew what sort of gymnastics Sean had to do to get this all set up. "I'm sorry. But I can't, I'm rubbish right now. I can't concentrate. "He climbed the steps with Sean trailing. Stepping onto the main floor and headed for the front door.

"You're going to have to handle it, mate."

"Handle it? I don't want to handle it. I want you there. You need to be there." Sean followed Perry outside, down the walk to the pavement, and into the street toward his car.

It would be a good two hours' drive back to London. On the way, he'd call Mrs Taggart and see what she could tell him. Then he'd plan his next step. She was more than keen to nurture their budding romance between him and Margaret. He'd hardly call it any kind of romance.

"You're mental!" Sean cried out in a burst of frustration. Perry wasn't about to change his mind. "Is it about her, is it? That girl—that American tourist?"

Down at the east end of the Royal Crescent, a few people exited from the townhouse. One of the women looked as if she somewhat resembled—

"Margaret?" Perry called out without thinking.

"That's not her, is it? That can't be—" Sean slapped his forehead with his open palm. "Unbelievable! Of all the places you both might be... how is this even possible?"

Perry recognized her at once. Her posture, the shape of her

head, the color of her hair. He raised his hand to shield the light from his eyes.

At the sound of her name, Margaret turned.

"Is that Lord Alison?" Katie descended the stairs of the museum and came up behind her friend.

Was it? Margaret moved forward to see if it truly was him.

"Margaret, it is you!" Perry jogged down the middle of the road toward her.

"Perry? What are you doing here?" Astonished was hardly the word she would have used...the odds he would have been here on the same day, at the same time she was...must have been astronomical.

I had an early morning meeting. What are you doing here?" He seemed to be as astonished as she at their unexpected meeting.

"We thought we'd spend our last day in Bath—" By his blank look, Margaret realized he had no idea to which house she referred. She pointed behind her. "We've come back to Bath to see No. 1 Royal Crescent. It's a museum—townhouse restored to the Regency era. It was closed when we first visited last week."

He glanced at the end unit of the Royal Crescent behind her that overlooked the city of Bath.

"You don't know what I'm talking about, do you?"

He chuckled. "Not really." He glanced behind her. "You're here with your friends?"

"Yes, several of us came for the day. We caught the train this morning."

"Is there any possibility I could persuade you to leave your friends and allow me to show you about this fair city? I have the feeling you know a great deal more about Bath than I."

"I don't think so." she demurred.

"Perhaps you would be so kind as to enlighten me?"

241

"I don't think I can, not really." She smiled. How could she tell him about his own country?

"Join me for tea? Coffee?" Such simple words and an easy question.

And Margaret wanted to accept.

"*Miss Holloway?*" Perry focused his attention on the small group. "Do you think you might continue your afternoon without Miss Swanson?"

"That sounds lovely," Katie replied, proving she had overheard every word. "I think you should go, Margaret. I hope you both have a good time."

"What about lunch at *Sally Lunn?*" They had already made plans for that afternoon.

"Paul will be with me, I'll be fine."

"I'd be happy to step in." Paul sidled up and wrapped his arms around Katie's waist.

"What do you say, Margaret?" The look on Perry's face made his request impossible for her to refuse.

It was the last day of her British trip. And she was in Bath, land of Jane Austen. Had she wanted to continue her day with Katie and the others? Margaret didn't want to forget Desmond.

Perry wasn't Desmond but there were times when a certain way he'd said something, a phrase, a look, or some mannerism he made reminded her of the man she loved. To see that familiar flash of that man was so irresistible, she didn't want to say no.

Why would he offer to spend more time with her if he didn't wish it as well? Was she only avoiding the inevitable? Life without him.

"Go on," Katie insisted, then whispered, "And don't forget to ask to see his etchings."

"Katie!" Margaret didn't need much encouragement and nodded her acceptance.

"Have a good time!" Katie waved. The rest of their small

group, the ones who just now exited the museum and had missed out on the conversation, joined Katie and Paul wishing their traveling companion well. "Take good care of her," Katie waved. "Don't forget the group has dinner plans tonight. Don't be late!"

"I'll make sure she's returned to Ashworth House quite safe," Perry promised Katie and mouthed to Margaret. "*Etchings?*"

"Have a good day and safe trip back to Town." Margaret turned and focused her attention on Perry, the two of them stepped away from the others. "She's trying to be funny."

"Right." Perry glanced over his shoulder. "Shall we be on our way? My car is right here but—if you don't mind, I think we should walk. There's his place just off Queen's Square." Perry smiled and with a sweep of his arm, gestured that he and Margaret move in that direction.

"*Jolly's?*" she guessed. It was an old department store that had a quaint tea room.

"No, it's right across the alley." Perry fell in step with her. "There's a nice path that takes us directly to Queen's Square from here."

"Lead on." Margaret would rather walk than drive.

They crossed in front of *No 1 Royal Crescent*, in the direction of The Circus, then turned right before reaching residential buildings on Brock Street. They eventually ended up strolling on a narrow, asphalt-paved path.

"How is it we both ended up at the Royal Crescent this morning?" Margaret wondered out loud. "I didn't even know I was coming here until yesterday after an extensive group discussion at dinner. Paul's the one who suggested we come back to see the museum."

"Sean, of the '*you're mental*' declaration you might have heard earlier, told me about this meeting late last night after the party we attended." Perry shook his head. "Which also happened last minute."

"Is that where you went after you left us in Green Park?"

"I was having such a splendid time at lunch. But when King and Country call, I cannot refuse."

"The King?" Could that be right? Perry had to leave because the King of England needed his council?

"Well, not the King exactly but it was Government business. On the other hand, it seems as if we meet at the most inopportune times and are purposely thrown together. Doesn't that sound mad?"

She didn't know what to say about that. The idea did sound a bit incredulous. Margaret was pretty sure the Universe wasn't acting against them.

She gazed at the rural area around them, the path they took, behind the multi-storied townhouses did not look familiar but suddenly she had a realization and stopped.

"Do you know where we are?" Her eyes widened in astonishment and she drew in a deep breath.

"I..." Perry glanced around. "No, not really." He probably saw the same trees, rocks, and shrubs Margaret had, yet they meant nothing special to him. But to Margaret the meaning of this place—

"This is the Gravel Walk!"

When he remained silent, she continued.

"It's where Anne Elliott and Fredrick Wentworth walked together and finally reconciled."

"I'm sorry, they are not known to me."

"They're from *Persuasion*," she said, expecting he would know after she reminded him.

"Is that a movie? A book?" He really didn't know.

"Jane Austen."

"Ah— *Her* I have heard of." He sighed when he finally

caught on. "Unfortunately I have not read any of her work, as far as I know. I may have in school but I cannot honestly recall. I am a rubbish Englishman, aren't I?"

"No, not really," Margaret reassured him. "There are a lot of people who have never read Jane Austen." However, growing up in England and not having read Austen was another matter.

He groaned. "I'm sorry. I must count myself as one of them."

"But you're nice enough to take me down the Gravel Walk." And he didn't even know how important a place this was. It's not only where the fictional Miss Elliott and Captain Wentworth strolled, it's where the real Jane Austen once spent time.

"I'm glad you can see beyond my ignorance and enjoy the iconic journey." Perry seemed not to have been so hard on himself. "I suppose I'm not a total loss."

"I wouldn't say so. You're just a normal guy." It might not make sense to him but it did to her.

"I've been to Bath many times but for some reason this time I've taken note of several period ornamentations. Buildings, furniture, interior design, which I never before noticed. I don't know if they were Regency or perhaps they are from the Victorian or Georgian eras, I can't say because I don't know the differences."

"Do tell." Margaret what she'd learned of this twenty-first century man is that he knew practically nothing of history.

"There was a moment after I parked my car and gazed to the hills across the Royal Crescent green thinking of how many people over the last 200 years who must have admired that very same view."

The rolling hills, the yellow Bath stone buildings, and the near-invisible *ha-ha*...did Perry even know what a *ha-ha* was?

"Then I stared from one door to the next, starting on one side of the Crescent and moved to the right, wondering about all the people who lived in those houses. Who were they? Not the current people but the original residents who first inhabited these dwellings."

"Rich aristocrats who could afford to live there," Margaret answered. "The servants had separate entrances."

"I wonder if my ancestors ever lived here?" He gazed at the buildings longingly. Even from the back, they looked amazing. "It doesn't matter really. Tell me what happened to Fredrick Wentworth and Anne Elliott?"

Margaret told him about the Elliot family and their financial troubles. How Frederick Wentworth, before becoming a wealthy naval captain was once engaged to Miss Anne Elliot. Miss Elliot had been encouraged to break the engagement because he was unsuitable. When he returned as Captain Wentworth and in a better social position, the two navigated through the trials and tribulations of the book only to realize they still cared for one another and finally confessed their true feelings while on the very same path they now walked. Miss Elliot and Captain Wentworth finally marry.

Perry smiled. So the story had a happy ending. She was so clever, he didn't mean Miss Elliot or Miss Austen, but Margaret. He was engrossed in, not the story, but her storytelling. He should have felt like a dunce but he didn't care, all he truly wanted was to be in her company.

PERRY LED Margaret up the steps to *Hall & Woodhouse*. He pulled open one of the tall, wood-framed, glass doors and they stepped inside, strolling up to the copper bar. The restaurant looked to be empty, only staff milling about and preparing for the day's business.

"Can I help you?" A male server came up to them.

"Is it possible to sit near the hearth?" Perry pointed some-where off to the left.

"Yes, sir." The server led the way to the back of the building and when they sat on one of the large Chesterfield sofas he asked, "Would you care to see a menu?"

"Not necessary. If you could bring us some tea." Perry requested and Margaret nodded.

"English Breakfast?"

"Fine, and a selection of muffins. Three, if you please. Surprise us."

"Yes, sir." The server smiled, possibly delighted at the chal-lenge. "Anything else I can get for you?"

"I think that'll be all for right now." Perry turned his atten-tion from the server, who left, to Margaret seated beside him with their backs to the tall exterior windows.

"This is quite a place." She admired the cozy atmosphere and the stack of recognizable board games sitting on the shelves, occupying a floor-to-ceiling, open bookshelf that flanked a large fireplace.

"I find it comfortable, and quiet at this time of day." He tugged at his tie, loosening it, and he unfastened the top button of his shirt.

"Is that why we're here?"

"I can't help but feel we were robbed of our time together yesterday."

Robbed of time... She thought that an odd choice of words for him to use.

"I can't tell you how nice it is to sit here with you."

A pot of tea, cups and saucers arrived along with a plate of a trio of muffins with utensils and two small plates.

"Shall we let the tea steep a bit longer?" Perry took his knife and circled over the three muffins. "What do you think we have here? Any guesses? Where shall we start?"

Margaret leaned forward inspecting their choices. "Hmm... I'm not sure. That first one looks like there might be a berry there. Might be blueberry."

"I do like a blueberry muffin," he said, sounding hopeful.

She pointed to the light-colored muffin. "Those are poppy seeds. This darker one... I'm not sure. Maybe we should taste that one first."

"If that's what you'd like." He slipped the tip of the knife under the muffin and lifted it carefully onto an empty plate. "Would you care to do the honors?"

"No, you go ahead." Margaret thought he was doing a fine job wielding the knife.

Perry tugged at the paper wrapping a bit then held it tight before slicing through the cake. He separated the halves and Margaret gave a little gasp of surprise at what she spotted sitting in the middle.

"What's that?" She pointed to the interior.

"The filling." Perry cut one side in half again and quickly popped it into his mouth. "Oh— it's spiced apple." He chewed it seeming to savor every bite.

"Filling?" These weren't cupcakes and muffins weren't filled— at least they weren't at home. The idea boggled. "Who fills their muffins?"

"Everyone?" Perry shrugged.

"Really? There's nothing wrong with that." She glanced at him, anxious to have a taste for herself.

"Here." Perry pushed the plate with the sliced apple-filled muffin toward her.

Margaret picked up the small piece and did as Perry had done, popping it into her mouth.

"Mmm." She nodded, approving of the flavor. It was apple, spiced apple with cinnamon, nutmeg, and a few others she couldn't quite identify. All of it good but she shouldn't have acted so impulsively as to fill her mouth. It wasn't until after she'd done it that she thought, how unladylike.

She chewed and chewed, trying to clear her mouth of muffin.

"Shall we go on to the next one?" He gestured with the knife. Perry seemed to sense her momentary difficulty and offered, "Or would you like some tea?"

She pointed at the teapot and would be grateful to cleanse her palate before continuing onto muffins two and three.

"Right..." Perry placed the tea strainer on her cup. "Milk? Sugar?"

"Milk, please." She managed but it sounded more like a mumble.

He slid the milk pot, handle toward her. Margaret poured a bit of milk into her cup while he finished pouring tea for himself.

She sipped her tea and swallowed. "Sorry." She brought her fingers to her mouth, embarrassed at her lack of manners.

Perry again offered her the knife, this time silently, turning the handle in her direction. Margaret took hold of it.

"Which one, do you reckon?" he said with a twinkle in his eye.

Margaret glanced between the two remaining whole muffins and pointed at the light-colored top with poppy seeds. She slid it to the last empty plate and cut into it, splitting it in half to reveal a yellow filling and it gave off a distinctive delicious lemony scent.

"Look at that!" Margaret offered Perry half, which he happily slid onto his plate.

"Lemon curd." He smiled. "Another one of my favorites." Perry sipped on his tea before taking a bit of the lemon-poppy seed muffin.

"You never did finish telling me what happened this morning." Margaret suddenly remembered that he'd started explaining what brought him to Bath but they were side-tracked with Jane Austen and her characters.

"Oh, that." Perry did not seem overly-excited to share the story. "I have a confession to make. As I walked into the hotel I kept noticing things, those details about the furniture and the architecture I was telling you about earlier...what honestly came to mind was how much you would like being here and seeing it for yourself.

"I thought you were back in London and I felt very far away from you. I knew you were leaving tomorrow and here I was stuck in a meeting and wasting the day while you were spending your last day... I couldn't sit there any longer. I had to find you and... I knew I had to see you again." He showed some relief when he got it all out. "I left the meeting."

"You just *left*?" She didn't know him well but she hardly thought he would do something so impulsive.

"Exactly." Perry sounded unapologetic about his actions. "There's one other thing I want to take care of." He pulled his cell phone out of his jacket and without checking his email or any message updates, he powered it off then returned it to its place. "Now I can guarantee we won't be disturbed. Now, where were we?"

"Our last muffin." Was he that serious about blueberry muffins or was it something else?

"Oh, yes. You go ahead." He brought his teacup to his lips. "I'm hoping the last one is what I think it is."

By the looks of it, Margaret would have been shocked if the last, but the not least anticipated muffin was most probably blueberry. And Margaret fully expected this blueberry muffin to also have blueberry compote filling. She cut the muffin in half and it had the expected blueberry filling.

"You knew didn't you?"

Perry smiled. "I knew."

"And it's your favorite."

"It is my favorite," he confessed. "It wasn't too much of a surprise, was it?"

"It didn't have to be. Everything doesn't have to be a surprise." Margaret merely enjoyed her surroundings and her company. Who could ask for more?

They spent nearly another hour enjoying the tea, the food, and the company before Perry said, "Do you think it's time we head back to London?"

Why did he have to say that?

"How long does it take to drive there?"

"Two to three hours, it depends on if we take the scenic route."

"Isn't every route a scenic one in this country?"

"I suppose they are. Would you mind if we stopped for lunch on the way?"

"Didn't we just have tea?" Margaret couldn't imagine having another bite to eat. "We can't just drive from one meal to the next? Can we?"

"It depends on how many times we stop and have a wander during our scenic drive. It could be hours until we return."

"Oh, so what you're saying is this could be an all-day adventure."

"Only if I'm lucky."

AFTER HAVING TEA, Margaret and Perry left *Hall & Woodhouse*. They walked up Gay Street and around The Circus, where they admired crescent-shaped buildings and the giant trees occupying the lawn in the center on their way to the

Royal Crescent where Perry had parked his car. He opened the passenger door of his dark blue Aston-Martin.

Dark blue? Margaret could have sworn it was green. Would she ever get the details right?

She slid into the passenger seat and Perry got behind the steering wheel.

"What's wrong?" Perry stilled after starting the engine. He had removed his tie and jacket and sat next to her only in his dress shirt.

"This feels weird. I'm in the driver's seat but the steering wheel is on the other side."

"Oh, well then, you don't want to watch me drive. It'll be on the opposite side of the road."

She cringed, hoping he wouldn't take it personally. It had to do with riding on the other side of the road. It just felt uncomfortable.

"It's all right. I'm an experienced driver, done this all my life...my driving life," he amended.

"I'll get used to it. It's just— this is new to me." Margaret tried to show that she was not distraught and calmly rested her hands on her lap.

"If you're ready we'll head out."

They had been driving for barely twenty minutes when Perry asked, "Would you care to go to Highgrove?"

"*Highgrove?* The country home of King Charles?" Margaret did not want to misunderstand.

"It's only another 20 minutes or so out of our way." Perry didn't even crack a smile. Margaret had no idea if he was serious. "If he's not in, perhaps we'll find Queen Camilla at home."

"You're joking, right?" Margaret hadn't the slightest idea. "You know King and Queen?"

"Not really." Perry chuckled. "I've met them but I'm sure they have no idea who I am."

"I think we can skip it and just head to London." Margaret scowled. There was nothing worse than a smarty-pants at home or across the pond.

"If you say so." He finally made the wide turn on to the M4 toward London.

It was strange that they rode mostly in silence. Merely being in each other's company seemed enough for them. Perry seemed to enjoy it as much as Margaret. It seemed to Margaret that sharing their company was all they needed.

They passed the exits for Chippenham, Cirencester, Royal Woolton Bassett, and Swindon. It was a nice drive. Looking at the passing landscape...the pastures, some horses but mostly sheep.

"Aren't they cute?" Margaret commented. "The sheep. We don't see that many where I live. We don't have much livestock."

"Let me know if they get any closer. Those *cute sheep* have been known to bring the motorway to a standstill."

The idea of sheep bringing a freeway to a stop seemed impossible to Margaret. They looked so small and fluffy.

"Do you think you're ready to stop for lunch?" Perry asked.

"Is it lunchtime?"

"I'd like to take you to one of my favorite out-of-the-way places."

"You're driving. I'm just a passenger." She would gladly go wherever he chose to drive.

They passed the Newbury, Oxford, Reading exits. Margaret began to recognize the names now they grew closer to London: Maidenhead, Slough, Eton, Heathrow.

The car turned off the freeway, or as Perry called it, the motorway, and onto a road. The farther they drove, the more rural the scenery.

"I must warn you, this place is not much to look at really. It's old, so I thought you might appreciate it as well."

The car came to a stop.

"Here we are," Perry announced. He laid his arm over the back of Margaret's seat and glanced out the passenger side window.

Margaret followed Perry's gaze and found herself staring at a small twin-gabled thatched cottage with diamond-paned windows set in thick stone walls. Outside the establishment read a sign: *The Poached Pheasant*.

Margaret's eyes widened and she drew in a deep breath at the coincidence...or was it? Maybe someone was trying to tell her something.

❧

WHAT HAD SURPRISED Margaret when she stepped inside was how little the interior had changed. After almost two hundred years one would expect a little redecorating—even after a scant hundred years had passed.

The dining room still had low beamed ceilings, dark paneling, and round tables. The tables were set with lace tablecloths, gleaming silverware, and sparkling crystal glasses. Perry looked completely at ease, while Margaret couldn't help staring at everything and everyone while they were being seated.

"I highly recommend any of the pheasant dishes. It's their specialty," he said, looking over his menu.

"Really? I sort of had the feeling the name *Poached Pheasant* had to do with—illegally acquired fowl." She shot him a sideways glance to catch his reaction.

Perry went absolutely wide-eyed. "What on earth would make you think that?"

She shrugged. "I don't know, it just sort of came to me, I guess."

Margaret ordered the Honey-Dipped Pheasant with a side

of summer vegetables, Perry ordered Bedeviled Pheasant accompanied by split peas with saffron.

He lowered the menu and leaned close to ask, "Would you allow me the liberty of ordering one of my favorite desserts for you."

"Sure." Margaret lifted her water glass and took a sip.

"Rice mould for two," he said to the waitress.

Margaret choked. It was the exact thing Desmond had ordered when he bought her here. *Desmond*, her *Pierce*. Now that Perry kept her company, it had been quite a while since she had thought of her Desmond. When she thought of him...it was odd that his image had not immediately popped into her mind.

Now that she thought about it, she could not exactly remember what he looked like. Margaret knew he bore a striking resemblance to Perry. But how the two men were similar and how they differed she could not readily recall.

"Are you all right?"

Margaret pressed the napkin to her mouth. "Sorry, I'm fine."

What was happening to her?

Perry gave a bashful smile. "I know it sounds horrendous, but it's a delight, really. You'll just have to trust me on this."

If she looked worried, it wasn't because she had doubts about what he ordered. It was because of what he ordered. The rice mould. History was repeating itself, and part of the history as she knew it seemed to be fading away.

"If I'm not being too indelicate—" He shifted in his seat. "There is something I'd like to know."

Margaret didn't like the sound of his voice. "And what's that?" She hoped she could answer him honestly. The truth was always best.

"You know the night we met?"

She nodded.

"As I stepped out onto the terrace that night you called me

Desmond. It was right before you fainted. I thought it might be because you thought I was a ghost."

He would have to ask that. "Did I? I don't remember." Everything had happened so fast, she really didn't remember everything that had happened exactly.

"Yes. I'm very curious to know why you said that particular name." He looked expectantly at her, patiently waiting for an answer.

How was she going to explain herself?

"Oh, look—the food is here." And just in time, too. Margaret was grateful for the momentary reprieve. And she knew it would be only momentary—by the look on his face, he intended to have his answer.

The opportunity for Perry to inquire about Desmond further was lost when their meal arrived. Once past their small talk, he would continue his questions.

"At the moment," he began. "Whilst work with Chapman Enterprises is ever ongoing, I have a side-interest in genealogy research of my family."

"Oh?" Margaret sounded not so much interested as guilty. Why on Earth should she feel guilty, he wondered, over his lineage?

"You might think it would be easy but you see, I've discovered that about two hundred years ago there was a shakeup in my family tree. A bit of pruning, no, I think grafting might be a better analogy."

Perry studied the expression on her face. Watching to see if she seemed interested, bored, or thought maybe he was off his rocker with all his talk of family history. But it was important to him and for some unexplained reason had grown increasingly so over the past few months.

"At any rate, something peculiar happened and the family records I've seen haven't been able to provide any answers. I've been doing my best to ferret it out but whoever has altered the past did a fine job of it and I seemed to have come to an impasse."

Her eyes narrowed when she asked, "What do you mean by 'altered the past?'"

Perry didn't know why but the phrase obviously meant something to her. He wasn't certain how much he should reveal. "I don't think my real family name is Chapman."

Margaret stopped chewing and said nothing. She did appear quite interested in what he had to say.

"It was only last week I came across the name 'Desmond' associated with my family. Then I heard you use the very same name: Desmond. At the time, I found it shocking. Now I find it fascinating." Resting his elbows on the table, he leaned forward. "I still can't seem to get the episode out of my mind. I'd be very interested in exactly how you came across that name."

"How?" She swallowed a bite of her honey-dipped pheasant and didn't answer right away. "Well, Katie and I visited a museum at Saffron Hall." The words weren't coming easy. "There was a painting of him, and well, I guess I must have thought I was seeing a ghost."

"Saffron Hall?" Perry set his fork and knife on the edge of his plate and directed his full attention to her. "Where exactly is that located?"

"It's not that far from the Hampstead tube station."

"Really?" He thought about it for a moment. "I know that area quite well. I can't recall a house by that name. I'm fascinated, though. Would you be willing to take me there when we're through with lunch?"

"Sure. I'd be glad to." She didn't mind helping him out, why would she refuse?

"Brilliant." Pleased with her cooperation, Perry's appetite returned. He started to eat again. "I've come across the name

Desmond several times in personal letters but I need some definitive proof that something out of the ordinary went on. Official written documentation from that era is not all that easy to come by, you know. Did you happen to see anything like that there?"

Margaret knew the tontine papers had been destroyed, maybe there was something else there that might be of some help to him. "Like marriage licenses, birth or death certificates, maybe?"

"That's exactly what I mean. If you had some insight that would be grand."

Moments later, the rice mould arrived with two small dishes. Perry waved the waitress away. He removed the lid of the casserole dish and with a dramatic flair, spooned out the dessert himself.

This time Margaret knew it was a dish made from rice and not something that grew on top of it.

THE DRIVE to Hampstead Station in London North took less than an hour from *The Poached Pheasant*. Having grown up there, Perry knew exactly how to get to Hampstead and on Margaret's behalf took the scenic route.

They drove Prince Albert's Road between the expansive Regent's Park and the grassy knolls of Primrose Hill. As they paralleled Regent's Canal, a tour boat slipped down the water toward Little Venice. Perry turned north on Haverstock Hill toward Hampstead.

The car came to a stop on Heath Street just outside the station for Margaret to get her bearings.

"It's strange driving around in a car...on the wrong side of the road and all." Pointing up the street, she directed him. "Go around this block and turn right. Then left at the dead end."

The car pulled out into traffic, and Perry slowed and turned right on Back Lane, then left on Flask Walk.

"There should be a sign somewhere around here." Glancing from one specialty shop to another as they drove by, Margaret searched the quaint street for a sign, guiding the way. "I think it's a left down here."

Perry turned down New End Square.

"Here." Margaret pointed at the flanking stone pillared entrance on the right. It was just as she remembered it. "Turn in here. This is it."

"Are you sure?" Pierce stopped the car.

"Of course I'm sure." Margaret sat back in her seat satisfied that she had indeed led him to the correct destination. "I was here just yesterday." She had as much confidence as he had doubt. "It's a big beautiful place. It's got huge Corinthian columns and a grand staircase in the foyer."

Perry shifted into first gear and inched the car forward. "Well, if you're sure." He shrugged and decided to humor her. "We'd better go see."

"It has this really long gallery. It's huge," she continued her description.

Perry imagined she was trying her best to prove to him that she wasn't making any of this up.

"And on the other end of the gallery is the dining room. Then there's the gold and white grand saloon next door."

"Yes, I know," Perry finally said when he slowed the car and made a wide turn, coming to a stop in front of the house.

"You know?" Margaret shot him a puzzled look. "I thought you said you'd never heard of Saffron Hall."

"I haven't." He pulled the car out of gear, set the parking

brake, and faced her. "I know because what you're describing is Alison House."

CHAPTER 19

THE BLUE ASTON-MARTIN stopped in front of the immaculately manicured grand country house. There was no visitors' parking lot, no public signs, no indication that anyone was here.

Alison House? How could this be Alison House?

They must have been sitting in front of the mansion for a good five minutes before Perry got out of the car.

The front door of the house opened. A tall, dignified dark-haired man dressed in a well-tailored suit, came down the steps and approached them.

"Good afternoon, Lord Alison," the man said. "The Viscountess is not at home presently."

"That's all right, Elliot. I'm not here to see my mother. We're just here to have a look at the house and gardens."

His mother lived here? How could that be? This was supposed to be Saffron Hall, not Alison House.

"Very well, sir." The man bowed respectfully and headed inside.

Perry's full attention was on Margaret. She stared at the house and still hadn't said a word. What could she say?

He led her down the side path of the house that ambled through the blooming rose garden. The path forked, the gazebo was on the right, off to the left was the house.

"Would you care to go inside?" Perry gestured to the left.

"No." Tears filled Margaret's eyes. She was losing her mind. Yesterday, this house was Saffron Hall. The *yesterday* before she went back to 1813. She was sure. But now, today... Margaret wasn't so sure.

Perry took hold of her trembling hand and gave it a slight squeeze. The gesture told her everything was all right.

"Margaret, look at me." He waited to speak until she looked from the house to him. "Every single description of every room you gave is true. You couldn't have described the interior any more accurately."

Margaret squeezed her eyes close, tears rolled down her cheek. "I don't know what to say."

"You don't know what to say?" Perry stepped into the gazebo. "You've never been here before. How could it be you know all those details?"

"I don't know." Margaret held her breath, trying her best not to break down in front of him. "Maybe it was all a dream?"

"I'm glad I'm not the only one doubting my sanity." He took her hands in his and held them tight. "I can't tell you how often I've doubted mine over the last few days."

"What?" Was he just trying to make her feel better? He couldn't possibly know what she was going through. He could never, ever dream of what had happened to her. Nor would he believe it.

"Nothing's been quite the same since I met you," he confessed, moving closer to her. "There are things I've done, known, felt... I can't... I don't understand any of them and I'm equally at a loss to explain why."

Margaret sniffed and blinked away her remaining tears.

"Don't feel bad, please don't." He gazed into her eyes.

She stared back, sensing a soft, familiar tug of her heart. But this time it was much stronger. The feeling told her he was not Perry but her Pierce.

How she longed to have him close and hold her in his arms. Perry brushed the pad of his thumb against her lower lip. She didn't think she could bear another touch—yet, ached for his kiss. Something to comfort her.

"It's you, isn't it?" He made a little gasp, taking in a breath of air and whispered, "You're quite a lady, Margaret."

The words sent a chill down her spine.

"I don't know what it is about you but I find I can't..." Perry never did finish his sentence.

He had leaned forward until their lips finally met. Margaret leaned into the kiss and Perry slipped his arms around her. It felt as it always had...right, heavenly, perfect.

He lifted her mouth from hers. "Please forgive me. I should not have done that. Completely uncalled for—I just wanted to comfort you. I'm sorry, I got carried away."

Margaret tried to act as if it didn't matter, but of course, it had. "It's all right, we just...got caught up in the moment, that's all."

"Yes, of course, the moment." Perry cleared his throat and turned away from her, directing his attention to the garden.

Was he her Pierce? She was nearly convinced of it, but Margaret wasn't completely sure.

"You're leaving tomorrow I understand." He sounded distant.

Did he want to be rid of her? "Our flight is at ten and we have to be at Heathrow early, two hours before take-off for an international flight." How could he shrug off everything that had just happened? Didn't he feel it too?

Turning toward her, Perry winced. "That does get one up and about a bit on the early side now, doesn't it?"

"That doesn't even give me a few morning hours for any last minute side trips." And right now Margaret wanted to find out more about Perry. If only she could spend more time with him. Yes, they had just spent nearly the whole day together but she wanted just a little more time.

"Well, in that case, I think you might want to see my etchings before you leave." He winked at her and one side of his mouth lifted in a smile.

"Your etchings?" she couldn't believe he really said that.

"I don't have any etchings as Katie suggested I show you." He chuckled and smiled. "I think you would find the old place interesting—it dates back to the 1700s."

"You mean, you don't live here?"

"No, not anymore. For some reason, I much prefer the Dower House. A month ago I convinced my mother to let me move into the Dower house while she remained here, in the main house." He shrugged. "That in itself sounds a bit odd, now, doesn't it? I really can't explain it myself...except that it's just the way I feel about the place. I just find the townhouse more comfortable."

It didn't sound that bizarre to her. "I'm looking forward to seeing where you live." Margaret smiled. "Even if you don't have etchings."

THE DRIVE from Alison House to the Dower House wouldn't take long. Perry glanced at Margaret, sitting in the passenger seat. After sharing a kiss, there should have been some sort of awkwardness between them, but there wasn't.

He may have apologized for kissing her, but he hadn't meant

it. Although they had only met recently, that small kiss felt...it meant so much. Everything inside of him said they were not strangers. And it was such an odd feeling.

The urge to take her in his arms was overwhelming—obviously because he had done so. And like so many other uncharacteristic impulses he had reacted to recently, he had no idea from where it had all come.

He was convinced that Margaret truly believed Alison House was Saffron Hall. When faced with the reality, she seemed truly shaken. The light in her eyes, gone. Parry wanted to lend her some comfort...had wanted to see her smile. But he never meant to kiss her. He still didn't know why he had.

❦

THE CAR ROUNDED a corner and pulled out onto Curzon Street. Curzon Street? Desmond's residence was on Curzon Street. Used to be on Curzon Street, Margaret quickly corrected.

What were the odds?

She looked around at the passing scenery. The neighborhood was not one she recognized, but then again almost two hundred years had passed since she had seen it last. The same large tree stood on the corner, now even larger with the passage of time.

The car stopped behind a building. An old iron fence surrounded the rear garden which held a profusion of colorful flowering bushes. Perry hopped out of the car and came around to her side, opening her door.

"It's really nothing special to look at. I imagine the pride of ownership I have is just some sentimental nonsense."

Sentimental nonsense? Margaret glanced from the back of the house to Perry. Had he really said *sentimental nonsense?*

She followed him to the back door and he urged her to enter first. Not five seconds later, rushing toward them, a tall man in—

He looked exactly like—

There was no mistaking, he was—

"Sorry, Maypink." Perry waved to the butler. "Came in from the rear."

"So I see, my lord."

Margaret skirted around the servant. Oh boy, did he look like the Maypink she remembered. Exactly like Maypink. She could not help but stare.

Desmond's Maypink—and she thought Perry's resemblance to Desmond was spooky.

"Would you care for anything to drink?" Perry asked Margaret. "Tea, coffee, lemonade?"

"I don't think so. We just ate."

He gestured in agreement. "I think that will be all for now, Maypink."

"Yes, my lord." The butler headed back in the direction he had come.

Margaret followed Perry down the hall. Talk about hints—somebody really was trying to get through to her and she was reading the message loud and clear.

"The Maypinks have been in my family's service for generations. Makes a swell posset—secret family recipe and all that."

Margaret smiled—*I know.*

Margaret peeked into every room they passed. The interior of the house had a definite feminine overtone. Of course, it had been the Dower House. There was a small drawing room flanked by the dining room. Continuing down the hall, she followed Perry past the large front parlor and caught a glimpse of a full-length painting.

"I see your portrait hangs in there," she commented, indicating the room they had just passed.

Perry stopped and motioned for her to backtrack, and led the way into the Victorian decorated parlor.

Pink and gold colors taken from the large floral print wallpaper were the predominant colors in the room. The curtains were lace, matching the decorative netting draped over the back and arms of each chair and sofa.

"That isn't me," he said, referring to what Margaret could now identify as a life-sized portrait.

If it wasn't Perry, then it must have been...Desmond. Margaret gazed into the portrait's face. Although familiar yet now somewhat unfamiliar because the man in the painting looked a great deal like Perry, she knew the subject to be Pierce Desmond just a bit older than she remembered.

She could not help but stare.

"Don't know who he is. I found the portrait in the attic. Must be a relative of some sort. My mum says he looks quite a bit like me. Although I can't see any resemblance myself."

He had to be kidding. Margaret looked from the portrait to Perry and back again. Looking at them side by side, the similarities were striking—his mouth, his hair, right down to the look in his eyes.

"As you can see, the nameplate has been removed and the painting isn't signed. Not only that, there aren't any identifying markings on the frame or the back. I've tried to research him through the painter, but all records of who this man was are gone. Looks like it's been deliberately done to hide his identity."

She knew exactly who he was, but should she tell Perry? She was sure but once she did, there would be no taking it back, and plenty of questions she would have a hard time answering.

"Come on—" he took her by the hand "—I'd like you to see my favorite room."

If Perry were really Desmond, Margaret knew his favorite room would be the library.

They stepped across the hallway to the next room.

"Just had it redone. What do you think?"

Margaret stood and stared. It was the library.

The small leather sofa centered between the two matching leather wing-backed chairs flanked the hearth. The inlaid Mahogany desk sat across the room, the walls were lined with books and wood paneling.

Redone? It looked as if it hadn't changed at all in two hundred years that had passed. Margaret couldn't help but stare at him from across the room. He busied himself by adjusting the items on his desk.

It was him, really him.

Every doubt she harbored had been erased. There was no question that this Perry was her Pierce. Once she admitted it to herself, it really hadn't shocked her. She knew—had known since she laid eyes on him. He was her Pierce.

He had promised her he'd come back and he did. Now they could be together just like he'd said, except... Perry didn't remember. Didn't remember...*them*.

Was there anything she could do about that? Hit him on the head with a frying pan? No, that was for amnesia. Perry didn't have amnesia, it was the opposite, he had lost life syndrome.

He might have suspected something going on between them. From what Margaret could tell, he only had moments of recollection. Like this room, for example, duplicated down to the last...

"Worn spot, you know," he pointed out.

Margaret looked at Perry and blinked. "What? I'm sorry I didn't hear what you said."

"On the carpet—there's a worn spot. It's an old Aubusson carpet I found rolled up in the attic. I'm quite partial to it, but I'm afraid there's a spot here where it's a bit thin."

Margaret looked down, then stepped aside. The worn patch

was in the exact spot where she was standing. Where she had stood. And where she had paced before Gerald's duel almost two hundred years before. She hadn't worn it out, although at the time Desmond had suggested she might. She wondered how...

"Let me show you a little secret. It's one of the small endearing things about this house." Perry pressed on the center of a medallion on the fireplace. "Look, it's a secret compartment." He reached in and retrieved several small items. "I can't imagine what these are doing here." He held out an almost hairless rabbit's foot, and a small, red box.

Chance's rabbit's foot and Sir Julian's snuff box.

"This small enamel snuff box dates back to the early 1800s, and this poor rabbit's foot has seen better days."

Desmond had told her he kept valuable items in here, but there was another.

But the small hidden box was only a ruse. There was a larger place she recalled, it was behind one of the panels. And to release the catch, the small box near the fireplace had to be removed first.

If Perry was looking for something important, papers on his family perhaps, that would be the place to look. She had to act now, Margaret had to push on the secret panel door before Perry slipped the small box back into place.

"Is that the only secret panel in here?" Maybe seeing the other secret compartment would jar his memory.

"I suppose it's possible, but I don't know of any others." He turned toward the fireplace, holding the box in front of him ready to return it.

"There are so many panels...maybe another one is hidden in here." Margaret pushed against one of the wood wall panels.

He paused. "I say there, Margaret, what are you on about?"

Then she tried another. "Perhaps it's this one." The third

panel she pressed moved with a loud, mechanical click, and the door swung open.

"What's that you've found there?" He was at her side in an instant. Perry eased her out of the way and had a look for himself. Another secret compartment. "I say, Margaret, you've found another one!"

"I have, haven't I?" She feigned surprise and watched for a reaction.

"Let's have a look inside, shall we?" Perry eased the door open.

The open panel revealed two shelves. There was hardly any dust on anything inside—the seal must have been close to airtight. It looked as if someone had been in here just yesterday.

On the top shelf sat a small, thin, brown box. It rested upon a piece of folded linen. Perry set the box aside and laid the material in his hand. It was a handkerchief, mostly made of lace with a faded blue embroidered M that faced up.

"No doubt this belonged to a lady-love." His eyes were positively glowing. "I wonder who she was?"

Perry set the handkerchief aside, pulled out the small brown box and brought it into the light. On closer examination, the box turned out to be tarnished silver. It looked like a cigarette holder.

He pressed the latch and the lid popped open. Inside lay a gold-edged, faded blue ribbon and a gold-covered button. Both sat on a small piece of folded parchment.

"I wonder who this belonged to? They must have been important to be locked up in here."

Desmond...he had kept them all this time. Margaret closed her eyes when she felt a lump form in her throat and she drew in a breath to keep her composure.

"My you are a sensitive one, aren't you?" Perry pulled his handkerchief from his pocket and held it out to her.

"Thank you." She braved a smile. "I'm sorry that I'm acting silly."

"You're not being silly at all. I find these sentimental snippets from the past quite touching."

Perry lifted the small parchment, taking care that the ribbon and the button did not fall. When he tried to pull it open, the paper protested, by cracking and threatening to break in half.

"Look, what's written on this—" His voice rose with excitement. "This is addressed to *Desmond*." Perry turned, angling the paper, trying for better lighting and read the faded print.

Desmond, wait for me in your room tonight.
Margaret

"That name again, your name." Perry glanced at Margaret and asked her in all seriousness, "You didn't happen to pen this *billet-doux*, did you?" then chuckled at the improbability. "It's such a strange coincidence."

"It is, isn't it?" She chuckled but she didn't find it very funny —especially since it was true. She had written it—a very long time ago.

"To have saved all these, he must have loved her very much."

Yes. And she hoped he still did.

Perry set the parchment and cigarette box next to the embroidered handkerchief before returning to the concealed compartment to search further. Next, he removed a thick portfolio from the lower shelf. "This looks impressive." He laid it on his desk and pulled the string on the bow, releasing the large envelope from its bond.

The mass of tri-folded papers held its position, unwilling to give up its shape. He tried to pull it open to read the top page and was careful not to force it.

"I believe these are some type of legal documents." Intent on finding the subject, Perry scanned the first page. "Can't make any sense of it really."

Margaret moved to his side to read over his shoulder.

He pulled the first page free, then the second. "Look here" —he pointed to the bottom of the third page— "It names—Pierce Desmond." Perry quickly replaced the first two pages and pulled the last one to the top.

The first name Margaret noticed was that of Joseph Bevans. Probably a relative of Desmond's solicitor Samuel Bevans. The next was the signature of James Chapman, third Viscount Alison.

"This is it. I think this is really it." He set the papers on the desk before wrapping his arms around her.

"Perry, that's wonderful." She managed, while in his arms .

He set her down and once again reached for the papers. "Of course, if they are referring to some sort of adoption, there may be questions about the legality of my inheritance. It's no wonder I couldn't find anything. Everything all locked up. It's all supposed to be kept hush-hush."

"You mean you might lose your title?" Wasn't that bad news?

The threat didn't seem to dampen his excitement in the least. "I'll need to consult with my solicitors. They'll know more after they've had a chance to go over it."

"Of course," she said with concern.

"But I think this is the link I've been looking for. You've done it." He gave her a squeeze. "I don't know what I would have done without you."

Margaret was looking for something more than excitement on his part. She wondered if he remembered anything. Had it jarred his memory?

"Let's, do, go celebrate!" he cheered. "First we'll stop off at the House and tell mother—I've got to show her these in person." He was very excited and spoke fast. "She's always humored me when it came to this, you know. Never said a word to discourage me, but—won't she be surprised when we show her?"

"Yes, I suppose she would be," Margaret replied, disappointed that nothing more came of his discovery.

"Then we'll drop these off at the solicitor's office on the way to... to... Where shall we go?" He stopped for a moment and thought. "Beef fillet at *Marcus Waring*? Lobster or lapin at *Le Gavroche*? Cod or sea bream at *Chiltern Firehouse*? Yes—I'll order champagne for us and we'll have a few starters and a fantastic pudding! I—"

She held up her hand. "Wait—I can't."

Perry stopped. "What's that you say? You can't? Why ever not?"

"There's a final group dinner tonight. I really should be there."

He looked disappointed...beyond disappointed. He looked as if she had abandoned him. "Well then...without you... I suppose, there won't be much to celebrate."

CHAPTER 20

Dinner for the Regency tour group was held at the *British Chop House*, a nearby restaurant. Seated in a private area in the back, the thirty-five members occupied eight large, round tables.

"Well? How'd it go today?" Katie ignored the others at her table and held her wine glass, focusing completely on Margaret.

"How'd what go?" Margaret pushed her glazed baby carrots from her chicken on one side of the plate to the rice pilaf on the other.

"Who do you think? Viscount Alison... You know, Perry. Geez, Margaret, out with it."

Everything had gone wrong. Margaret didn't want to dwell on her loss. "There's nothing to tell, really."

"Just the fact that you're not willing to talk about it tells me there's a story. Come on—come on, I want to hear."

Margaret shot her a hard glare. "Instead of becoming a psychologist you should consider becoming a tabloid reporter."

"Well, I am minoring in Journalism," Katie said, seeming to give it some thought. She turned back to Margaret. "Now don't try to change the subject."

"We aren't on any subject," Margaret insisted.

"Yes, we are. You were about to tell me all about your day with Perry."

Ignoring the question, Margaret pointed at Katie's plate with the tip of her knife. "Your Yorkshire pudding is getting cold."

"It's only food." Katie leaned toward Margaret and whispered, "I read in the *Evening Standard* that Viscount Alison was somewhat of a recluse and that recently he's been seen about town in the company of an unidentified woman. It was in today's paper. They're talking about you, aren't they, Margaret?"

Why did she fight it?

Tomorrow they'd be closed up together on an airplane across the Atlantic. Katie was going to get it out of Margaret one way or another. She might as well answer all of Katie's questions now and get it over with.

Margaret set her fork and knife down and gave Katie her complete attention. "Okay, what do you want to know?"

Her eyes widened. Katie must have thought she hit the jackpot. "I want to know everything. Don't leave one thing out. Start at the part when you left the Royal Crescent this morning."

This was going to be like living the day all over from excruciating minute by excruciating minute. Except Margaret was going to omit certain details when she relayed the story to Katie.

Margaret took a breath and told the story starting from the drive to *The Poached Pheasant* and ending at the time he saw her back to Ashworth House, at the exact stroke of five in the afternoon.

She left out the Saffron Hall/Alison House episode. Since it seems to have never existed, she was pretty sure Katie wouldn't remember going there the day before, the visit was probably erased from her memory as well.

Katie munched at the baby carrot on her fork. "It's too bad you had to miss out on champagne and lobster."

"It doesn't matter. I'm not all that hungry anyway." Margaret's current dinner plate was still full, while Katie had cleaned hers.

"Can I have your baby carrots?"

Margaret slid her plate over to Katie. "Here, knock yourself out."

"Thanks. Now tell me—"

The room's lights dimmed, interrupting Margaret's tale. A spotlight illuminated the microphone at a podium on one side of the room. Linda Cameron, their English guide who had been with them over the last three weeks, stepped up to the microphone.

"Is this working?" She said too close to the mike, sending her voice booming over the speakers in the room. She moved a respectful distance away. "Sorry, is this better? Yes? Good evening fellow travelers. I want to tell you how much I've enjoyed your company over the last two weeks.

"There's something special about the Regency era. I know you all realize that, but as a tour guide, it has a special meaning. It narrows the area of study to a scant ten to twenty years—for your strict Regency buffs, that would only be nine.

"It makes it quite nice, really, to enjoy only a thin slice of British historic sights. I just wanted to thank you for allowing me to show you the cities of Bath, Brighton, and London. I hope you will have a chance to return someday." Finishing her speech, Linda moved away from the podium.

Jean Robertson, the tour coordinator, stepped up to the microphone. "Good evening, I hope you're enjoying your last night in London. I just want to remind you before we go on much further, we have a flight to catch tomorrow. So watch the time, eh, folks?"

The audience erupted in bursts and chortles of laughter.

"Will you be seeing *him* tonight after dinner?" Katie asked.

"No, I'm not planning to." Would it matter? He didn't remember her. "Besides, I need to start packing."

"What about the two of you?"

"There is no two of us." Just thinking about it made Margaret want to cry. "He's got a life here. And I have things to get back to—you know, finishing college and the rest of my life." And the rest of her life would be without him.

It might have been hard for Katie to accept, but Margaret had to adjust to the fact she was really going back home. A life without Perry. How could she face going back to the same old routine of friends and school? How could she face attending another Regency Society meeting?

"I was really hoping for a fairy tale ending here." Katie nearly looked as bad as Margaret felt. "I just thought that maybe you and he would—I don't know. Somehow, maybe you were in love in a past life and found one another again."

"Katie..." Margaret's mouth dropped open in disbelief. "You've got to be putting me on." Katie was a well-educated Psychology student, how could she be talking about fairy tale stuff?

But as much as Margaret made fun of Katie's idea, she never would have admitted that she had wished for the very thing herself. Except it was her present life and Perry's past. Without a doubt, Margaret now knew Perry and Desmond were one and the same. Her thoughts and feelings for them were becoming inseparable. The feelings she had felt for Pierce were merging with her feelings for Perry. He was *figuratively* stepping into Pierce's Hessian boots.

Katie pushed her wine glass away, and she'd lost her smile. "It's really sad to think you're never going to see him again."

"Never is a long time. I do have his card." It didn't make Margaret feel any better but it might cheer Katie up.

"His business card?" Katie's smile returned. "Why don't you give him a call?"

"I can't do that." It was too late. One phone call was certainly not going to make a difference.

"Yes, you can. Just tell him you called to say good-bye. Maybe he'll want to see you one last time."

"Katie, we've already said our good-byes." Why would she ever want to play that scene out again? It was hard enough the first time.

Jean stepped up to the microphone and continued. "We're also here this evening to recognize the Regency achievements of our members."

There was mumbling from the audience—some confusion about what was about to happen.

"Every year we take notice of some of our guests' certain qualities and equate them to behaviors of the Regency period. This first award is the *Beau Brummell Award*, given to the man most conscious of his attire." Jean held up the quizzing glass statuette. "Linda…"

Linda stepped forward. "Although there are no real dandies in this day and age, there are still a few men who tend to be a clothes horse. One young man stands out in my mind.

"Besides his excellent Regency costume, which was authentic to the smallest detail, this young man managed to find a fashionable men's clothing store in each of the cities we visited."

A bout of chortles, chuckles, and finger-pointing of likely candidates followed.

"I don't know if any of you noticed, he never wore the same thing twice." Jean pointed out into the audience. "The award goes to Jonathan Montgomery."

The Sir Julian Montgomery look-alike.

Amid the applause, Jonathan went up to claim his award.

It was true. Always immaculately dressed and, come to think of it, he did wear a distinctly different shirt every day.

"He has those two tiny carry-ons. Where does he put it all?" Margaret wondered aloud.

"I bet he ships all his dirty laundry home," Katie suggested.

Jean stepped forward again with another statuette in hand. "This next award is called the *Beau Nash*" —this statuette was adorned with a gentleman's hat and walking stick— "awarded to the gentleman who has made the effort to go out of his way to see to the comfort and general welfare of others."

Linda took Jean's place. "This young man made sure everyone had plans for the day whether on a walking tour, visiting a museum or just shopping. I think I'd better watch out, he could be after my job. Anyway—I'm getting off track here. This award goes to Paul Davies."

The Sir Cornelius Poole look-alike.

"Hey!" Katie waved at Paul who stood to accept his award. "Paul won—who would have thought? He was awfully nice to everyone, don't you think?"

"Always," Margaret replied. *And especially nice to you.* She thought if a romance were to develop during this trip, a more likely one would have been between Katie and Paul.

Jean stepped forward to announce the next award. "This award is basically the counterpart to the *Beau Nash*—it's called the Patroness of Almack's, *Lady Sally Jersey Award*. Given to the lady who so eloquently stuck her nose into everyone's business and with her charming ways, dug up every rumor that threatened to plague us."

Linda stepped forward, interrupting. "Of course we mean this in the truest sense of fun."

No one was surprised when Katie's name was called—except Katie.

Katie returned to the table with her award topped with a closed fan. "Can you imagine? They're accusing me of sticking my nose in everyone's business?"

Margaret shrugged and hid her smile. "I don't know where they could have got that from."

"Just because I feel everyone should—"

Katie was shushed from the next table before she could finish defending herself. Not that anything she would have said could have changed any one's opinion of her.

"With their love of antiques," Jean began. "Karen and Thomas Bean clearly qualified for the *Prince of Wales Award*. This signifies the person, in this case, persons, who dug the deepest into their pockets during our trip."

Linda presented the statue bearing the traditional three plumes emblem for the Prince of Wales. "They'll need to take out a second mortgage to pay for the souvenirs they shipped home."

"Now to our final award for the evening."

"It's a very prestigious one," Linda prompted.

"Yes, it is," Jean replied. "This is what we call the *Explorer of the Realm*. It's given to the person who did the utmost to seek the sights, smells, and sounds of the Regency period whose only boundary from the past was the barrier of time."

Linda continued. "I remember this young lady who in Bath marched from the Pump Room to the Assembly Room and from one end of St James Parade to the other.

"In Brighton, she visited the subscription rooms and the Pavilion. Even those areas off-limits to most tourists, I heard she managed to sneak by and conduct a solo expedition."

Jean leaned forward and spoke into the microphone, "This award goes to Peg...Margaret Swanson."

Explorer of the Realm stopped only by the barrier of time...
If they only knew. Time hadn't been a barrier for Margaret.

❦

RETURNING to Ashworth House after dinner, Margaret spent
the next several hours packing. She wrapped her statuette, an
emblem of a rolled-up map and clock, in a shirt for protection
and tucked it away before zipping up her suitcase and set it by
the foot of her bed. Everything else was ready to go.

Everything except her.

He really was nice, kind, considerate, and understanding.
He never made her feel bad or called her crazy. Perry was everything she'd thought he would be...he wasn't Desmond and
Desmond...when she tried to recall his image, it wasn't a man
dress in a high-point collar and a carefully crafted cravat she
saw, it was a man in a dress shirt and with a Windsor knot.

It was Perry...and she loved him.

Did he ever feel the connection between them? There were
times Margaret thought she had seen a hint of it in his eyes.
While spooning out the rice mould at *The Poached Pheasant*,
examining the blue ribbon and gold button, and the moment
before he kissed her in the gazebo. He must have, at least a little.
As time went on, would he remember more?

Tomorrow morning, Margaret was going home, home to
America. Her eyes filled with tears, and she cried, knowing that
this was their last chance to get it right.

She was really leaving...leaving London...leaving England...
leaving him....

This time it would be forever.

CHAPTER 21

PERRY CHAPMAN PACED on the worn spot of his library carpet. He couldn't sleep. His mind was a torrent of muddled words and tortured thoughts, replaying the final five minutes he had spent with Margaret.

"Let me at least see you in," he'd said and leapt out of his side of the car to open the passenger door for her. "I don't want to be that unfeeling cad you met on the walk."

Once they had stepped inside the lobby and it was time to say good-bye, he wasn't quite sure what was appropriate. Gad, it had been awkward. Worse than a first date.

Shaking her hand seemed inadequate, and kissing her would have been out of line. Although, he could secretly admit to himself that he would have loved to kiss her again.

Their kiss this afternoon had taken him by surprise. He still didn't know why he had done it. The fact that he would attempt the intimacy with a near-stranger had shocked him.

Something inside him insisted Margaret was not a stranger. But how could that be? They had only met a—that much he knew. It was a question he couldn't puzzle out.

There was something about her...something about the two

of them...if only he knew, could remember exactly what it was. Whatever it was felt right as if they belonged together. He was equally as sure.

The more he thought about it, the more he was certain he should have pulled her into his arms there and then.

Had he done that? No.

And what did he do? Perry slapped his forehead and fell back into the leather sofa, groaning. *Numpty.*

He shook her hand and produced his card. Why on earth did he hand her his card?

What did he expect her to do with it? Write him a Thank You note? Then he could write her back—thanking her for her *Thank You.* He sat up and raked his hands through his hair.

The chances were good she might never come back to the UK. The chances were excellent he might not see her again. Ever.

The idea of never seeing her again bothered him. It more than bothered him, it frightened him. It suddenly occurred to Perry that it wouldn't be long before he would pay her a visit. He would find her again.

He would travel to the States to see her and tell her he was there for—what? How would he explain his presence? He came because he missed her? Someone he had only known for a few days?

What would he do? Follow her around the college campus? Carry her books home for her? No, that wouldn't work out at all.

And nothing would be resolved by him standing here and torturing himself about what he would do after she left—and what he could do to see her again.

Not even Maypink's posset had helped calm his nerves. He had refused his supper, yelled at his PA and his secretary, and isolated himself in his library. That was at six last night.

He glanced at the mantel clock—it was almost half seven in

the morning. Perry sat in his chair feeling irritable and grumpy, doing nothing but count the minutes and curse each passing half-hour. Margaret would leave for the airport soon and in another two hours—gone. And here he sat.

Maypink wasn't surprised to find Perry, who never came downstairs until eight. "I was told by one of the housemaids that your lordship was already up and about." Maypink had brought a coffee tray and filled a cup.

Perry remembered that twenty minutes earlier he had given one of the servants the fright of her life when she came into light the hearth.

"I haven't been to bed yet." Perry stood and took the coffee.

If the butler was going to pry, he might as well have the facts, Perry thought irritably.

"I do not wish to involve myself in personal matters, your lordship, but you do not seem in the best of spirits this morning."

"I'm not, Maypink." Perry rubbed the bridge of his nose and then his tired eyes. "Nowhere near, I'm afraid."

"Does this have to do with the young lady you had lunch with yesterday?" The butler inquired politely while attending to his duties.

"Yes, the *American* tourist." Perry gave it the same inflection of disdain that the butler did to everything he considered unacceptable.

"I am not your father. However, after serving under the previous viscount for many years I can impart some advice he provided quite often that would seem to have a direct bearing on your present situation."

"And what would that be?" Would it help? Perry was willing to listen to anything.

"When in doubt, one must follow one's destiny."

"Did my father really say that?" Perry looked at Maypink over the rim of his cup.

"He did, sir. On more than one occasion."

"Does this have anything to do with that fairy tale business?" Perry doubted his father knew anything about that.

"I cannot say, sir."

It did sound like something his father would have said. Something along the lines of advice but nebulous enough to have allowed for the decision maker's preference. He knew exactly what it boiled down to...do what you think is right.

Or do in your heart what you think is right.

Would his father have approved? Probably not, but he would have supported Perry's right to make a decision and encouraged him to do what he thought best.

And what did Perry think was best?

He sat, thinking for a moment. He had been torturing himself over Margaret for the last twelve hours. He would never hear her, see her, or touch her again...and that's not what he wanted.

What he wanted was a second chance.

He launched out of the chair to his feet. "I'm off to Heathrow."

Maypink cleared his throat. "My lord, if I may draw attention to your...your appearance. It is not exactly suitable for—"

Perry looked at his previous day's wrinkled attire he still wore. He fingered the open collar of his shirt and rubbed his unshaven, stubbled face. "Don't worry, I'm certain she'll fancy me just as I am."

"As you say, my lord."

Perry jogged toward the back door.

"Sir?" Maypink held up Perry's passport. "You may have need of this."

Perry jogged back to retrieve it. "Good idea. I might, now that I think of it."

"Also, I would like to inform you, my lord," Maypink added.

"There is a high probability that if your lordship chooses to be seen in public in such a state, your valet may resign."

"It's a chance I'll have to take." Losing a valet wouldn't be the end of the world. Losing the woman he loved would.

⁂

PERRY SPED down the M4 toward Heathrow. While driving to the airport, he had called Mrs Taggart at Ashworth House for Margaret's flight information.

Mrs Taggart knew. Of course, she knew. She knew the comings and goings of all the guests in that house.

Perry then called the air carrier and purchased one of the few remaining tickets. If he couldn't catch the plane in time, he'd take whatever flight left next.

Pulling up to the curb of Terminal 3, he dashed out of his car. He fully expected to find his car clamped and impounded when he returned, but he would gladly pay the exorbitant price of his illegal parking spot if he could make it to the departure gate on time.

Jogging through the Departure terminal, Perry headed for the American Airlines ticket counter. He patted his coat pockets. He must have left his mobile on the passenger car seat. Well, it didn't matter now. Reaching the American Airlines area, he ran up to the *First Class* counter.

"Good morning," Perry huffed out of breath. "I'm Pierce Chapman, I called about a half-hour ago and purchased a ticket for Flight 6118, nonstop to San Francisco" —he recited from memory— "and I've requested that you already book me a seat— anywhere."

"Yes sir, I need to see your passport." the ticket agent responded.

He pulled out his passport, flipped it open, and handed it to her.

"Viscount Alison?"

"Yes, that's right." He knew her reaction well, one of why-didn't-you-tell-me-you-were-titled.

"That flight is boarding now—at Gate 23." She handed his passport back to him.

"Yes, thank you."

"Do you have any luggage to check?"

"No." But he did wish she'd hurry.

"Just let me print your boarding pass."

His fingers drummed on the counter.

The ticket agent finished and slid his boarding pass over the counter to him. "You'd best get a move on, your flight is boarding now. I'll call ahead to Security and tell them to expect you. Have a pleasant flight, sir."

"Thank you." Perry took his travel papers and rushed to the Security area. He traveled up the escalator and jogged down to the corner of the building where the queue for the turnstiles lay.

Once through the turnstiles, Perry stood at the end of a queue waiting to move through Security and onto the waiting area for departure information.

How was he to get through this and find Margaret before the doors closed on the plane?

"Lord Alison," a uniformed security officer called from the side. "If you will come this way, please, sir."

Perry made his way forward, wriggling his way past many, many others. "Excuse me, please... I'm sorry... I beg your pardon..." His expedited journey to the front of the line did not exclude his need to pass the Security check.

He removed his jacket containing his Passport, boarding pass, cardholder, and wallet, folded it and laid it in one of the gray bins. Everything from his trouser pockets came out next—money clip, loose change, and keys.

After stepping through the metal scanner, Perry left the security check area and kept going.

"Sir...sir, you've forgotten your jacket! Your personal items. Sir!" the security guard shouted after him.

Waving them off, Perry kept running. "I'll be back for them later. Later!" he yelled back. He ran past the Duty Free stores selling perfume, alcohol, tea, and chocolates toward the enormous status board in the middle of the largest waiting areas.

He read the top for the flights that listed the green BOARDING status.

08:25 American Airlines - San Francisco
Flight: 6118 - Gate 23

If things went the way they always did, Gate 23 would be at the very end of the terminal. Perry turned toward the long wide corridor where all the departure gates lay. He went off to the right and continued down the corridor. He ran past Gate 16 and 17, 18 and 19, then on to the 20s, finally making it to 23.

"We are inviting our Economy passengers to board," an airline employee announced over the loudspeaker. "At this time we are asking for rows fifteen to nineteen to come forward."

MARGARET AND KATIE wheeled their carry-ons into line, had their boarding passes in hand, and stepped toward the jetway.

"I can't believe you're leaving England and him." Katie was still talking about her favorite English subject—Perry Chapman.

Margaret was holding back her tears and had tried not to

think of...or about leaving him. She reminded herself that Katie didn't win an award for nosiness for nothing.

"It's not even ten in the morning, Katie, can't you give it a rest?"

"Give it a rest?" Katie gawked. "We're talking about the rest of your life, your future happiness. You can't leave now."

The way Margaret felt this instant, there was no future happiness for her. "I'm only supposed to stay for two weeks." She reminded Katie. "My time's up. I have a return ticket and I'm supposed to go home."

"But you could—" Katie started up again.

Margaret cut her off and continued, "If I don't leave him alone, Lord Alison will bring me up on charges of stalking and Immigration will have me bodily removed."

"Stalking—I'm sure!" Katie made a face.

"I don't know why you're so worried about him." Margaret was ready to scream. No one was more aware than she that she'd never see Perry again. Katie really had no idea how painful it was for her. "He's probably at home tucked in his warm, comfy bed, asleep."

"Dreaming about you," Katie added with a smile.

Margaret glanced skyward. "And some people think I'm a romantic."

"Margaret! Margaret!" a voice called in the distance.

Standing in line ready to board at Gate 23, Margaret and Katie stood on tiptoe, faced back toward the waiting area.

"Excuse me, sir, you cannot cross this point without a passport and boarding pass," a uniformed airline employee warned.

"Margaret! Margaret!" came the call again.

"I think it's *Per-ry*," Katie said in a singsongy voice. "What are you going to do?"

He *came*. Margaret thought her heart had stopped. She turned on tiptoe scanning above the other passengers in line, trying to catch a glimpse of him. Maybe she only imagined he'd called for her.

The call came again—louder and more frantic.

No, she hadn't imagined it. He was here. "I suppose I should see what he wants."

"Wants? Silly—" Katie gave Margaret a playful shove. "He wants you."

Katie was right. What other reason could there be?

"Go on. I'll be fine." She slipped her arm through Paul's and smiled up at him. "I have Paul to keep me company, remember?"

"Margaret—Margaret Swanson!" The frantic call came from the front of the gate again.

Okay. I'm going. Margaret pushed her rolling carry-on forward and stepped out of line. She waded back through the passengers. She collected a few, "All right, Margaret" and "You go get him" encouragements along the way.

Perry reluctantly stepped away from the airline counter and leaned against the glass partition for support, unwilling to break eye contact with the woman he came for.

Margaret abandoned her bag and passed back through the airline check-in door to Perry. He wrapped her in his arms and hugged her.

"Margaret, I can't believe it—Margaret! I caught you in time."

Of course, she was glad to see him, and secretly hoped he had come for her—to stop her from leaving. But that couldn't happen, she was sure he hadn't remembered who she was, or who he was, and what they had once meant to each other.

Or did he? Margaret wondered. "What are you doing here?" she whispered, suspiciously.

She pushed away and held him at arms' distance. His usual

immaculate, groomed self was now rumpled and unkempt. His hair actually stood on end in places.

"You look…" She eyed him from head to toe. *Terrible* is what she wanted to say.

"Haunted—" was the word he supplied. "I'm sorry, I'm so very sorry. I know I must look a fright but I had to see you." He ran his hand down a wrinkled pant leg which didn't remove the wrinkles.

The waiting passengers were more interested in what was going on between the couple than boarding the plane. They didn't even pretend to ignore the touching scene.

"We need some privacy, come on." Apparently, Perry didn't want an audience. He led her into a corner across from the boarding gate doors.

Margaret wondered if he had slept at all. He looked pale and his dark brown eyes were ringed with red—and he was also acting a bit odd.

"I know this shows very bad form, but I've come to stop you from leaving." He drew his fingernails up his unshaven neck, the rough stubble making a raspy sound from the underside of his chin. "I can't let you go."

"I don't know what you're talking about." Margaret stepped back.

She gasped as he caught hold of her by the arms.

"What is it?" He sensed that something was wrong but she didn't want to tell him.

"You're acting weird and it's scaring me," she said with deliberate calm.

"I apologize. I'm terribly sorry. I don't mean to." Perry loosened his grip. Margaret pulled free and rubbed her arm.

"American Airlines Flight 6118 to San Francisco is now calling for the remaining passengers for all rows and remaining seats to please board," a voice from the loudspeaker announced.

Wringing his hands was the only gesture missing from his performance. But it was very clear that Perry was extremely uneasy about her departure.

"I don't know how else to put this but I don't want you to go back to the States."

"What?" Where had that come from? "But I have to go—it's my flight home."

"Yes, I realize that." He pushed his hands into his pockets then pulled them out and took a deep breath. "But I don't want you to leave. I want to be with you. I want us to be together."

They were the same words Desmond had used.

"I know, I know—this is so bloody difficult." He ran a hand through his already disheveled hair. "I can't say I understand it myself and you'll think I'm barking mad but I just know we're supposed to be together... We belong together." He groaned, probably at his own words.

Margaret couldn't believe what she was hearing. What had happened to Perry? How did he know?

"I didn't realize until I left you yesterday," he whispered.

"Realize what?"

His voice began to strain with emotion. "I realized that I cannot go on living day after day knowing I will never hold you in my arms, never see your gentle face, and never again hear your sweet voice." He studied her eyes and mouth, watching, waiting for her reaction. "I know I love you." He gently held her hand. "If you leave now, I'll only follow you—I have a ticket."

He made a motion to reach into his jacket pocket only to realize he wasn't wearing one. "I suppose I've left it at Security. I was in a bit of a hurry to get here." He offered a weak smile. "Say you'll stay, please."

Yes, she wanted to say yes, but Margaret couldn't just do it. "I can't just stay with you."

"Of course not, we will marry." His smile broadened and he watched her expectantly.

"We will?" This was moving too fast. Margaret was only trying to make the decision to stay or to go, not to get married.

"It is what you want, isn't it? It's what I want," he declared. "Will you marry me?"

She wasn't Mrs Margaret White, this time she had a choice. She could have the man she loved. "I think it's a bit soon to be talking about that, don't you?"

In the background an airline employee announced over the loudspeaker, "This is the last call for American Airlines flight 6118, calling for final boarding. This is the last call."

The woman on the loudspeaker only stood ten feet away from the couple. And obviously, the announcement was meant for Margaret, the only person who had yet to board the plane.

"Ma'am?" the airline employee pointedly spoke to Margaret.

"I don't know what to do," Margaret whispered to herself. If he was really her Pierce, he'd know the answer to that. "What do you think?"

"Really? Really?" He smiled wide, his eyes lit up at the possibility that she would consider staying. "I think you're about to miss your flight home." Perry drew Margaret into his arms.

Their lips met with a century-long passion. Her arms twined around his neck and caused havoc with his already chaotic hair.

"It is you," she whispered, giving a little gasp, taking in a breath of air. "All right. I'm staying."

"I love you, Margaret. I think I always have, ever since I first set eyes on you."

And someday she would tell him the truth about how it all came about.

About the Author

California-born Shirley Marks lives in Silicon Valley with her husband and unpredictable Australian Cattle Dog-mix.

Shirley dreams of returning to London, Paris, and Florence to research settings, develop new characters, and stories to weave together for her upcoming novels.

When at home, she spends time reading, writing, gardening, and trying to get the odd knitting projects completed

Shirley writes Traditional Regency Romance stories (clean/sweet), Romantic Comedies, and a couple of paranormal novels

You can visit Shirley at:
www.ShirleyMarks.com